mavis a.

the world's hugest oil platform—standing on towering legs above the icy waters of the North Sea, commanded by a man who is part genius, part slavedriver; and peopled by a force that includes secret traitors and smuggled-aboard prostitutes

the american enterprise

the sea's newest, most gigantic supertanker, its crew captive, its one female a sexual plaything and vital pawn, its new captain an Irish terrorist brilliant and strong enough to dominate any man and use any woman for his staggering scheme

the assault on mavis a.

Don't try to guess who comes out on top!

"Pressure-cooker intensity, all the more explosive because of the credibility of the characters and plot"   *—Business Week*

"Superb, imaginative suspense, with depths that the normal thriller doesn't bother with"
                                      —Houston Chronicle

the
assault on mavis a.

norman stahl

Fowler's Books
Buy - Sell - Trade
323 N. Euclid
Fullerton 92632
or
2634 W. Orangethorpe
Fullerton, 92634

POPULAR LIBRARY • **NEW YORK**

The excerpt from "The Host of the Air" by W. B. Yeats is reprinted with permission of Macmillan Publishing Co., Inc. from *COLLECTED POEMS* of William Butler Yeats. Copyright 1906 by Macmillan Publishing Co., renewed 1934 by William Butler Yeats; and by A. P. Watt, Ltd., London.

THE ASSAULT ON MAVIS A.

Published by Popular Library, a unit of CBS Publications, the Consumer Publishing Division of CBS Inc., by arrangement with Random House, Inc.

ISBN: 0-445-04500-0

Printed in the United States of America
First Popular Library printing: November 1979

10 9 8 7 6 5 4 3 2 1

to people who stick

PROFILE COMPARISON ~ AMERICAN ENTERPRISE
AND ORDINARY SUPERTANKER

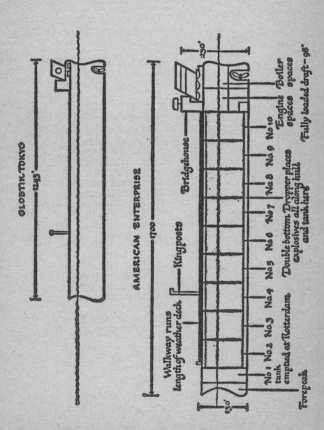

GLOBTIK TOKYO

1243'

AMERICAN ENTERPRISE

1700'

930'

Walkway runs length of weather deck — Kingposts

Bridgehouse

230'

Forepeak

No1 No2 No3 No4 No5 No6 No7 No8 No9 No10
tank
emptied at Rotterdam

Double bottom. Dropper places
explosives all along hull
and tank here

Engine Boiler
spaces spaces

Fully loaded draft ~ 98'

AMERICAN ENTERPRISE FROM ABOVE

Manhole access to empty no. 1 tank
Target of Ethel Browne

Walkway traveled by Ethel Browne

Door from bridge-house to weather deck walkway

Bridge-house

No. 1 tank   No. 2   No. 3   No. 4   No. 5   No. 6   No. 7   No. 8   No. 9   No. 10

Oil tanks divided (except for no. 1) into 3 parts for stability — center and port and starboard wing

PROFILE OF MAVIS A.

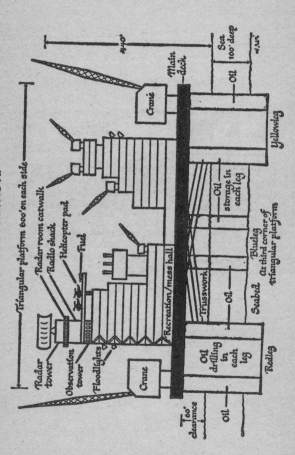

Triangular platform 600' on each side

Radar tower
Observation tower
Floodlights
Radar room catwalk
Radio shack
Helicopter pad
Fuel
Crane
Crane
Recreation/mess hall
Main deck
440'
Sea 100' deep
Oil
Yellowleg
Oil storage in each leg
Trusswork
Oil
Blueleg
At third corner of triangular platform
Seabed
Oil drilling in each leg
Oil
Redleg
Oil
100' clearance

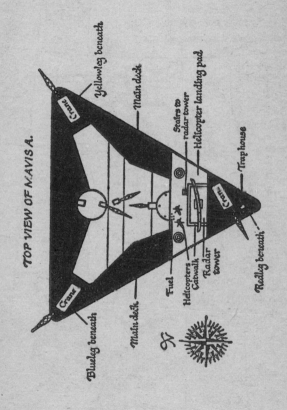

TOP VIEW OF N.A.V.I.S. A.

Crane

Yellowleg beneath

Main deck

Stairs to radar tower

Helicopter landing pad

Trap house

Crane

Redleg beneath

Crane

Blueleg beneath

Main deck

Fuel

Helicopters

Catwalk

Radar tower

N

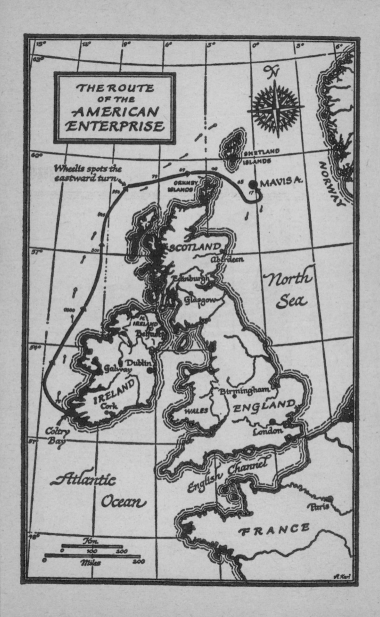

prologue

The north sea is a poor thing, as great bodies of water go. It is really only an arm of the Atlantic, a flat plate held between the mainland of northwest Europe and the British Isles. Glacial sands race restlessly across its bottom, propelled by terrible tidal currents, forming high sandbanks that are swept away and raised with such speed and regularity that they seem to be adrift. The Admiralty charts have never been able to stay up to date with the shifting bottom, and deep-drafted ships use the sea only at hazard.

Like many of the insignificant, the North Sea has a vile and dangerous temper. The weather over its sullen face can change four times in a day, and a week-long storm can boil out of it in hours.

North Sea sailors hardly think it worthwhile to mention winds of seventy-five miles per hour piling up fifty-foot waves. Indeed, the blow that was moving down from Norway and that had already crossed southwest Ireland was now hurling such winds and waves between the Norwegian and Scottish coasts.

But when in a true temper, the tiny sea could skew up what no work of man could ignore; ninety-foot waves and a hundred-and-thirty-mile-per-hour winds have been recorded, and undoubtedly there are bones on the shifting sands below that have seen worse at their last awful moment. Hence, except during the wars of seven centuries, this ugly stepchild of the oceans figured only lightly in men's interest, until one day in 1961, when some Dutchmen working for the Shell Oil Company pricked the ground at Groningen in Holland and found the second largest gas field on earth.

Even a schoolboy geologist can tell you that the floor of Holland matches precisely in structure the floor of the North Sea, so undersea drilling for natural gas was begun beneath its surface. Some drilling for oil was done, too, but nothing came of it until 1969, when Phillips Petroleum hit the huge Ekofisk Field. Hardly a year later British Petroleum, working largely by chance, dropped a drill into the Forties Field. Its reserves were estimated to be above 2 billion barrels, and with this discovery, the North Sea turned into the treasure house of the West. Its key was Mavis A.

chapter 1

As platform master of Mavis A., Noel Cullenbine commanded a machine as vast and expensive as the Aswan Dam. In brilliance, daring and importance, his charge was the greatest individual work of man.

Mavis A. was so called because it was the first rig to stand in the Mavis Field, a 900-million-barrel cache of oil beneath the North Sea. There had never before been an oil-drilling platform like Mavis because there had never been a crisis like the one that compelled its construction.

Cullenbine and the men who stood with him in Mavis A.'s darkened observation tower, two hundred and fifty feet above the thundering waves, were not merely at the center of a storm sweeping down from Norway; they were at the center of a storm sweeping down on the Western nations. And thus at the center of the world. Through the rain smearing the tall, thick windows, they watched the peaks of the waves moving toward them from the tips of mountains sixty feet high. Despite all the unimaginable tons of steel and concrete beneath their feet, they still felt the drumfire shocks of the sea.

13

The mind of Noel Cullenbine had been kept prisoner by the community, like the body of a queen bee. What was in his head was simply too valuable to be kept in his own care. He had been a child wonder—a Mozart of science. At the age of seven he had been brought to Edinburgh, at the university's request, to be studied by wondering professors. While his railway-engineer father and seamstress mother fretted in a hotel room, the phenomenal ability of their only son to retain, process, organize and transmit information astounded his examiners.

Noel Cullenbine never really went home again. He was taken from his parents almost as effectively as if he had been kidnapped. After his mind had been plumbed and exclaimed over, he was placed in a series of special schools, none of which seemed to be near his home.

The sheer utility of Noel Cullenbine's mind had encouraged a peculiar kind of academic greed. From the start, the teachers of physics, mathematics and chemistry had the advantage. He was never in a music or history class for more than a few days before his program was amended to replace these courses with more physical sciences. Always it was arranged that what would come out of Cullenbine would be machines and systems, not art or literature.

By the age of eighteen Cullenbine had grown to feel that he was unable to touch anything that breathed, and to try and save himself as a man he rebelled. He disappeared from the university and from England by buying false papers and shipping out as a sailor on a freighter. Bored immediately with that life, he jumped ship in Mexico and drifted to work in the oil fields. Here he found the first task he'd ever loved: the brutal challenge of wresting from the earth a running treasure, the energy stored by a hundred million years of suns. He had felt its power beneath his feet as he now felt the shock of waves, and ever since he had wanted to unleash and command its power.

At first he had been content to work, to learn and to make his way slowly up through the lowest backbreaking, limb-crushing jobs. But within a year he yearned to multiply his energies and to be a leader.

By this time his body had made the same startling genetic leap beyond his parents that, earlier, his mind had. Though neither his father nor his mother stood more than a wiry five feet eight inches, their prodigious son grew to a thick-shouldered six feet three. But for all his bulk he was hugely agile, a combination that made him a terror in bloody oil-field brawls. With this indispensable credential, he was a foreman in the toughest fields of Mexico and Texas by the time he was twenty-four. The Limey, as the other workers called him, commanded hard men by becoming a walking terror. He punished with his voice, which was loud, metallic and abrasive when he raised it. Directed at a cringing workman, it had the effect of the curdling yells used in Oriental fighting arts; it paralyzed. He punished with his fists, which were ridged with knuckles so massive that they might have served for models of a gladiator's glove. And he punished with his scorn. It shot out of his eyes like venom; men who felt it once would perform wonders rather than face it again.

Now, just past forty, Cullenbine needed all these savage talents as the operating boss of Mavis A. Brilliant, computer-nurtured plans flowed into operation largely because of the fists and tongue of this spectacularly effective man.

He had attained his present position as inexorably as though God had determined it. When he returned from his exile after eight years, even harder than he had left, society again sponsored him where it had left off, but now he was willing because the world was after industrial growth, and a major part of this growth hinged on the recovery of oil.

Third Officer James crawled up the bed along the bone-white nakedness of Mariclare Brady and sat upon the Irish girl with her chest between his knees. "Now how the hell did you do it?"

Mariclare ran her hands along the soft thickness of him, and his lips lost the words they were starting. So

15

James never came to ask how a brothel, even one so fine, was able to use the tightly controlled company frequency of Petromarine to call the *American Enterprise* at sea. Or how the call went unentered in the supertanker's radio log. Or how the call came to choose Will James for its invitation to the hospitality of the grand new brothel on Coltry Bay. Indeed, Will James was now in the transport that makes of a man a beast viler than any mounting in a field, for the beast would look to its danger. Will James, kneeling, the ankles of Mariclare Brady tight in his hands, lifting and pulling and spreading the sweating, reddened pelvis tight against his penetration, saw only the wide blue eyes locked on his. He did not in time perceive it as the blinkless gaze of a hunting cat, nor feel the paw upon his back. As he rose to his climax, the snarl of the gale against the looming cliffs ringing the bay rose higher.

Coltry Bay, rolling sharply in the rain and darkness under the ever-accelerating wind of the long-fronted blow rolling from the north, is one of those geological wonders that slice the tall western headlands of Europe. This needle of ocean thrusting between sheer, vaulting walls of rock in southwestern Ireland is a fjord as mighty as many that enter the coast of Norway.

With cliffs too high and sheer for comfortable shore installations, the bay had lain for a thousand years scarcely used for the shelter of shipping. But now its age had come.

None of your mud-bottom harbor dredging here to get another five feet for deeper-drafted hulls. Here the chisels of the heavens had deep-split the rock beneath the sea for more hundreds of feet than anyone would bother to measure. Only in a rift like this could the shores of Ireland contain the incomprehensible mountain of steel that now rode at anchors the size of small houses.

The *American Enterprise* resembled an oil tanker only in the sense that a whale is a mammal like a mouse. She was a supertanker built so far beyond the scale of her sisters that there was no adequate terminology for her bulk.

The surge in oil-tanker size from 50,000-tonners to 125,000-tonners had hastily been covered by the acronym VLCC: Very Large Crude Carrier. But with the Suez still closed and the Western thirst for Persian Gulf crude growing fiercer, 200,000-, 300,000- and even 400,000-tonners had slid down the ways of the vast Japanese dockyards. The bigger economies of bigger ships were irresistible. The new term ULCC, Ultra Large Crude Carrier, was used for the new giants, but it served only until the building of the *American Enterprise*.

This floating oil field stretched 1,700 feet, almost a third of a statute mile. Her beam of 275 feet far more than doubled that of the old *Queen Mary,* which could have ridden comfortably on the tanker's weather deck. And in her ten arena-sized tanks lay 1.2 millions tons of high-grade crude petroleum. It had been taken on two and a half months before under the broiling Persian Gulf sun at Kharg Island. The cargo was scheduled to deliver to Petromarine, the American owners of the *Enterprise,* a profit of just under $11 million.

Nature itself seemed to take special notice of the ship's grand numbers, for the *Enterprise* was among the first of man's vehicles to feel the effects of the earth's rotation. The vessel's almost unimaginable mass came into the pull of the Coriolis effect, being tugged to the right of course in the northern hemisphere, to the left in the southern.

Although none was philosopher enough to articulate it, the officers of the *Enterprise* found much to dread about the ship. Even on nights when the gale did not howl across the empty prairie of her decks, the terrible loneliness of man lost in space exacerbated the crew's nerves.

A man might find himself in an alleyway so remote that his step would be the first on it in months. A figure appearing at the far end would shimmer like a ghost, its features, its clothes unrecognizable in the distance. Even a loud shout could fail to gain its attention, and it might disappear so suddenly up a forgotten ladder or down a lost manhole that the chilled viewer would become uncertain that he had seen anything at all.

The great Atlantic liners had complements of close to 1,300 men serving thousands of passengers. But man, the great exterminator, had all but exterminated himself in the design of the *American Enterprise;* she sailed with a crew of forty-nine.

Jim Sam Cody stood on the port bridge wing, staring sixteen stories straight down to the savage chop pounding the hull. He was still called captain by his crew. They did not yet know that what they stood upon did not require a captain. But for the fact that it floated and moved, it was not truly a ship. It was an office building, a warehouse, an automated space station. Cody, who had swum away from the burning *Atlanta* off Guadalcanal and the crippled *Gambier Bay* in Leyte Gulf, was carried on the payroll books of Petromarine as ship's manager.

Now, with the rain driving down his neck, he closed his eyes and imagined that he was a young third officer on a wool clipper running for Cape Horn, or on a 10,000-ton tramp driving, bows under, through Macassar Strait. No good. With the wind climbing near fifty knots, not a ventilator or radar mast rolled a hundredth of an inch against the sky. Cody stood on an island that did not ride the waves, but broke them with its bulk.

The broad, gray-bearded Vermonter took off his cap to the storm, feeling the need to refresh himself. Through the rain streaming in front of his eyes he saw a light on shore change color. It was in the upper window of a new white building that stood on the main street so recently gouged out of rock. The light flashed from white to green four times, and then, after a pause, flashed again. Cody thought it a lover's signal, which seemed to be the most comforting way to think of it.

Seeing the green light from far down the street, the two old men drove their tiny automobile into the high-walled drive behind the brothel. When they unfolded from the front seats and stood listening and watching, one could see that they were old men of a type common to the west coast of Ireland. They were both near seventy, but the years had not slackened their great-boned bodies. The passing of time had burned away the beer bellies, slack jowls and bar-stool bottoms, and they stood all sinew and muscle, stronger than men thirty years younger and far more knowing and terrible.

One of them reached into the back seat, pulling and rolling onto the pavement a teen-age boy who had been tied, jackknife fashion, with his wrists to his ankles. He whimpered like a small animal as they picked him up by his bindings and carried him through a double door to the black cellar below. Two floors above, Will James dimly heard the doors close.

James was uneasy now. Like many a good Catholic boy before him, he had small power to deny his loins. But with the physical insistence past, memories rose of dark mutterings through confessional screens, and hard floorboards on young, trembling knees. This girl was beautiful. This place was beautiful. The welcome was warmer than any he had known at home. But now he wanted to be back on the ship, soaking in his tub, contritely contemplating the betraying pink mass floating at the bottom of his white belly.

"How do I tell that man to return my clothes?"

"He's going to have them all nice and pressed for you."

"He's had two hours."

"You've got all night."

"The hell I do."

"Theres nothing else in the town."

"The ship. I've got to get back."

"You don't. Not till the afternoon tomorrow." She faced him on the bed, sitting tailor-fashion. It opened her wide.

He tightened. "You've got a man aboard us, haven't you? Or somewhere else inside Petromarine?"

"Who cares, Will? You've not eaten. You'll dress in a while and come to our dining room. It cost a hundred thousand pounds, they say. The chef was at the Hotel Connaught. Then we'll come up here again." She ran a fingertip idly down the side of his flaccid member.

19

He nodded. "Still as a guest, Mariclare?"

"And as a friend, Will."

The power of a girl without her clothes continued to move the earth.

Colonel Willem Lustgarten and his adjutant, Captain Rolfe Zamke, were different from the men with them in the observation tower of Mavis A. They were not technicians like Noel Cullenbine or petroleum executives like Admiral Sir Devereux Magnus. As commander of the North Sea Security Forces, Lustgarten, along with his aide, was simply a policeman.

As was his custom with any new acquaintance, Lustgarten was cataloguing Cullenbine. Although the German was no expert on accents, he realized that Cullenbine's had become as much American as anything else. Lustgarten saw a man of about forty-five who moved like a boy. The build was much like his own: tall, broad and with much of the weight carried in hard slabs in the legs and shoulders. The face must have been almost pretty once, but now it was scarred. The nose had been broken several times, and the lips and eyebrows often split. Nevertheless, the result was not unattractive. Yet, Lustgarten thought, he himself, though more than fifteen years older and entirely gray, was a better-looking man.

Lustgarten had no knowledge of the power of the sea or of the strength of this structure, so he was glad when the blond, cherub-faced Zamke asked the question first: "How much of this pounding can your platform take, Mr. Cullenbine?" His English was as good as Lustgarten's, but the German accent was much harsher.

"All the rigs in the North Sea are built to withstand what we call a hundred-year storm wave—that is, a wave that could occur in these waters once in a hundred years. We estimate such a wave as being ninety feet above the level of the sea when it's calm."

"How much force would that be?" Lustgarten asked.

"Readings have been taken by lighthouse builders on coastal rocks of wave forces of above seven thousand pounds per square foot. Of course, coastal waves don't tell us all we'd like to know about the biggest sea waves, but Mavis A. can withstand shocks of fourteen thousand pounds per square foot."

Cullenbine clapped his big hand on Lustgarten's shoulder; he felt the German stiffen, but out of perversity kept his grip on the braided epaulet. "Don't worry about getting your feet wet, Colonel. This thing's built to last a thousand years. Just like the old German Reich. Doesn't even have survival capsules."

"Just like the old *Titanic,* with not enough lifeboats, perhaps?"

Magnus barked an unpleasant laugh. "If Mavis A. founders, there will be a lot more going to the bottom than a bunch of millionaires. We will very likely have lost England, for a beginning."

"Oh, I think your country has survived harder blows than that, Admiral Magnus," Zamke said. He was much younger than Lustgarten, and not above deprecating the past military adventures of his country.

"I can see that you have not been with Security for long, Captain."

"Less than a week, sir."

Lustgarten broke in quickly. "I had planned to brief Captain Zamke more fully on the importance of this installation during our helicopter flight from Ostend, only the weather made prolonged conversation impossible, Admiral."

"Had the same sort of trip myself. Came in just ahead of you. Another hour and neither of us would have been able to land. Damned stupid time we picked for inspection touring."

"Perhaps, Admiral Magnus, you would do Zamke the honor of telling him something of what we have on our hands here." Every old German soldier knows when rank wants to hear itself speak.

Zamke nodded. "I would appreciate it, sir." Every new German soldier knows what every old German soldier wants him to say.

21

Magnus was torn between still not trusting any damned krauts and wanting to voice the torments that had dogged him recently. "You know who I am, Zamke?"

The young German looked into the surprisingly clear blue eyes of the old man, who, though small and white-haired, radiated energy and toughness. "Admiral Sir Devereux Magnus. Retired from the Royal Navy. Served with high distinction in the Mediterranean, notably at Taranto. Winner of—"

"That's who I *was,* damn it. Do you know why I left a very comfortable seat on the board at British Petroleum at the age of seventy-two to sit at the middle of the North Sea in a force five gale?"

"No, sir."

"It's because my country is falling apart. It's because I have been given, as the last big responsibility of my life, a chance to make the British National Oil Corporation something more than a cruel joke."

Magnus stalked around the observation tower, speaking as though Zamke were the ears of the world. "In this sea tonight stand over four hundred oil platforms, each disastrously expensive and critcally important. But none is so expensive and important as Mavis A. On this structure rides the political and economic fate of Great Britain. With the sickest economy and one of the worst inflation rates of any industrial nation, Britain's only real hope is this oil gold mine: the richest of the North Sea strikes— the Mavis Field. With this field fully exploited, the brutal foreign-exchange losses brought about by the Arab oil squeeze and an undercapitalized economy would vanish. The nation's industrial base could be rebuilt without the insupportable unrest that would be caused by cutting back on our social system. And most vitally, the political upheavals inherent in a collapsing economy would be controllable for the foreseeable future.

"But the timing is critical, Zamke. We are trying, I must confess, to keep what may be too great a share of the oil for the government. We have antagonized the bloody oil companies. Until the deal improves, they have

22

slowed the staggering investments necessary to bring the oil up. I'd do the same thing myself. But every day of delay sees the price of the work still to be done climbing, and Britain sinking toward international bankruptcy. I doubt if a dozen people know it, but even now the government cannot afford to recover the oil on its own. Neither its funds nor its expertise is anywhere near sufficient.

"The answer to all of this is to be Mavis A." Magnus stood for a moment in front of Zamke, holding him by each elbow; it was the way he stood when he was addressing prime ministers. "We have rushed an enormous amount of our immediately available financing—perhaps too damned much of it—into this single platform. All by itself it is capable of supplying the cash flow needed to develop the rest of the Mavis Field. And that means the rest of the North Sea." For emphasis, Magnus poked Zamke's chest, and the young officer took a step backward. "And by God, we may succeed. Right now this platform is pumping three hundred thousand barrels a day, twice what any concrete deep-water structure has ever before produced. If Mavis A. can finance ten more of its kind by the early nineteen-eighties, Great Britain will become the world's fifth largest oil producer. We'll be pumping more oil than Kuwait. By the mid-eighties we could be *exporting* a million barrels a day."

"But that is wonderful, Admiral."

Zamke's voice had broken Magnus's elation. "We are still far from anything wonderful. So delicate is the balance of time that a single major setback in operations could put the national situation beyond salvage. The political repercussions of a British social and economic collapse simply cannot be calculated."

Lustgarten, who had been Field Marshal von Rundstedt's youngest general in the 1944 Ardennes offensive, allowed himself the moment's luxury of savoring this thought, then said to Zamke, "That is why I have brought you here. Half the job of protecting something is knowing more about it than the people who will be trying to destroy it."

In the dining room of the brothel fronting Coltry Bay, the glassware and chandeliers were of the heaviest Waterford crystal, fully one-third lead, and it could be seen in the sparkle. One member of the string ensemble would have been recognized by name at New York's Lincoln Center. Many of the diners were recognizable too, in Irish and English government circles and in those of international oil, and big-tanker shipping. At a table in a large, high-windowed alcove sat officials of the local police, chatting easily with members of the local press. It took no quick mind to connect the continued flourishing of Dominic Quinn's questionable establishment in the Land of the Church with their frequent presence.

Dominic Quinn was one of those beautiful black Irishmen. As little more than a child he had learned that the eye he sought was likely already upon him. And his own eyes were the dearest of his gifts: violet-blue plates rimmed by a broad, sudden band of black that made them snap and bite. His hair—lashes, brows, even that on his hands—had the glow of sable.

Watching Will James and Mariclare Brady finish the fine meal he had ordered for them, Quinn signaled to an elderly waiter—one of the men who had carried the human package to the cellar—to bring the handsome couple a cordial. Then he went back to his small leather-bound Yeats. It was still fashionable for leaders of the Irish Republican Army to know their Yeats, and some could quote him by the page. Not Dominic Quinn. His mind was formidable only in its simplicity. He did not understand the elegant locutions, but, by God, he felt the music in the words. They brought tears to his eyes, so shallow in him lay gentle sentiments. " 'O'Driscoll rode with a song' . . ." he intoned under his breath. By the time he had read down to the last " 'And never was piping so sad, and never was piping so gay,' " his love for all things Irish knew no bounds.

Quinn was one of the most dangerous men in the world.

"Do you mind if I sit with you for a moment, Mr. James? My name is Quinn. I'm your host, as it were."

James stood to shake his hand. "Yeah. Please do." He was surprised that the Irishman, whom he had taken to be an enormous man as he watched him cross the room, stood half a head shorter than his own six feet. James had this trouble with people by whom he felt intimidated. In his mind, his own tiny mother loomed far above him.

"We know you have enjoyed yourself, young man, for what we intend a person to experience here is pretty well what he experienced." It seemed perfectly all right for him to call James "young man," though Quinn could not have been more than five years his senior.

"Then you won't be surprised to know that you're right, Mr. Quinn. I want to thank you."

"You can thank me, indeed, Third Officer." Like many Ulstermen, Quinn spoke with little trace of the southern brogue and a good deal of burr, which suited the insistent edge of command that he slid into his voice. "Since you are truly satisfied with our hospitality, we wish you to pass your pleasure along to your fellow officers on the *Enterprise*." He handed James a typed card. "That's all of them, isn't it?"

Apprehension rose in James as he read the list. "Danenhower is missing. The electronics officer."

"A technician. But if you think he should be along, then he should." Quinn took back the card and added Danenhower's name to it with a gold mechanical pencil. "Do they keep full-time radio watch in port? I've heard they do."

"Of course."

"Fine. I'll show you our own radio room right now." He checked his watch. "If we call at once, givin' them an hour or so to tidy up, they should all be here by nine o'clock. Have them back aboard by nine in the mornin'."

James did not like the pressure. "They can't leave the ship without officers on the watch. Not in this blow."

"I understood that your Captain Cody and your first officer, Mr. Browne, often stand all the overnight watches in port." Quinn seemed to remind himself to smile. "And what the hell, your friends are in port maybe twice in six months."

"Sometimes not that often. We were at sea three hundred and forty-five days last year. The only ports where we set foot ashore were Coltry and Rotterdam. The sea berths are getting so far offshore that you can hardly see the lights of your port."

"When a ship costs sixty thousand dollars a day to operate, you'd damn well better keep her steamin'. And with a hundred feet of loaded draft, she's not goin' into many harbors."

"You know something about ships, Mr. Quinn."

"Only about this one. The pure size of it gets you interested."

Mariclare Brady forgot the value of her quiet. "But you used to build ships, Dominic."

"I was a welder at Harland and Wolff in Belfast for some years. I am hardly a shipbuilder."

"But you know a great deal about ships, Dom. I listen to you."

"Mariclare, now that you have finished your dinner, do please go and have the girls I asked for here in one hour. Have them, and no one else, in the Charles Street wing. Now go, please. You'll be seein' Mr. James again later."

James rose for her as she left.

"You're very polite to your whores."

"I don't think of her that way. Honestly."

"Men keep makin' that mistake. Honestly."

The young officer did not like this contempt for the receptacle of his sacred seed. "I suppose a man in your business must have that attitude." It was the noblest defense he had ever made of a woman.

"While you're on your feet, let me show you somethin' that might impress you."

Quinn guided James through a heavy curtain at the rear of the dining room, and down a spiral stairway. The only light came past a thick metal door standing open at the end of a short hallway. A low-pitched electronic hum

26

could be felt as much as heard. James walked inside and clapped a hand to his head in wonder.

"Good Christ. Can you call Mars?"

The room was small, but packed full with first-rate radio gear. There were three men in the room. Two were operators, at the moment engaged with heavy incoming traffic. The third slid a pile of loose-leaf books into a pilot's flight bag. One page, removed for convenience, was late following. James recognized the print-out of a machine code. A whorehouse using a machine code?

"These men are all named Murphy, Mr. James. Everyone you meet in this buildin' except me is named Murphy."

"I understand."

"Our clients are very important men who must stay in touch with their interests all over the world. Our radio is a great convenience to them. One of the Petromarine lads ashore has been able to arrange for us to tie into that wonderful six-hundred-foot antenna of theirs. We can reach anythin' from here that your company can."

"It would make a better story if you were just using that thing to call in new business."

"Then we'll change our story, James. It's a rare story that doesn't need improvin'." Quinn placed the typed card of officers' names in James's breast pocket. "Who has the radio watch on the *Enterprise?*"

"Brand, until eight."

"That checks. One of our Mr. Murphys will raise Mr. Brand on the radio and tell him to skip enterin' anythin' in the radio log. Don't worry about that. He's done it before, and is a case of fine whiskey ahead for it. Now we reckon that your fellow third officer, Goldman, is scheduled to come ashore at eight, and with him both second officers, Goslin and Danenhower, as well as both second engineers, Queen and Case."

"That seems right."

"But we think that good Captain Cody and Mr. Browne will stand all the watches if the other lads have a fine place to go."

"They might."

"That would mean we could also expect the other engineers, Larsen and Engelberg."

"Probably."

"What about Traskin, the chief engineer?"

"He's a very old man. He almost never goes ashore."

"Possibly he's never been asked to the right place."

"Quinn, I don't think I'm going to do this."

"My friend, you do understand that you are not pimpin', if that's what's on your mind? Your friends will pay nothin'. It is their good will I want, as I wanted yours. You are not bein' paid to do anythin'."

"I have been paid very well, thank you."

"As many a pure lad in the twenty-six counties is bein' paid on a front-parlor couch at this exact minute. The cunt is always buyin'. Fur coats, food, security, husbands."

James looked at Quinn unblinkingly. "You're a homosexual, aren't you?"

"You've a fine pair of eyes if you can see that."

"It's nothing I can see, except you're a bit too pretty."

"Oh, is that how you can tell?"

"No. Mostly it's your whole disgusting view of people."

"I do get a disgustin' view of people. Take you and that fancy tongue of yours. Not two hours past, I had a view of it four inches up a slut's pussy."

James whitened, but his voice dropped lower. He had been brought up to believe that the power of a boy who never missed mass was God-given and illimitable over Jews and homosexuals. "The natural weaknesses of a man are forgiven. The unnatural ones are not."

"I can tell that we share a religion."

"I share nothing with you, you goddamned fag."

"Murphy, get the ship."

"I will not become an occasion of sin for any of my friends."

There was a long, barking laugh from Quinn. "Good sufferin' shit, who the hell is the Irishman here?"

When James put his hand flat against Quinn's chest to

28

push past him, the man caught the fingers and bent them backward.

James dropped to his knees. "I'll have this place closed in the next hour, you sonofabitch."

"Don't forget to confess callin' me a sonofabitch. And you're goin' to be very busy in the next hour."

One of the Murphys canceled the call to the ship. The other wrapped a policeman's short cuff-chain around James's wrist, which made it easy to get him quietly into the cellar.

Desmond Hanley lay coughing the last of his lungs into the thick air of a military hospital in Belfast. "Hey, you British shit," he wheezed to the soldier who stood at the door, "give us a smoke. What the hell, you'd like to see me dead a little faster anyway."

"Right about that, Hanley. But the intelligence boys want more chatting with you."

"What a pea brained bunch of bastards they are. Even you must see that, Bristol."

"If you told 'em what they wanted to know, you could go home to your family and die like you were a decent man."

"It would be a little damp under all that spit, would it not?"

"Why not give your kids or grandkids a bit of yourself to remember."

"Yeah. My tuberculosis." Hanley coughed dryly, then convulsively. "Goddamned fever's comin' higher again. You'll have a new assignment in just a few days, Private."

"Thank God for that. What I have against the IRA is not so much that they shoot innocent men in their beds or blow up women and children, but that they're so bloody boring."

"Applied with skill, even a tiny weapon becomes deadly."

There was a rush of feet and a babble of swearing outside the door. Bristol jerked it open to find the guards from the front gate and lobby carrying the ravaged body of a soldier still wearing the tartan bonnet of the Argyles. A doctor trotted behind shouting with frustration. "There may be spinal damage, you flaming idiots. He must be flat on a stretcher."

The raging soldiers stopped. "Well, then, get the mucking stretcher," one of them roared.

Three bleary-eyed civilians, showing evidence of having dressed in a great hurry, caught up with the group. The doctor grabbed the first one by the elbow and pointed to a room.

"There's a rolling stretcher in there. Get it out here fast."

The man rushed out, and in a moment reappeared with the stretcher. As the soldiers gently lowered the injured man onto it, one of them pointed to the bewildered and intimidated-looking civilians. "Has anybody given them Paddies a pat-down?"

"I have, Sergeant-major. Just a little penknife on 'em."

"Like as not it was them in on this. The boys will be wanting to talk with them."

"It's why I brung 'em along, you know."

The oldest of the civilians gathered himself together. "This is not fair. Here we pushed ourselves out on a dangerous street to help a hurt man not one of our own, and—"

The doctor, now aided by two nurses, was cutting away at the injured man's tunic with a scalpel. "Why in hell didn't you get this shoulder bag off him?"

"Damn buckle is jammed, Doc."

The doctor cut the shoulder strap and pushed the bag off the stretcher. The tallest of the civilians caught it.

"We're ready with the operating room," a nurse called from down the corridor.

With both the doctor's hands holding pressure points on the man's shattered body, the nurses and two of the soldiers rushed the stretcher away through distant swinging doors.

"Miserable Irish shits," spat one of the two soldiers remaining behind.

"How'd it happen?" Bristol asked.

"How does it ever happen? Probably watching the roof line two blocks away for snipers, and some bum lying in the alley rolled a grenade between his legs."

"Why these kid soldiers keep slipping off alone in streets like these—"

"You can bet your teeth he had the invite from some cute little quiff to slip over tonight and jam her. You can bet on who she was working for, too."

"These blokes seen any of it?"

The oldest Irishman spoke up. "Aye, we did, sir. There we was, my brothers and me sleepin' sound and we got woke by this big thump around on Royal Avenue. We hardly stopped to get on a bit of clothes." He held open his dripping overcoat to show he wore only an undershirt and suspendered, unzipped pants underneath. "We found the young man pretty well blown up. I suppose nobody else heard the noise over the storm. So we sent Brian here runnin' over to the guard at the hospital here, and they come speedin' over in the little Army car."

Bristol looked around quickly. "Where's your other brother? The tall one?"

The tall one stepped out of Hanley's room, his big hands all but engulfing a tiny Israeli submachine gun with a clip twice as long as the rest of it. "Stay away from the side arms, boys, and keep it awful quiet."

His supposed brothers pushed the three soldiers into the room ahead of them.

"Brucie. Michael," Hanley rasped happily. "I like to keeled over when Brian slipped in here. I thought I'd go under without seein' another face that wasn't on some English baboon."

The one called Michael went down on his knees in front of the wounded soldier's discarded shoulder bag, which had found its way into the room with Brian. Ammunition clips and pieces of three more submachine guns spilled out of it. "We weren't going to let you out of it that easy, Desmond." He swiftly assembled a gun, clipped it and threw it to Hanley. "There's one more job."

Hanley could scarcely draw back the bolt cocking the gun. "It better be a job that's short, Michael. There's not a hundred breaths left in me."

"Short enough. Take this, Brucie, and stick your head out for a watch." He handed an assembled gun to Brucie and started on the last one in the bag.

"You're wasting your time," Bristol hissed. "The old bastard'll never tell us a thing, and he'll be dead before morning."

"As a matter of fact," Brian said, "so will you," and he expertly killed the soldier with a steel-knuckled commando knife.

Before the body even sagged, Hanley put three rounds into the chest of the soldier nearest him. Michael shot the other through the back as he turned for the door.

"Ah, Brian, you sonofabitch, you could have just coshed that Bristol. He wasn't a bad sort."

"None of us are bad sorts, Desmond. Here, your friend would want you to have his nice raincoat. It's comin' down like the world's end out there."

"I can't walk, boys. Carry me, Michael. I weigh like a baby."

Watching down the corridor, Brucie saw the soldiers who had gone into the operating room burst through the swinging doors, running so hard that they were half on him before he could bring up his clumsy little Uzi. The sergeant-major, screaming curses, fired a pistol so wildly that the bullet sliced the ceiling. Brucie started to shoot him but saw the other soldier fight loose the jammed bolt of an automatic weapon. He swung his fire that way, his spray of bullets fanning the soldier's trousers like a high wind. The man's legs collapsed, but he brought the gun up again from floor level. Brucie tried for his head with the second burst. Dark pieces bounced along the corridor. Metal. He was blowing the man's weapon to bits like some comic-book sheriff. A laugh leaped in his throat. But then the sergeant-major placed the barrel of his pistol against Brucie's cheek, just under the eye, and blew him off the world. The body jerked away from the door, and the sergeant-major jumped inside, crouching with his gun held out before him as he had been taught. Brian stepped from behind the door and jerked the outstretched firearm from the soldier's hand. To his astonishment, the sergeant-major found himself being shot to death by the frail old prisoner who was being carried in the arms of another man.

Brian said, "We've got two minutes to catch the lorry."

chapter 2

"What are the platform's defenses, sir?" Zamke asked.

Cullenbine swept his arm around the circle of rain-battered windows. "That. The North Sea. We have little to worry about from an outside attack. We keep a thorough air-and-surface radar screen operating. Before anything suspicious could get close, the Royal Navy or Air Force would have intercepted it easily."

"In a storm like this, though, wouldn't interception be seriously interfered with?"

"No; the storm itself is our shield. What would hamper our operations would hamper theirs. There is no man-made object on earth that this sort of storm can't hinder."

"I take it then, Mr. Cullenbine, that the threat is an internal one?"

"Very much so. I hired every man on this rig, and I can tell you that half of 'em belong to the Scottish Nationalist Party. Using other nationals is politically unacceptable, of course; we've got to keep all those Scots happy."

35

"You're bloody right we do," agreed Admiral Magnus. "The Scottish Nationalist Party has one out of three Scottish votes already. The two major political parties of Britain know that it wouldn't take much of a shit to give the Nationalists the power balance in Parliament. Make no mistake; a great part of Scotland wants this oil for itself—all of it. With Mavis A. out of action and Britain in financial collapse, those people could probably get the votes and the foreign help they need to put us out of the picture. There are only about five-and-a-half million Scots. With this oil and independence, they would shift from one of the poorest to one of the richest nations on earth."

"The Nationalists have got a nice slogan," Cullenbine said. " 'Rich Scots or poor Britons?' "

"I understand," said Zamke. "Then all of the men aboard this platform must be subjected to the strictest regulations."

Cullenbine grunted. "This isn't Germany, Zamke—not even the new Germany. If we tried to restrict them the way we should, we'd have a strike every half hour."

"What about infiltrating them?"

"Most of them have known each other for twenty years. They'd smoke out an infiltrator in a week."

"I see, Mr. Cullenbine. Still, we are dealing only with the men and space on a single oil platform. It should be possible for a small number of trusted foremen to keep an effective surveillance."

Lustgarten waved his hand negatively. "Zamke, you have not yet understood the size of Mavis A. or the scope of its operation."

"If the weather ever clears, Captain," Cullenbine said, "you will be able to see that Mavis A. is not so much an oil platform as a densely populated industrial city." He flicked an overhead switch that illuminated, in red battle-light, a table onto whose glass top were projected diagrams of Mavis A. from four sides, top and bottom. "Our main deck is a triangle, with each side a bit over six hundred feet long—about twice the size of previous plat-

36

forms. The main deck is supported by three cylindrical legs, one at each corner, which support the platform one hundred and sixty feet above the sea bottom. Here we have sixty feet of clearance between sea and platform. The tidal range in the North Sea is negligible, amounting to only about ten feet.

"Now these columns, which are one hundred and forty feet in diameter, have a double function. They are actually a column within a column. The inner section, a hundred feet in diameter, contains the oil wells. There are thirty wells down each leg, either producing or being drilled. Don't look so surprised. We've learned to make space work. Through a device called a whipstock, we are able to slant our wells outward to tap the oil at great distances from the platform. We can drill three miles deep, and a single well can draw oil from four productive layers simultaneously. As a result, this single platform can tap into over three hundred and fifty oil-bearing formations. So this is no frivolous investment. Mavis A.'s production makes the wealth produced by all the legendary gold and diamond mines look like peanuts.

"The second function of the legs is oil storage. The outer forty feet of each leg's diameter holds a combined total of a million barrels of oil, or about thirty-one-and-a-half million gallons. A good shipload all by itself. A pipeline system to shore is not economically feasible from here; we off-load the stored oil onto tankers and lighters."

Zamke was impressed. "Destroying your platform would mean spilling a million barrels of oil."

Cullenbine's face moved into the glow of the battle-light. "I'm afraid it would be far more serious than that. The wells we're tapped into are all high pressure—meaning that we don't have to pump them. High internal pressures from inside the earth—perhaps a ton per square inch—force the oil upward. We prevent disastrous blowouts only by keeping special mud continuously in the boreholes while we drill, to apply counterpressure. We might have installed choke valves below the sea bed, but they're often troublesome, and given Mavis's extra strength and other precautions we've taken, we thought it more efficient to do away with them. That's a mistake that will have to be corrected someday. We were thinking too much about nature and not enough about men. Anyway, if the producing pipes were ever sheared off below the water, Mavis A. would be pouring three hundred thousand barrels of oil into the sea every day. It would be months before we could get divers down to clear the wreckage and cap the flow."

"My God. You couldn't begin to estimate the consequences."

"But we have, Zamke." Cullenbine hit the overhead switch again, and the projection on the table top became a map of the Mavis Field and the adjacent Scottish and Norwegian coastlines. "The coastlines to the south—British and French, principally—would be very hard hit; there would be incredible damages. But that would be a minor annoyance compared to what would happen as the slick moved down into the southern oceans. Crude oil contains tars and asphaltenes that are simply not biodegradable, and in the sea they last virtually forever. They would move down on the prevailing currents to the south coast of Africa."

Another flick of the switch produced a projection of the South Atlantic. "These waters are the master link in the world's life chain. The tiny plants and animals that float near the surface are amazingly rich and abundant. The fish come up to eat them, and the birds come down to eat the fish. Our oil slick could poison everything in that chain."

"What it adds up to," Magnus said, "is that we would greatly damage the ability of the world to feed itself over the next fifty years."

Shivering in the bloody raincoat, Hanley tried weakly to brace himself in the back of the careening truck. The beam of Michael's flashlight flickered over eight olive-colored fiberboard cases weighing fifty pounds each. In each case were ten five-pound boxes of the plastic ammo-nium-nitrate-based explosive called gelignite 60.

"I've got the detonators in, and all the wires set," shouted Brian, who was driving, over the racing engine and drumming rain. He was using all his boyhood knowledge of the back streets of Belfast to avoid the roadblocks—except the one he wanted.

Michael handed Hanley a small metal box that was at-tached to the fiberboard cases by a coil of wire. "Not much of an exploder. One of the old twist types. But it will do fine. The firing key's already in it. You'd better get up front with Brian."

He helped Hanley climb into the passenger seat, care-fully uncoiled the wire and rechecked the exploder lying in the old man's lap.

Hanley's teeth could be heard chattering above all the other sounds. "Those cases are sittin' right over the petrol tank, aren't they?"

"They are, Desmond."

"Oh, my, it's goin' to be a fine thing for me to be warm again."

The light from the unfrosted bulb was so bright and fo-cused down so narrowly by its small shade that Will James could see nothing outside its cone. The dirt floor told him he was in a cellar, but how big it was he could not guess. Every voice came as a fresh surprise to him. He thought there were six men in addition to the three at his back. One of the Murphys held his arm up behind him on the cuff-chain and the other had a hand under the back of his uniform jacket, holding him by the belt. Quinn stood between the Murphys, his fingers lightly squeezing the nape of James's neck, like a kindly teacher directing a favorite pupil's attention to something of un-usual interest.

Voices began from the darkness.

"On with it."

"On with it."

"Right, Commandant."

The old man who had served James his cordial, still wearing his waiter's uniform and bow tie, appeared in the cone of light with another big-boned ancient. Between them they carried an old kitchen table with sturdy legs and a porcelain-coated top. They set it down, and lifted into position the extension leaves that hung from each end, so that it became a gleaming, six-foot-long rectangle of white in the bulb's glare.

Back into the darkness the old men went, and soon they all heard the small-animal whimper that most in the room knew well from other times.

They reappeared, one on each side of the jackknifed boy, carrying him by his ropes as though he were a coal scuttle. They thumped him onto the table on his back with such disdainful force that he almost slid over the far edge.

The boy beat his head against the table and his drawn-up knees. "Jesus, Jesus, Jesus. For Jesus' love, don't do it to me."

"Shut your yawp, McCarthy. You're havin' your trial."

"Shall I belt him quiet, Commandant?"

"No. Just get movin'."

One of the old men opened a drawer in the table and took from it two flat, white packets of cloth, and handed one to the other man. When they shook the packets out, each proved to be a carefully pressed, immaculately white butcher's apron. These they solemnly tied on, protecting their clothing from knees to collar. The waiter carefully tucked his bow tie inside the bib.

The voices came from the dark.

"Who reads the charges?"

"I do, Commandant."

"Let them be read for the judges, Pomeroy."

"Yes, sir. The charge is that this here Philip McCarthy, one of our own, has now gone over to the enemy."

"What will the evidence be?"

"McCarthy came to us back eighteen months, out of Buncrana."

"Over the border, then?"

"Yes, sir. Just a bit into Donegal. But he come out of excellent people, so it seemed. His great-granddad was holdin' the Post Office with Pearse in the sixteen risin'."

"It's not likely the boy had many long, patriotic chats with the great-granddad, is it?"

"No, sir, but the family's been with us every step."

"Surely not all of the family? Surely some of them drifted to that nice Ulster civil service?"

"Say a half-dozen over the years, sir."

"That will finally be the weak place. Go on."

"He did good messenger work, and seemed able to take a hard chance without doin' anythin' reckless. A good man for the delivery squad, we thought."

"First thing they try to sneak onto."

"He did well at first."

"Just bringin' in pick-ups. Not settin'?"

"Yes, sir. Not settin'."

"Well, not settin' never proved a thing, did it? He might've been deliverin' cheese for traps."

"We brought him for a settin', sir. The big store on York Street last June. Took the front wall out proper."

"But don't I remember that they were searchin' around for a gas leak just before it? Had the street and the store well cleared. One of them convenient miracles that keep happenin' in this country."

"We should've been a bit more leery of it, I suppose."

"He knew who the setters were by now?"

"He wasn't supposed to, Commandant. But you know how it is when you've been inside for a while. You get the feel for who's what."

James saw one of the old men slowly reach a hand into the dark and whisper to someone unseen. The hand came back holding a large military revolver. He broke it, checked the load and eased the gun closed. Then he held it behind him, out of sight of the boy on the table.

"What did they start to hit? Your deliveries or your sets?"

"They started pickin' up big shipments. Anythin' over a hundred pounds they'd grab almost as sure as hell."

41

"What's the proof you have on the boy?"

"We gave him the chance to get himself hung and he jumped at it. We got this delivery off an ore carrier from the States, a full two tons of stuff. Plastergel, it was. Biggest load we had in two years. We sent the boy to deliver."

"You went too far with such expensive bait."

"It was an expensive leak, and we figured to get his connections, too. We set it up with Commandant Quinn there."

"Hello, Dominic," the hidden commandant said.

"Hello, Malachey."

"Don't get too attached to your sailor boy, whoever he is. He shouldn't be here. And before we leave, speakin' in a fatal sense, he *won't* be here."

"He'll be where I want him to be, Commandant. Stay in your own division and run your trial."

From the dark, the other commandant's voice stayed even. "What was your set-up with Commandant Quinn, Pomeroy?"

"McCarthy didn't know any of Quinn's boys. You know how close Quinn is with his moves."

"I know that well."

"We had Quinn's boys all around that lorry. In cars ready to set up blocks if they came in on wheels. On foot for a couple miles in the most vulnerable places. Plenty of rapid-fire weapons, including heavy machine guns up in windows on key corners. We could have handled half a regiment."

"And you still lost the lorry?"

"Yes, sir. I think Commandant Quinn can give witness here."

Quinn said, "I don't know it all myself. All I can say is this McCarthy made a sudden turn off the route he gave you boys. Down a loadin' alley. If a bus hadn't blocked him at the other end, just by chance, he'd have been away. He stuck with the lorry too long. We caught him on foot."

"But you lost the load."

42

"Commandant, a big dumper movin' slow came onto the street just then. Twenty-five strong lads with short haircuts all standin' in the bed and makin' a show of their shovels and picks. I couldn't think of a better way to bring up soldiers myself."

"Were they?"

"Caught in a damned alley, we didn't stop to see. We hustled back to the others with the boy and got away in cars. We circled a man to check not ten minutes after, and there was no lorry."

"What does the boy say, Quinn?"

"That he's as innocent as new snow. Even when we gave him some rememberin' help, bendin' his fingers way back and such."

The trussed boy now seemed to waken. His voice was as young and clear as an altar boy's. "A man on a corner stepped into the street and gave me our emergency signal. A cap under the arm. He pointed me into the alley and I turned down it. They grabbed me by the lorry because I didn't try to get away. I was standin' waitin' for what was next."

"Quinn?"

"The signal? A dream."

The commandant called Malachey grunted in the dark. "The men in the dumper, McCarthy? You didn't know them?"

"I never saw them. Our boys were runnin' me back up the alley the minute they had me."

"So a lorry with two tons of plastergel in it is taken by the fairies. Pomeroy, you asked people all along that street, of course."

"A windin' blind street with empty warehouses, sir. No people but what happen past. Couldn't find a one was there."

"Then we know all there is for evidence. Anythin' else?"

"Sir, there was nothin' in the papers, as you know. Usually when they grab off a couple pounds of firecrackers it's all over the papers."

Quinn stepped in. "Two tons of stuff? That's embarrass-in' to have got here in the first place. Tells the people we can get in all we need."

"Maybe, Quinn. All right, McCarthy, stick by your tale. We'll get our verdict now."

There was a scuffling of chairs in the shadows and less than a minute of coarse whispering.

"You're guilty as hell," came the voice of the commandant, Malachey.

"Not death," Quinn said. "You don't have enough on him. And it's been a good family in Buncrana."

"Not death. Kneecap. One kneecap."

An old man taped a pad of gauze over the mouth of the boy.

"Which way?" asked the man with the pistol behind his back.

"Straight on."

Quinn spoke again, more sharply. "No, Commandant. It's too strong."

"Stay in your own division, Dominic."

"If I stayed in my own division, Malachey, you and a lot of your friends back there would be sittin'—or maybe lyin'—in another kind of dark. There you were, last August, ready to jump on that armored payroll wagon with your tear gas. And you the last man in Belfast didn't know it was packed with Sutherlands wearin' gas masks and prayin' for your knock on the door. Were it not for that handsome policeman stoppin' your car for a look at your papers and a word of advice . . ."

"You made a lovely copper, Dominic. We'll take one more vote."

The chairs scuffled on the hard dirt floor again and there were more, harsher whispers.

"All right, Quinn," the other commandant finally said. "Nobody likes it, but we'll do the side job on the knee."

Now the cellar seemed to send up a sweet, acrid odor, the near-ejaculatory rush of apocrine-produced sweat that runs out of men when they are about to punish.

One of the old men opened a clasp knife and cut away

44

the rope that was keeping the boy's legs drawn up, but the stiffened muscles still held them under his chin.

Three red bricks were thrown softly out of the darkness into the dirt. They were picked up, stacked and placed on the table so they were under the boy's left knee when the other old man drew the leg down.

A "side job" gave its executioners more difficulties than a "straight-on." In a straight-on, the purpose would have been to maim permanently, to destroy the knee joint and leave the boy's leg fused as stiff as a rail for the rest of his life. The leg would simply have been held flat against the table and a shot fired directly down into the kneecap, through the joint and out through the bottom of the table. A side job took some precision.

"Will you men clear that wall, please," said one of the old men.

The bullet would now fly out and hit the wall. It would have been possible to roll the boy on his side and still fire straight down while sparing the joint, but experience had shown that the effect on the audience was nowhere near as moving.

As one old man leaned over the boy's head and pressed the hips down against the table, the other held in his left hand the ankle of the leg to be punished, stretching the limb taut over the stacked bricks. With his right hand, without putting down his pistol, he split the boy's corduroy trousers across the knee. He then cocked the Webley, placed the muzzle broadside to the kneecap, angling slightly upward, and fired.

Urine shot into Will James's trousers at the splitting crack that was half detonating gunpowder and half the shattering of bone. A jet of red and white blew into the air over the boy, and its haze seemed to settle with unnatural slowness in the cone of light. James observed the last of the blood spray the once-white butcher's aprons. Averting his eyes, he saw a piece of bone lying on his highly polished shoe.

The last thing he knew before he fainted was that he was going to do anything that these men asked him to.

It was one of the big, permanent roadblocks. It had not only the barbed wire and welded anti-vehicle tripods, but also sand-filled drums, a scissoring strip of tire-rippers across the front and a mounted heavy machine gun looking through a sandbag embrasure.

Stopping the truck a foot in front of the rippers, Brian counted eight men behind the barricade, seven of them armed with Patchett guns.

A lieutenant in the Sutherlands came forward, carrying a boxy portable searchlight that he kept beamed on the windshield of the truck through the blowing rain. He carried no visible weapon, relying on the corporal behind him who was carrying a Patchett at ready. "Who the hell are you? How the hell did you get this far? There's a half-dozen other blocks behind you."

Brian leaned out the window, shaking his head. "I'm so damned lost with not bein' able to see the signs, I could be in hell for all I know."

"Drive one inch further and you *will* be in hell. You're in one of the most restricted areas in Belfast."

"Shit, Lieutenant, I'm sorry about that."

"Corporal, take careful aim at that man's head. If he does anything too quickly, kill him and the man next to him."

"Shit, I said I'm sorry."

"Driver, I'm going to find out why a man who doesn't know the streets well enough to get through them without signs is driving a truck in the middle of the night."

"Middle of—Hell, it's not eight o'clock yet. Hey, where am I?"

The corporal walked slowly forward until the thick muzzle of the Patchett was just a yard from Brian's face.

"You're at the South End Detention Building."

Brian broke into his widest smile. "Well, then, we've found the place. You hear that, Desmond? We're there, after all."

The lieutenant stepped up alongside the corporal. "We've had our list of callers for the night, and none of those two hundred bad boys in there is expecting anybody."

"Bad boys, my ass," Hanley wheezed. "Try givin' 'em a decent trial."

Cautiously, under his poncho, the lieutenant fumbled an automatic out of its holster. "All right. Down out of there at once. Both of you. No, stick your hands out of the windows. Open the doors from outside."

Brian opened his door and stepped to the pavement. "My friend with the big mouth is sick. He'll need some help."

The corporal motioned Brian aside so that the lieutenant could lean into the truck and fix his searchlight on Desmond Hanley.

The withered hands held up the wired exploder, thumb and forefinger cocked on the firing key. "I suppose you've seen one of these before?"

The lieutenant's light flicked along the wire. The beam found Michael crouching behind Hanley in the body of the truck. Michael pointed to where the end of the wire disappeared into one of the eight fifty-pound cases. To give the officer a better look, he tilted a case forward and gingerly patted the bags inside. "Gelignite." He threw one of the five-pound bags onto the driver's seat. "Check it to be sure." When the lieutenant did not move, he said, "If you dropped what it was you was holdin' under the poncho, you'd have your hands free." The pistol clattered down onto the cobbles.

"Is it okay, sir?"

"Yes, Corporal. Stay right there." He picked up the bag, examined it closely in the light and sniffed it. "Yes. Gelignite." He threw the bag back to Michael. "You look awfully young to be killing yourself."

"He ain't holdin' the exploder," Hanley said. "I am. Now get Brian in out of the rain."

A flashing yellow light, urgent but no emergency, summoned wrinkled old Sergeant Brewster from his pile of magazines in the second-floor guardroom. Bloody Lieutenant Samuels, he thought. When they left him in charge of the camp he fancied he was Monty of Alamein. He let himself into the first-floor guardroom and saluted.

The lieutenant, shivering, his uniform soaked, stood dripping at the desk. Corporal Collins and a civilian stood near the door.

"You're wet, sir. Let me—"

"It's all right, Brewster. I loaned my poncho to Mr. Taylor here. Mr. Taylor is from the government. We must do something for him. Very quietly, very, very quickly."

"As you say, sir."

"I want the following six men brought to this room dressed for traveling. I want it done in fifteen minutes." He pushed a blank pad and a pencil at Brewster.

The civilian spoke the names from memory: "Molaise Mullins . . . Patrick Costello . . . Roland O'Driscoll, Junior . . . Eamon O'Driscoll . . . George Barton . . . John Devlin."

"What sort of guard, sir? And what restraints?"

"We'll take a guard from the roadblock," the civilian said. "For restraint? Cuffs with a waist chain will do." Michael had the little Uzi under his poncho on the sergeant's middle.

Brewster reached for the phone. "I'll put some men on it, sir."

Samuels took the receiver from his hand. "Do it alone."

"Alone, sir? They're a mean bunch. Well, here, Corporal. Lend me your squirter." He grabbed up the corporal's Patchett. "Now a helluva lot of good this thing does you without a clip in it, Collins. We're all terrible sorry you have to carry that extra weight all night, but these are hard times." He unlocked a metal cabinet, took out a thirty-round clip and slammed it into the breech. Slinging the gun across his back, he unlocked a second cabinet and produced a tangle of cuffs and chains. Brewster felt better about everything now. To a jailer, the clank and heft of all tools of submission are heartening. In another moment he was out the door, his nailed boots ringing, his chains jangling up the steel stairway to the second floor.

"Corporal," Michael said, "go to the motor pool and bring us two automobiles with as much military shit painted on them as possible. And remember I can see you all across the yard in that nice big floodlight."

Desmond Hanley watched the cars being moved across the yard. The metronome tick of the windshield wipers made him ache for sleep. He looked at the eight soldiers standing in a tight clump in front of the headlights. All of them had their clipless, impotent weapons gripped tightly in both hands, as though they might squeeze out of them some of their former power and reassurance.

Most of the faces were incredibly young. Hanley had grandchildren older than some. He saw the fright, the look that always wrung a smile or a toy out of you. My God, he thought in his fever, maybe they're not the British soldiers at all, but their children. He reached under the raincoat and felt the breast pocket of his pajamas. "Brian, I left my beads at the hospital. Have you got a set?"

Brian, in the driver's seat, brought the hand that was not holding the Uzi out of his pocket. Rosary beads were twined through the fingers. "I couldn't, Desmond. These were my mother's and grandmother's."

"That's right, you can't be givin' those away. You'll be givin' em to kids of your own, God hopin'."

Brian stuck his head out the window and called to the soldiers huddled in the headlights. "Who there is a Catholic?" A hand went up. "You got your beads, boy?" A head nodded.

"You can't, Brian. You can't take 'em now."

"Desmond, he probably took 'em off some poor sod he shot for chasin' a hat in the wind."

A white face with the pathetic straggle of a first moustache appeared at the window in Brian's searchlight.

"Hand them beads here, boy. My friend wants to thank Mary for bringin' us all through this without loss of life."

49

The private handed him the beads in a leather case and tried to smile. "You wouldn't really set that shit off, sir, would you?"

"Not if you stay as sweet as you are." Brian handed the beads to Hanley.

The old man read the boy's name on the case. *Paul Heenan.* "You kin to Red Paul Heenan in Ballymena?"

"A granduncle, sir. I'm named for him. Never saw him until six months ago when I come over from Scotland."

"Well, I'll be . . . We was in the sappers together in the first war. Remember to say—"

"We're thankin' you for the beads. Now back in the bunch," Brian said. They watched him walk away. "Nice boy, Desmond. Red Paul is goin' to miss him."

Molaise Mullins, known to all as The Dropper, woke to the sound of chains being thrown into his cell. Brewster stood silhouetted against the dim light coming through the open door, holding a submachine gun. "Get 'em on, Mullins."

The Dropper rose naked and went for the chains.

"Hold it," Brewster said. He turned an electric torch on The Dropper. "Hands up over your head and do a slow full turn."

"I ain't in the mood for one of your midnight romances, Brewster." The Dropper knew that the jailer, who was married and also had a girl friend, often invited sex from prisoners.

In fact, The Dropper was not Brewster's type. Young enough and well-made, but too hard and stringy-muscled; red-headed as well. Brewster merely hated the uppity Irishman, and sexual humiliation always served that cause well.

The Dropper finished his turn. "See. No bombs but the two under my gut."

"Maybe. Turn your back to me and bend over with your hands on your knees."

"Brewster, if you try—"

"You've had body searches before." The sergeant thrust a finger into The Dropper.

"You better be careful about pickin' your nose after this, Brewster."

"Shut your yawp."

"You goin' to stay in there for the night? Then order some wine."

"Mullins, if you can spare me a minute, no more than a minute——"

"If you do not back that finger out in one second, I'm goin' to blow somethin' into your hand."

Brewster gave the finger a painful twist and pulled it out. He wiped his hand on The Dropper's hanging clothes and tossed them to him. "Get 'em on fast. Then the waist chain, then the cuffs."

A terrible look passed between them, the look of men who know that they will shortly be in separate worlds. For they both believed that Molaise Mullins was on his way to a bullet in the neck and a hot bath in quicklime.

When he had dressed, chained and cuffed himself, The Dropper was prodded along the cellblock to the solid steel door of the floor's main receiving cell.

Brewster turned the lock, stepped back and leveled the Patchett. An eye looked out of the door's slid-back peephole-cover. "You inside. Open it very slow and walk out here the same way. Stand off to the side there, Mullins."

The door opened, and out of the black receiving cell filed five roughly dressed men, each chained in the same way as The Dropper. They blinked in the strong ceiling lights.

"Hey. The old Dropper's comin' to hell with us."

"Then I ain't goin'."

"Unless you get word there's a full glass and a cunt down there, Father Costello."

"Or even half a glass and a young boy."

Brewster cut off the beginnings of a laugh by thrusting The Dropper into the midst of the men with a knee kick in the small of the back. "You all know the way down to the guardroom. Start moving."

At the end of the line The Dropper's quick mind focused on what was happening. Why *these* men? He had thought that there might be others: maybe Loughlin, Greenwood, the leaders. But these were nobodies. With the exception of Punchy Devlin and himself, none, so far as he knew, had ever killed a man. Something in common? He let his mind dwell on the names of the men.

Punchy Devlin? No real commitment to anything. Born without a hair on his head or body, his viciousness was merely that of the physically hideous. A sailor when he wasn't doing the Army's work.

The O'Driscolls were nothing more than village fishermen who had come to Belfast and moved up to sailing on bigger ships. Roland had the real stuff in him, but Eamon thought it was all just another game his big brother had dreamed up.

Father Costello had stopped being a bad priest twenty years ago, and instead had become a good sailor and deliverer of explosives. He would try anything, although he had never been on a big operation. Another sailor? Was that the tie-in? Sailors?

George Barton, the last of the other five, was a seaman, too. The tankers he'd been on had brought half the guns in the city from the Middle East.

Only he, The Dropper, had not been to sea. What was his part? Maybe none. The British had plenty of reason to shoot the best explosives man in the Army. But the sailors?

Entering the first-floor guardroom, they saw the lieutenant sitting stiffly behind the desk. The corporal was standing so closely in front of someone sitting in the corner that only the edges of the man's poncho could be seen.

Brewster saluted. "They're ready, sir."

Standing up, the lieutenant came around the desk. "Give me your gun, Brewster." He took the Patchett. "And you can unlock all of them."

52

Slowly the sergeant drew out a key ring. He started for the arms cabinet. "I'll check out another weapon for Collins, sir."

"Just unlock them, damn it."

"As you say, sir."

A look flew between the chained Irishmen. In the lieutenant's voice they had all heard the same thing. He was not in command here. Brewster had heard it, too. The Dropper felt the sergeant's hand tremble as the cuffs were unlocked.

Held only by its pistol grip, the lieutenant's gun pointed to the floor. The Dropper saw that he could take a fast step and tear the Patchett out of the man's hand. The side arm was gone from his holster, too. Collins? The corporal stood with his hands behind him. Was there a gun in his hand? Or in the hand of the man he was purposely hiding?

The Dropper slid his foot a quarter step nearer the officer as his elbow nudged Punchy Devlin toward the men in the corner.

A good jailer, Brewster sensed their intent. Removing the final chain, he wrapped it in his hand as a flail and lashed it in a short, savage rip against the side of The Dropper's head.

His ear split open and running blood, The Dropper lurched against Devlin and spoiled the bald man's spring at the corporal.

"Got to watch these Irish snakes, sir."

Michael braced the back of his chair against the corner, placed his foot against Collins's back and sent the corporal sprawling onto the floor.

"Very good, Brewster. I'm sure you're going to get some sort of a decoration for that one." As Michael said it, he lifted the poncho from in front of the Uzi so Brewster could see it."

"Michael Hare. Jesus Christ, boys. It's Michael Hare."

"Michael."

"Oh, God bless you, Michael," with a sob.

Michael had breathed a magic draft on the weak spark

53

of their lives, and it roared up in the room like a terrible bonfire.

Before the corporal could rise from the floor, the men nearest him were making his head fly with grunting kicks. Devlin kicked the lieutenant's gun so hard that it flew against the ceiling. Picking a metal water carafe off the desk, he slammed it wildly into the retreating officer until the handle broke off and the container sailed away. The Dropper tore the chain out of Brewster's hand, wound it around the sergeant's neck and pulled it tight. The hands of Barton and Costello joined his in the pulling and twisting. Murder was still the first opiate of the oppressed.

Michael barreled into their midst as if he were in a Rugby scrimmage. "Get the hell off 'em, damn it." Most of the men were so weakened by the months in cramped confinement that he was able to throw them aside like children. "We've got a lorryful of blasting gel out there and soldiers all around it. If we don't show 'em these men alive, they'll know that they might as well rush it. We'd never get out of here."

The Dropper was so weakened by both passion and exertion that he could hardly wind the chain off Brewster's neck. "Just the one thing more, Michael."

Half dead, the sergeant had fallen, coughing and wheezing. With a letter opener grabbed from the desk, The Dropper ripped the seat of the man's trousers. "No underwear. Wouldn't you know it about this sonofabitch."

A thick rubber truncheon hung by a leather thong at one side of the kneehole of the desk. The Dropper lifted it out and spat on the end of it. "Brewster, this is the first time since I've been in here that I wished you boys used bigger billies." He worked the club up the writhing, choking sergeant.

Devlin laughed like a banshee. As quickly as drunks, the men turned playful.

"Now be careful, Drop, you'll be givin' the poor fellow the piles."

Crouching down beside Brewster, Eamon O'Driscoll

gave him a loud kiss on the cheek. "Is it makin' you feel like marriage, darlin'?"

"Lucky it ain't mine, Brewster, 'cause it's a lot longer and harder than that."

They howled and thumped each other on the back.

Growling with impatience, Michael pulled The Dropper away. "We've got cars right outside the door. I want everybody to tuck their hands up under their belly like they were chained. Our English friends here are goin' to push you along in case we got anybody lookin' out of a window somewhere."

"Well, Brewster, I can't be leavin' my dick behind." With that, The Dropper jerked the truncheon out of the groaning sergeant and pulled him to his feet by the collar.

Roughly, Michael shoved his men into a line, with the lieutenant and Collins at the head and Brewster and himself at the rear. Devlin held a Patchett tight against his body.

"Okay. The lieutenant and the corporal in the nearest car with Devlin, Barton and Costello. The rest of us in the other. Get walkin'."

They marched into sheets of rain to find the two cars standing with lights on, doors open and motors running.

"We'll be stoppin' at the front roadblock to pick up Brian and let out the Englishmen."

"And then where to, Michael?"

"A little stop in town to pick up a lorry we'll be needin', then down to Coltry Bay. The wheels will never touch the ground. It's part of a job. You'll be there in time for a good briefin', Dropper."

"We ain't in any shape for a job."

"You'll like this one. Lots of noise, I hear. Your kind."

The cars filled, closed and rolled slowly across the yard to the roadblock. Brian was there to lift a striped barrier so they could pass through. Michael drove past the soldiers standing motionless in the headlights' glare, stopped opposite the cab of the lorry and got out, dragging Brewster with him. Lieutenant Samuels and Corporal Collins came up quickly, pushed from behind by The Dropper.

"All right," Brian said, "you will tell your men to stand just as still as they are for twenty minutes. That's until eight o'clock. Remind everybody who wants to stay in one piece what's in that lorry. If someone comes up to see what's goin' on, let them in on your little secret and invite them to join you."

"And we'll not be hurt?"

"I've known that old man who we're leavin' in the lorry for most of my life. Anything that happens to you happens to him."

That seemed to brace the lieutenant. "Collins, Brewster, we'll wait with the men. It's all we can do." The officer and the corporal helped the collapsing Brewster walk to the group of soldiers.

Through waves of fever, Desmond Hanley saw Michael's dripping face at the window of the lorry, then felt the strong young hand on the bone of his own withered arm.

"Desmond, they'll be namin' kids after you. You've been part of the great blow that'll put England on her knees and get 'em out of Ireland after three hundred years. Think of it."

Hanley's hand was seized and shaken. Then he was left, as old men usually are, to die alone.

"Oh, Desmond, how did it all happen to you? Mary, Mary, Mary." Tearfully he kissed Paul Heenan's beads, praying as quickly as he could.

The car doors slammed, gears ground and the living left the dead with the usual speed.

The hard seat of the truck had become intolerable to Hanley's shrunken buttocks. Grasping the steering wheel, he heaved up his weight to ease the ache. Then something was sliding from his lap; there was a thump on the floorboards. The exploder. When he bent to look for it, the blackness below ran together with the blackness rising inside his head. He sagged sideways onto the seat opposite, saving himself from going flat only by a desperate downward dig of his elbow.

Sit tall in the seat, he told himself. Keep your head above the dark; it's coming up fast.

If he could just see. There would be a dome light. He fumbled at the tangle of knobs on the dash. The headlights went out. The knob he turned to put them on again stopped the windshield wipers.

The sweat running into his eyes stung, blinding him. Grinding the heels of his palms into the sockets only blurred his vision more. The clear, individual faces of the soldiers he had been able to watch in the headlights between sweeps of the wiper had now melted together into a dark distorting lump.

When the headlights went out, young Paul Heenan, standing close to the front bumper of the truck, was able to make out the man in the cab. The floodlight in the yard spilled in just enough for the soldier to sense the old man's agony. Heenan nudged Lieutenant Samuels. "Sir, the old crock is in some kind of trouble. Let me go have a look at him."

"We can't frighten him. They've got what they wanted. I think he'll surrender when the time is up."

"I don't know, sir. He was so hot to borrow my beads. I don't like it."

"You talked to him?"

"Yes, sir. He's every day of seventy-five and sick, I think. Pajamas on under his coat."

"It will make a difference if he knows you, I suppose. Move very slowly. If you see anything like panic, get back here."

Hanley got the headlights back on, and then the wipers. By the feeble light of the dash he tried to read the dial of the watch Brian had strapped to his wrist, but the numbers would not hold still.

Shit, a soldier was moving. Paul Heenan, his hands raised to his shoulders, was shuffling cautiously to Hanley's side of the cab. Get back there, you limey bastard, or— Or *what? Or I'll cough on you? That goddamned ex-*

ploder. Reaching back toward the boxes of gel, he found the wire. His fingers followed it back to where it dropped down to the floor. *Mustn't pull too hard, or I'll jerk the wires right off the terminals.* He felt the weight of the exploder dragging along the floorboards.

Heenan was at the window now. Something under the seat caught the exploder and held it.

"Sir, it's me. I want to speak to you a minute."

"It'll be the last of your minutes, Heenan, if you don't go back in that bunch right now." He moved the wire gently about, tugging from different angles like a fisherman trying to free a fouled hook.

Heenan moved closer. "I can see you're a sick man. You do things when you're sick that you wouldn't if you were thinkin' clear."

"Son, this exploder in my lap will do all the thinkin' for me. Get the hell away from here." Hanley felt the exploder come free, pulled it rapidly into his lap and took the firing key between thumb and forefinger again.

"Sir, Lieutenant Samuels promises that he'll wait the twenty minutes. Let me help you out of there in the meantime. It's warm in the infirmary. They'll have some whiskey." Heenan put his foot on the running board. A bony fist jerked out of the window and drove weakly against the soldier's forehead. "Aw, there's no need to be doin' that, sir." The fist did not withdraw into the cab, but struck out again, with the private dodging its slow-motion advance. Was this the beginning of the panic that the lieutenant had warned him against? Another feeble swipe of the fist. A paragraph of his Army explosives training manual nudged at Heenan's mind. Some exploders had a safety button that had to be depressed with the other hand before the firing key could be turned. Was this one of them?

The hand started to go back through the window. With a wild lunge, Heenan caught it by the wrist. Leaping onto the running board, he drew the arm straight out and twisted it. His other hand went into Hanley's lap after the exploder. The ancient face was tight against his, convulsing with pain. Their sweat ran together.

Heenan found the clawed hand on the exploder; the fingers fought to turn under his desperately restraining grip. Slick now with the rain on his palm, the wrinkled skin began to slip under his fingers. The soldier felt his rosary beads still twined around Hanley's knuckles, turning, turning. Was there a safety button? Paul Heenan looked sidelong into the wide, dimming eyes of Desmond Hanley and knew that there wasn't.

Both of the hands on the exploder closed imploringly on the beads. The last thing printed on the flying atoms of the men's minds was the searing white flash they had last seen at the moment they were born.

The shock wave of the blast struck the heavily loaded automobile so hard that Michael felt the steering wheel jerk in his hands. Before the blaze in the sky had faded, store windows folded in and vomited canned goods and draperies onto the sidewalk.

Michael pounded the rim of the wheel. "Too soon. Too bloody soon."

"They might have rushed him," The Dropper said.

"If he'd held that exploder where they could see it, he could have held them for a week."

The men in the back seat were turned around, looking through the rear window.

"Look at that fire against the sky. It must have flattened the whole place."

"And will you listen to the sirens? We're goin' to have plenty of company, Michael."

"We should have been through all the main trouble before the blowup. It's goin' to be a near thing now."

"Michael, we'll never make it in this thing anymore. Stop here and we'll each go our way."

"You're full of shit if you think we lost Brucie and Hanley to give you boys a vacation. You're goin' to be in Coltry Bay in under five hours. If you don't like it, there's the back of my head. Do somethin' about it."

"Better slow up, Michael. You almost lost Brian on that last turn."

"Can't. I figure we've got just a minute or two before they have us blocked off from where we've got to go."

"We're more than a minute or two from Coltry."

"There'll be a stop before that, Dropper."

The car took a tire-screaming curve so fast that the wheels bounced over the opposite sidewalk. They could hear Brian's car taking the same turn behind them. Now they were speeding down a street of warehouses that dead-ended against the River Lagan. At the last building, Michael stood on the brakes. Behind, Brian's skidding car almost destroyed Michael's.

"Barton, jump out and get that door lifted."

The big overhead door had been barely rasied before both vehicles were inside.

The men found themselves in a black cavern with gray blots of light from windows high in the rear wall. They heard Michael let himself out of the car, and in a moment a series of dim and dusty bulbs strung along a low overhead wire came on.

Just in front of the automobile stood a very large truck. Chained to its rear bumper sat a big, sick-looking dog.

Michael motioned them all out of the cars and over to the back of the truck. He let down the tailgate and switched on two strong dome lights that thoroughly illuminated everything in the body.

The Dropper whooped with delight. "Plastergel. It must be all the goddamned plastergel in the world. I could drop the Houses of Parliament, Westminster Abbey and the Marble Arch, and still have plenty left for Buckingham Palace. Tell me, Michael, who'd we steal this lovely stuff from?"

"From the IRA."

"What's your meanin'? That's ourselves."

"The load came in by freighter from the Middle East, a whole container of it brought with a contribution from Boston. They took it away in small boats off Rathlin Island and landed it at Ballycastle Bay."

"Who picked it up?"

"Malachey Coyle's division. He's sailin' high in the Army now; he asks for the big shipments and he gets them."

"And, I take it, your Commandant Quinn doesn't like it."

"Dominic doesn't mind that as a rule. He's not much of a blaster himself."

"If you'll forgive me for sayin' so about your friend, Dominic Quinn is not much for anythin' except runnin' a whorehouse down in the South. Very long on the philosophy and very short on the boom-boom. Nobody even thinks he's worth arrestin'. Maybe he should stick to his pamphlet-writin' and leave Malachey to the plastergel."

Barton nodded. "I won't fool you, Michael. I don't like this business of the Army stealin' from the Army. If we don't stand together, we're less than nothin'."

Michael's cold voice went high and hard. "Now listen close, you sons-of-bitches. While Commandant Coyle's been so busy shootin' up pubs, children and chicken coops, Dominic Quinn's come up with somethin' that's goin' to put us all on marble monuments."

"Or under 'em, more likely. I don't like his kind of dreamer."

"What's this big hit?" The Dropper asked.

Even in the bad light they could see Michael redden. "I don't know that."

"Then what the hell are you tellin'—"

"If Dominic wanted everybody in the six counties yappin' about it, he'd have asked Coyle for the gel nice and proper instead of liftin' his lorry."

"I don't see why the hell we should do this, boys," The Dropper said.

A knuckled commando knife appeared in Michael's hand, its tip wavering under The Dropper's chin. "You should do it because Dominic just now gave you back twenty years of your life, you little bastard."

"I need a better reason."

"There's the reason." Michael pointed into the truck.

"Tons of plastergel. And it's all goin' to go off in one load. I don't know what it's goin' to go off in, on, or under, but I know it's all goin' off at once. So you know it's nothin' small that we're about."

Michael had read his men well. Molaise Mullins was one of those born destroyers, without whom war would present little artistry. His life had been nothing more than an incredible history of vandalism, arson and mayhem. The happiest three years of his life had been spent as a quarryman in the South, where he had fallen in love with the lore, literature and virtuoso application of high explosives. In certain quarries, men still spoke of the mighty facings he had brought down with his cunningly placed charges, and of how the tears of delight streamed on his cheeks as the rock, which had stood fast for ten million years, broke, screamed and tumbled under his shattering hand. His dreams were of Number-8 detonator caps, and of venerated bridges of the world spewing their foundations and settling in a single intact piece into the rivers they spanned.

The Dropper licked his thin lips. "It would be shameful not to be in on a noise like that one." He looked around for nods, and finally got them. Offer a man a grand enough chance to destroy, and he'll follow you anywhere.

Outside the warehouse they could hear the sirens howling as police, troops and firemen mobilized.

Eamon O'Driscoll was sitting with the dog, patting his head and rubbing its flanks. "They'll be stoppin' everythin' on wheels. We won't get this lorry out of here for a month."

Michael climbed into the bed of the truck and pushed a large medical-supply box bearing British Army markings to the edge of the lowered tailgate. "Dig all the bandages and adhesive tape out of here. Wrap each other up like you'd all been just blown up. Cut off some pants' legs. Some of you get down to your skin. Here's some splints. Use 'em. Make up some slings, too. We're goin' to make this look good."

While the men began to rip, bandage and tape, Michael

jumped off the truck. "Take the dog over there by that tool rack, will you, Eamon."

The dog came willingly with O'Driscoll, who scratched it approvingly behind the ears. "You know, Michael, this is an expensive dog. I'll bet if I took him to the vet and got him some shots and got him combed and fed, he'd be a beauty. My father could keep him for me."

Michael sat a bucket down alongside the tool rack and with his commando knife cut a length of electrical wire from a spool on one of the shelves. "Never get too attached to a dog or a woman." Kneeling, he swiftly tied the dog's hind legs together with the end of the wire.

"What the hell are you doin', Michael?"

"Lift him up in your arms."

Placing his arms gently beneath the stumbling animal's body, O'Driscoll picked it up, cradling it like an overgrown baby.

Now Michael tied the other end of the wire to a brace on a high shelf of the tool rack. Then stepping behind O'Driscoll, he grabbed him by the collar and jerked him sharply backwards. Pulled out of the cradling arms, the dog fell; it flopped and yowled, hanging upside down from the rack. With his toe, Michael moved the bucket beneath the dog's muzzle, briskly drew the shaggy head down with a grip beneath the jaw and used the knife to open an artery in the throat. The animal's blood rang on the galvanized metal as Michael directed it into the bucket.

"You awful sonofabitch," O'Driscoll screamed. Brian bear-hugged and smothered his lunge at Michael.

Without looking up from his work, Michael shook his head. "Hardly a couple of hours ago that same knife did the same thing to a good-lookin' young soldier at the hospital. Can you tell me why nobody called me a sonofabitch then?" His head motioned to a pile of paper cups on a workbench. "Everybody take one of those cups."

More shaken by what they had just watched than by anything else during the terrible evening, the men, like schoolboys under the hard eye of a commanding nun, quietly lined up to take their cups. "When you've got yourselves bandaged, have another man pour a cup of that blood where the wounds are supposed to be. Don't be stingy. The more awful you look, the less likely they are to be pokin' through and holdin' us up. Take an extra cup or two in the lorry with you. When we get stopped, pour it over your head or down your chest so they can see it run and truly believe you're bleedin' to death."

They waited until they were in the lorry and ready to roll before they poured the first blood. It was already cool and thickening; each man felt the thinness of the shell that separated his own warm blood from this spilling liquid. A blackness settled on their spirit.

Sprawling with the others in the back of the lorry as it started to roll, Father Costello looked bleakly at the scarlet apparitions around him. "Christ's eyes. Is this what we do to people?"

Captain Umfrax and Lieutenant Barstowe watched the taillights of the lorry disappear down the road.

"Poor buggers. There'll be a lot of arms and legs off in that lot, if they live at all," Umfrax said.

Barstowe signaled the armored personnel carrier back into its position blocking the street. "Captain, I don't think we should have let them through at all. Reports are that the bomb was in the South Detention. The wounded would be soldiers—which that lot weren't—or prisoners."

"We've had other reports. One that the bomb was in a pub, two that it was in a church, and another that it was in a bus station."

"They do that for the confusion."

"Barstowe, for all I know you were right. You can't know anything for certain in this city anymore. They may use that pass we gave them to run a bomb under every Army post for twenty miles. On the other hand, half of them might have died while we were keeping them away from a casualty center."

"Still, we can't be making snap judgments on sentimental feelings, sir."

Captain Umfrax smiled a little at Lieutenant Barstowe.

"And why not? What else do we have to tell us we're still human? Barstowe, when I looked in the back of that lorry and saw that poor, broken bugger with the tears rolling down his face, clutching his dead dog in his arms . . ."

It speaks well of the race that compassion still remains a fearsome weapon.

chapter 3

Zamke was deep in his homework. His cap set far back on his head, he switched the table-top viewer from projection to projection, scribbling notes rapidly in a leather-bound notebook. "How many men are aboard, sir?" he asked Cullenbine.

"About six hundred and sixty. But we rotate 'em ashore for two weeks after a month, which means three hundred and thirty replacements. So you've got security to run on over nine hundred men."

Lustgarten interrupted. "Are there good surveillance points, Mr. Cullenbine?"

"Surveillance? Just about impossible. There are hundreds of men working, and not a place on the rig where you can see more than twenty of 'em at the same time. With six hundred feet to a side, the main deck covers hundreds of thousands of square feet, and it would be hard to keep an eye on even if it was empty. But look." Cullenbine flashed an isometric view of the platform's upper structures onto the table viewer. "The deck module alone goes up as high as the observation tower. We're two hundred feet above the main deck and two hundred and sixty above the sea."

"I see equipment up above us."

"That's our radar and radio. Those things that look like masts at the deck's three corners are the booms of cranes. We keep 'em vertical when they're not in use."

"I can't imagine a crane that big."

"Imagine three of 'em. Among the biggest ever made, and one on every corner so we can use two on the same lift. That way we can raise whole lighters out of the water and bring 'em up on deck."

"Give you a fine opportunity for sabotage. You have not overlooked that?"

"Only I and the foremen are trained to operate those cranes. But the truth is they've made it so damned simple that anybody who can operate an erector set could figure out how to work them in five minutes—at least enough to make one let go of whatever it was carrying."

Zamke was studying the isometric diagram. "Above this tower is the radar room?"

"Right. That's our first line of defense. Anything approaching to do us harm, accidentally or on purpose, we'll see; we can warn him off or have him taken care of."

"The radio room is part of the radar level?"

"No, radio is in the level just under it, which is also the helicopter landing pad. That's a big convenience because so much of our radio traffic has to do with dispatching helicopters. From the pad on down there's all the stuff you'd expect to find in a helluva big onshore oil field, except it's piled up instead of spread out. And of course there has to be a lot of room to house, feed and entertain the crew. The crew quarters are an the first two levels. Four-man rooms, mess hall, game room, movie theater, library, even a shopping center.

"No exposed part of the platform except the copter pad is flat for more than a hundred feet. The module is seventeen levels high right here, but at other points on the platform it may be only five or eight levels. If that doesn't make things hard enough to watch, we've got a thousand tons of drill pipe, casing, valves, blowout preventers, acidizing systems and you name it stacked everywhere. Perfect to hide behind. Then there are the men working down inside the legs, where they could do the most damage. With thirty wells operating in a space only a hundred feet across, it's impossible to keep track of everyone."

"Don't look so discouraged, Zamke," Lustgarten said with what might have been a grin. "We wouldn't be here if there was nothing we could do."

"I fail to see what we *can* do, sir."

"Plotters always have a weakness: their love of plotting. The bigger the plot, the more people in on it, the more they commit to paper, the more they commit to the airwaves, to codes, to couriers. And the more time they take. Finally one thread catches somewhere, and then we take hold of that loose end and unravel their fine scheme before it's ready to happen."

"Suppose," said Zamke, "that your plotters understood that as well as you do, Colonel?"

"We policemen have only one advantage over the criminal system: We are a continuity. We die, but our files live on. Even a very talented criminal has a career of only twenty years or so, and he writes no books and keeps no records. The next criminal does well to equal the skills and knowledge of the one before him. But *we,* in effect, have been watching the same man for two hundred years. Given the faintest hint—and we know where to look for them—we can tell you what he's going to do before he knows it himself. We have *method,* Zamke. And method—system—can overcome any individual spurt of brilliance."

Dominic Quinn had covered an oak-paneled wall with enlarged photostats of exactly the same diagrams being studied at that moment by the command crew of Mavis A. He had made elaborate plans to extract them from the files of the British National Oil Corporation, but providentially a popular magazine had printed them in full as part of a fifteen-page article on the remarkable platform.

Also on the wall was a large blowup of the S.S. *American Enterprise* under full steam.

Quinn had staged the scene beautifully. There were no bare rooms with lanterns and packing-crate tables for this meeting. The men before him were being made to understand that this wasn't one more plan to shoot up a police station in Strabane. They sat in deep leather armchairs, warmed by the heat and bathed by the light of a crackling hardwood fire. There was fine brandy in their glasses. Each was a Monty or an Ike planning to move a hundred divisions across the English Channel. The paneling, paintings and thick carpets of Quinn's grand room on the top floor of the brothel told them so. Merely being shown what it is like at the top is a motivator of great deeds.

The first half hour of Quinn's talk set the men totally at ease. An Irishman loves a nice story nicely told, and he had given them that. Relaxing in the warm, clean clothing that had replaced their decoy bandages and prison rags, they had been struck by the epidemic of nodding agreement that can sweep through men like cholera. Looking out over the room flickering with pleasant firelight and filled with the melody of his voice, Quinn could see the heads making a never-ending ripple, as one might observe a row of those dolls whose necks are on loose springs that are set moving by the slightest breeze.

Quinn had removed the shade of a floor lamp to throw more light on the diagrams. "The code name of this operation, my friends, is 'North Sea Gunman.' It will begin in less than one hour, will be completed in a little over thirty hours, and will end forever the power of Great Britain." There was no reason for any of them to ever use the code name, but Quinn knew the men would enjoy the ring of it. He rather liked it himself. "I have told you in detail about the importance of Mavis A. to the United Kingdom; I'm sure you already sense that it is our target." The "our" seemed to slide down easily. "Here is a look at the entire operation."

He taped a map that included the North Sea, the British Isles and parts of the Northern European continent to the wall beside the diagrams on Mavis A. The picture of the *American Enterprise* sat just under the map. With a red felt-tip pen, Quinn began to make markings. "Mavis A. sits here in the North Sea at this circled X. It is one hundred and fifty-five miles off the coast of Scotland and about one hundred and eighty miles from the Norwegian coast." He tapped the picture of the tanker with the end of the pen. "Those of you who are seamen will recognize this gigantic vessel. She's the *American Enterprise,* the largest oil tanker ever built. She sits a half-mile from this room, right out there in Coltry Bay. Except for a few hundred thousand barrels that she pumped out at Rotterdam, she's brimmin' with Arabian crude oil—almost three million barrels. She's due to begin pumpin' a million barrels ashore here when the storm lessens, then is supposed to sail for Halifax, Nova Scotia. We mean to see to it that neither of those two things happen.

"Almost all of the ship's officers are in bed below us without their clothes on, enjoyin' the hospitality of this poor inn. We will take them in just a few minutes, and through them we will take their vessel. You men were picked for this work because most of you were tanker sailors. You'll be able to supervise the officers who will be operatin' the *Enterprise* without havin' them pull anythin' tricky."

"I knew it," The Dropper cackled. "I knew you was after the sailors."

"Yes, Dropper. Except for you. You're with us for your fine touch with high explosives."

"They sail 'em, I sink 'em, eh?"

"Yes, but there's a bit more involved than that." Quinn began to extend a red line from Coltry Bay. "Under cover of this storm—the like of which we've waited on for a good three months—we sail not west, but north." The red line moved up the west coast of Ireland, crossed the fifty-eighth latitude and swung around the top of Scotland into the North Sea. "We'll sail wide of the Hebrides and the Orkneys. At an average speed of seventeen knots, we'll cover seven hundred miles in between thirty and thirty-

71

five hours. That means we'll reach Mavis A. sometime around dawn on the day after tomorrow."

"How will we get aboard it in this muck, Dominic?" Eamon O'Driscoll asked.

"We don't get aboard it. You don't think we're stealin' a ship this big to use as a taxi? Boys, we're goin' to drive the one-and-a-half-million tons of the *American Enterprise* straight into Mavis at flank speed. We'll cut the legs out from under it and spill it into the North Sea like a tray of dishes."

The men gave a startled yelp, like a pack of romping dogs over which a whip had just been cracked.

Quinn drove on hard. "There are fewer than ten ships in the world heavy enough to do this. We're lucky enough to get the biggest, and with it, a bigger storm than we could have prayed for. God Almighty is with us, boys."

Ah, the former Father Costello thought, it's heartening to know that God still spends most of his time with scoundrels.

Quinn continued. "Immediately after the collision, we split our tanker wide open with explosives, sink her on the spot and spill her oil into the sea along with what will be pourin' out of the storage tanks and broken wells. The loss will run to billions of pounds that Britain doesn't have and will never have again. They'll be out of Ireland in a year."

There were whoops, cheers and applause from the men, who were well into the brandy.

Roland O'Driscoll, who had turned as white as Dominic Quinn's shirt, came forward to stand with his face a foot in front of the commandant's. "To drown like dogs seems little pay for such fine work."

The room became dead quiet as the thought of cold sea water mingled with warm alcohol. As the two men's eyes locked together, Quinn's voice became as gentle as that of a mother in a child's sickroom. "Roland, there's barely a hundred feet of water where Mavis A. stands. She draws better than ninety feet loaded, with maybe forty feet of freeboard. When she sinks, she'll settle down on the bottom with her upper decks standin' out of the water like a big island. We'll be as safe and dry as a bunch of lords."

"Until the sea breaks us up like a sand castle."

"Or until they come get us," Barton said.

"But we *want* them to come to get us, George," said Quinn. "We could never hope to put together the string of rescue boats that the government keeps around that platform. Six big barges on station at all times. We're absolutely *dependin'* on them to pick us up. And of course we'll be well-armed and take them over at once. We'll have them radio the appropriate confusin' messages about what's supposed to have happened, and then send them on a long swim in their life preservers. We've got plenty of sailors here to get us to a rendezvous point with a fast launch. Then we'll sink the barges and lose ourselves in all the oil-field and fishin'-boat traffic. We'll be warm ashore in Scotland twelve hours after the collision."

Barton pulled the curtain next to his chair away from the window so that Quinn could see the storm outside. "Rescue boats? Rendezvous? Fishing boats? I've been thirty years at sea and I can tell you that you'll find none of those things in a norther like this."

"It can't keep on goin'. We must be at the top of it now. In thirty hours most of the force will be gone out of the wind."

"Is that what the Meteorological Office says, Dominic?"

"They're wrong more than they're right, George."

"Maybe we don't have enough goin' for us in this thing," Punchy Devlin said. The hairless man always moved in opposition.

"We've got *everythin'* goin' for us, damn it. First we've got surprise. Until this hour, only one other man but me knew about the objective of this operation, so there won't be any leaks. Second, we've got simplicity: a takeover that'll be child's play and a collision with somethin' that can't run away. It will be the easiest job of demolition we've ever had. And last we've got luck. This storm is *luck*. We've got a ship that can cut through the weather like it wasn't there; the other side doesn't. Nobody will know that we're steamin' north, not west, until we're right on top of the platform. By the time they know what we're up to, they'll never be able to get a warship near us in that kind of sea. Not in time. And boys, you'll never have to go out again. It will be over. This is the end of England." A tear rolled down Quinn's cheek. He had them. They rose and rushed toward him, and he folded them one at a time in the arms of death.

Commandant Quinn had failed to mention one other possibility, but Tiny McArdle and his five Scotsmen were on Mavis A. to take care of that. McArdle lay on his bunk in the crew's quarters. In the four-man room on the second level above the main deck he could feel the tremors of wind and sea more clearly than Cullenbine and the others high above him in the observation tower.

A wire snaked from a plug in his ear to a small portable radio sitting on a metal chest of drawers behind his head. But he was not listening to the never-ending newscasts and rock-and-roll programs. He was listening to every word of the radio traffic to and from Mavis A. Patiently he went through the weather reports, requests for medical advice, confirmations of drill-pipe deliveries and the undecipherable number-and-letter gibberish of the oil-company codes. He did not fret under the tedium. Like many stupid men, McArdle was blessed with monumental endurance.

McArdle was the only one besides Dominic Quinn who knew the whole of Operation North Sea Gunman. He would not tell his own men the cataclysmic end of the plan until their part of it was completed and it was time to save themselves. Feeling the furies of the sea beneath him, he was thinking now that he might never tell them, for there could be no rescue in this sea. They would behave better if they never knew what awaited them. As for himself, he never gave doom a thought.

Tiny McArdle was a Highlander born almost in the shadow of the Cape Wrath lighthouse. He came from a

74

breed of streetfighters who would maim without mercy, and who never truckled to quarter or cost. To die was of no consequence to him; to keep his word to Quinn was everything. For this was Tiny McArdle's fame: his wild devotion to his word had made him a legend across County Sutherland, had made him a leader whom men followed without thought, had impelled Quinn to choose him over a dozen men just as strong and steady. The secret that the commandant had put in the wiry little Scot's head was as secure as if it had gone to the grave.

During lulls in the radio traffic, McArdle tried to play back every word that Quinn had said to him. He was intensely aware of the honor of having been chosen, but the scope of the operation dizzied him.

He had his heroes: Napoleon, Churchill, Roosevelt; men who led with the power of their minds; geniuses who could grasp and weave a thousand details into plans that changed history. He knew that Quinn was one of these and Quinn had given him the responsibility of blinding and deafening Mavis A. when the time came. Quinn had told McArdle that the platform's formidable radar and radio capabilities were the only things that could stop the operation cold. Mavis A. could track the immense bulk of the *Enterprise* forty miles out. If her purpose were guessed, R.A.F. jets, precision bombing through the weather by radar, could send the ship to the bottom within an hour. So large were the chips on the table that the cost of the ship and her crew might count for nothing.

McArdle almost groaned aloud at his responsibility. Just as Quinn had not been able to tell the high leaders of the IRA of the operation, so, too, had McArdle not been able to tell the leaders of the Scottish Nationalists. Men as close to him as brothers had been kept ignorant on the word of Dominic Quinn. He pressed the plug tighter into his ear, afraid that he might miss a sound.

Checking to make sure that the bulk of Fat Tom MacCrummon still sat in a chair against the door, McArdle grasped a key he had hidden in the springs of his mattress, leaned over the bunk and unlocked the large chest beneath it. Almost every inch of the drawer he slid out was filled with a powerful radio receiver which Mac-Crummon had smuggled aboard piece by piece and assembled over weeks. It was into this that the earplug ultimately ran. Several circuit-tester lights had been built in. McArdle pressed the tester buttons one at a time, grinning with relief as each glowed green. Then he fished a black box the size of a loaf of bread from behind the receiver. This he handled much more gingerly. He set it on his pillow and got a green light by gently pressing the tester. With even greater care, he lifted a hinged guard cap to look at the switch beneath it. This time a red light winked on.

If he now moved the switch he had exposed, a radio signal would knife through fourteen decks above him, pass into the radio room and enter a small receiver planted behind the main transmitter. This in turn would pulse an electrical signal into four wires radiating from the receiver and detonate four twenty-pound packages of a high explosive called Cyclotol, a 60/40 mixture of RDX and TNT. The packages had been hidden in the radio room over a period of several days by a McArdle man named Fred Morrison, who had been able to violate security with an offer of one of the women the crew kept hidden aboard. While the watch officers had labored over her in the emergency-generator room, Morrison was placing the charges meant to pulverize their equipment and kill or maim them.

McArdle poised his finger over the button, almost ecstatic at the power of this toy that he did not really understand. Aware of MacCrummon's eyes on him, he faked a fast stab at the button and made a loud explosive sound. The way the fat man jumped in his chair sent McArdle into a giggle that collapsed immediately into a scowl. The box on his pillow was going to do only half the job it was meant to. They had not been able to penetrate the radar room. That would have to be stormed. Or would it? With the transmitter out, there could be no radio call for help even if the radar saw the need. Signal light? Distress rockets? Who would see them? Nobody. Defenses? There were none. What could the crew of Mavis A. do with the knowledge that they were about to be rammed? Try to save themselves, surely. Part of the job was to get as many of the crew off as he could before the tanker struck. If the men could accomplish the evacuation on their own, so much the better.

As ever, the mists in McArdle's mind lay thick, and he struggled to see through them. He ran down the job of every tool-pusher, roustabout, welder, mud engineer and mud logger. What order could an alerted command give any of them to impede the operation? He covered his eyes with his fingertips and slowly pictured the rig deck by deck, room by room. He saw it from a workboat, the three thick, round legs rising from the sea to support the main deck and its wedding cake of structures and cranes bristling against the sky. He thought his way around the legs, each of which was painted a different color to help helicopters and workboats make the correct approaches: Redleg, at the tip of the triangular deck that pointed due south, Blueleg and Yellowleg at the tips pointed northeast and northwest.

He let his inner eye drift up the iron rungs that climbed from the sea along the outside of Redleg. He floated through the steel door that led into forty feet of tunnel along the column's hollow heart. This passageway went past the hundreds of thousands of barrels of stored oil that circled Redleg's drilling shaft. He saw the miles of drill cables hanging as thickly as jungle vines, suspending drill bits into the wells that moved down into deeper formations in the earth. The cables soared a hundred and sixty feet from the seafloor to the main deck above, and among them men swarmed, shadowless in the worklights, like demons in a filthy, clangorous hell. They scurried along catwalks and ladders, rose and plummeted on an open elevator bucket running along the wall in an open frame, and gathered like a heap of ants around the slowly revolving drums of wells being drilled. McArdle's plodding brain searched through them among the nightmare of pipes that carried the oil from the producing wells up into the storage tanks. In all this, what could hurt the operation? Then he saw him, standing where he always stood, on the narrow supervisor's platform circling the seafloor: Cullenbine.

Noel Cullenbine was a man who manipulated steel pipe wide enough to drive a Land Rover through, and he did it as easily as a plumber replacing the pipes under a bathroom sink. Given warning, he could secure the wells. The unstaunchable hemorrhage of oil that Quinn demanded could be reduced to the spill of a teacup. McArdle saw Cullenbine staying the hand of God, averting the twist of destiny. This was the threat he had to meet.

McArdle slid the drawer closed on the large transmitter; the small one he kept out. Producing a clasp knife from his pocket, he slit the end of his pillow along the seam. Cutting a cavity in the foam rubber the size of the black box, he carefully closed the guard cap and worked the box into the cavity. When he lay back on the pillow he was able to put his hand inside the slit unseen, for he had it facing the wall. He rested his fingers on his murderous little friend.

The earplug crackled with a message and McArdle stiffened, listening. It was only a question sent in the clear, not in company code, concerning drilling mud. But if the words had held a hint of warning about North Sea Gunman, either to or from Mavis A. . . . softly he made the explosive sound again.

chapter 4

The officers of the *American Enterprise* were captured one at a time at their moment of greatest helplessness.

Electronics Officer Robert Danenhower, entering his kneeling woman from behind, felt The Dropper's pistol in the angle of his jaw in mid-orgasm; he sagged against the Irishman more as a spent lover than a captive.

Second Officer Harold Goslin had his eyes closed, his legs spread over the arms of a leather Morris chair and his manhood lodged in a woman's mouth when his chest was tickled by the muzzle of Eamon O'Driscoll's Webley. The woman jerked away and spat on Goslin's belly.

Third Officer Gilbert Goldman started up from a pleasant postcoital nap to find the hideous Punchy Devlin lying alongside and grinding away on top of his erstwhile partner. The pale, lashless eyes sighted a revolver in the center of Goldman's face.

All of the engineers, Peter Case, Wolfe Engelberg, Arthur Queene and Arvid Larsen, were taken while asleep.

Stark naked but not otherwise discomforted, the ship's

officers were herded into the cheerful and impressive room where Quinn had addressed his own men. Gone from the beautiful oak-paneled walls were the pictures, diagrams and maps that had covered it. Their bodies blotchy with fright, the officers were motioned to the leather armchairs, which had now been pulled into a cluster in the center of the room. The chairs faced Dominic Quinn, seated smiling on the edge of a writing desk in the corner. His men stood against the walls, their weapons nowhere in sight, just as ordered. What could have been taken as expressions of good cheer on the Irishmen's faces were actually the expressions of contempt that may be justifiably directed to young men suddenly stripped naked of uniforms, authority and courage.

It amused Quinn to see how fright drew the male genitals back into the pubic hair in a trinity so tight and tiny that the wearer seemed turned into a woman. And even though the fire had by now made the room almost unpleasantly warm, there was gooseflesh on the captives' pale bodies. First, he must reassure them. "Throw one of those nice big logs on the fire, George. We must look after the good health of these fine specimens." He kept the tone gentle, jibing, a little coarse. Just rough boys at play. "Although from the looks of some of these jelly bellies and big arses, you boys would do well to start lookin' after yourselves. If I didn't know better, I'd say you'd been hangin' about too much with loose women." A ripple of giggles, pitched a little too high, rose from the center of the room. Quinn drew a pack of Players and a gold cigarette lighter out of his jacket pocket and tossed them to the American closest to him. "Light up, boys. We're goin' to have a little chat, so we might as well get as comfortable as we can, considerin' not all of us are dressed for the occasion." Another ripple of giggles.

"You are the prisoners of the Irish Republican Army. But you needn't fear about your safety because you are not our enemies. We'll tell you our real names because if we succeed in our operation they will be well-enough known, and if we don't—well, who cares about dead men's names? I am Dominic Quinn. My men will introduce themselves when the time comes. We'll be together quite a bit over the next day or so.

"We need two things from you: your help and your ship. We are after nothin' more than ransom—twenty million dollars of it."

Danenhower, who was still a little drunk, spoke up. "Why an American ship?"

"Because the English don't have one worth stealin'."

The laughter came easier this time. "A guerrilla organization must raise its money by going where the pockets are deepest. The volunteer fund-raising in the United States has been very impressive, and we are in your country's debt. But we have good reason to hope that the involuntary fund-raising will be an even greater success. I assure you that the Petromarine Company will weep tears of gratitude at the reasonableness of our asking price. A ship that size . . . all that oil . . . the cleanup costs if anything happened to be spilled . . . widow's payments for you and all your friends on board if the scuttlin' got out of hand . . . As it is, their insurance will hand them their money back before we have the ransom counted. At worst, you've got involved in a family argument—with a mild robbery of them what's already too rich thrown in.

"What we're goin' to do is almost too simple to call a plan. You boys are goin' to get your clothes back on—hell, you can even finish what you were doin' if you want—and sneak us on board. That'll be easy enough; your vessel is the size of a city, and right now you can't see across the beam. You'll get us to your captain, first officer and chief engineer, and you'll tell them in your own way why it will be no more than a little adventure for them to cooperate with us. As soon as they agree, we'll raise steam and move out. It won't be all that hard, because there's no channel to follow in Coltry and the *Enterprise* has those fancy new side thrusters to help her maneuver without tugboats."

"The shore's going to see us go," said Danenhower.

"The people outside the company won't give a damn.

Inside the company? There's only a handful of them in this town, and most of those are off duty at night in this weather. Besides, they know that a sudden change in the oil market can shift a ship's unloading plans and destination in five minutes. And a lot of those shifts are as secret as the atom bomb used to be. If they call us up when we're under way, we tell them something like that."

"Why would we leave in the middle of the night?"

"Why wait around when the other traffic inside and outside the bay isn't movin' and you have radar? A ship like the *Enterprise* loses thousands of dollars just sittin' around for a few hours. What would be a more natural move for an experienced captain than to use his good judgment and take off as soon as he could?"

"Where will you sail us?" Goldman asked.

"Where the threat of a good spill will do the most good. Where a lot of countries would be in on the mess. I thought I'd let you take us up around Scotland and out into the North Sea somewhere. That would make 'em all nervous—Holland, Belgium, England, France. They'll put the pressure on to pay up fast."

"But you'll never be able to escape with what they pay you."

"Why not, Mr. Goldman? I have reason to believe that the government of Libya will be happy to entertain us. From there we'll see that the money gets back to the Army. Also, in the fullness of time, when the Republic is one again, we can expect to go home in very fine standing indeed. Probably tell our life stories on the telly and get a hell of a lot more than a paltry twenty million out of it."

Quinn felt a thrill like a fighter who had struck a perfect blow. He had hit the Americans precisely square and true. Using only his tongue, he had turned the frightened captives into comrades. The spirit of mischief and adventure—always underrated as a shaker of events—had hold of them; he could see it plainly in the sly grins that they exchanged, first with one another and then with him.

What stories they would live to tell. Days or weeks in the hot eye of a watching world. Poking a stick in the eye of their millionaire bosses and not having to pay for it. Jesus, they might have pulled this off themselves. Libya. So long, straight world; sorry, tired wife and girlfriend.

The prisoners tried their smiles on the men along the walls, and the O'Driscolls and Father Costello smiled back. The Dropper, Punchy Devlin and George Barton did not. The warmth wavered and became confused.

"Open that door over there, Dropper, and have that young man come in and say hello."

One of the old men was holding Will James by the elbow when he stepped into the room. He looked fresh and scrubbed; his uniform seemed to have been pressed. Quinn motioned the old man away and held out a hand to James. The officer instinctively stepped forward and shook it. The action had just the right effect on the tanker men.

"I'm sure you'll forgive your friend, Mr. James, for gettin' you here. But we threatened him with an awful thing so he'd make that call on the radio." No, mustn't bring back the fear. "We threatened to give him a girl with both legs in one stockin'."

It worked. James and his shipmates got to laugh together, and the thin cloud of betrayal that he had brought with him into the room blew away easily.

Quinn folded his arms and strolled around behind the seated men, so that James was left alone facing them. He saw Quinn make a small talking motion with his thumb and fingers.

"Okay, guys. I think we all agree that the best thing we can do is go along with these men. They're not asking us to do any fighting, or to hurt anybody, or even to take sides. But we have to give them some help. The smoother we can get them on the ship and under way, the less likely there's going to be any strong-arm stuff. Getting aboard won't be any trouble because we're not at a sea berth, for a change. We'll drive out along the big pier in a truck. There's a scaffold near the bow where they're checking out those plates we sprung coming around the Cape. We'll board from there.

"I'll take some of these IRA men to Captain Cody, who should be in his rooms. Mr. Danenhower will take another group to the bridge to get Mr. Browne, who will have the watch.

"Mr. Goldman, as soon as Quinn has the ship, get some men together and run the truck ramp over the side. We're going to drive up on deck. Mr. Goslin will round up another bunch with some fork-lifts to get the truck's cargo transferred. There are several tons of fifty-pound cases." Some of the officers exchanged whispers. "Yes, it's explosives. But God willing, we'll be pitching it all overboard off Tripoli next week when they give us back the ship."

James was now actively enjoying his part. It was nice to see the commanding Danenhower, the supercilious Goslin and that cocky little bastard Goldman nodding their "yessirs." The naked bodies in the chairs were shifting into new attitudes now. There was a brazen submission among them. It brought to mind the waiting room of a brothel less elegant than the one they were in. They seemed eager to be taken.

Owen Browne, first officer of the *American Enterprise,* should have remained standing his watch on the bridge. To be technical, it was actually Will James's watch, but it was one that he and Captain Cody had volunteered to stand while the other officers took the night ashore. Besides, the electronic army of sensors would guard the ship better than any pair of eyes straining against the dark and rain. But Browne was one of these model people who, by God, followed their plan, and it was his plan to be the best damned ship's officer that Petromarine ever had. Naturally his deviation was on behalf of a woman, in this case his wife.

Even so, Browne could only leave his post by degrees, and with the agonizing ratiocination to which he subjected every act. He started his departure from the bridge with a slow stroll from wing to wing. The two-hundred-and-ninety-foot walk took him five minutes because he paused to peer out of each of the windows looking forward. But if there had been a five-alarm fire roaring up from the forepeak, it is doubtful that he could have seen it.

When he reached the far wing, he turned to look back along the incredible width of the bridge. A man standing at the other end would have been as far away as an outfielder from the batter in a baseball game. Slowly he retraced his steps until he stood among the control consoles. He grasped the wheel as though he might hold himself where he belonged, then walked into the chart room, an alcove behind curtains at the after end of the bridge house. It was only in the few feet that encompassed this room, the wheel and the engine controls that the scale of the *Enterprise* could be grasped. In this space a single man could still hold together the basics that for four thousand years had made a ship a ship: a helm, a system of propulsion and a system of navigation. But now these basics, and the men who pretended to command them, were merely part of a crude backup arrangement. In this chart room Mr. Browne and his colleagues mostly checked on, marveled at and offered diffident suggestions to the true master of the *American Enterprise:* the long, high banks of computers in the control room. The room lay beneath Browne's feet, which put it directly behind the captain's quarters on the captain's bridge deck. In an emergency the skipper could reach the computers before he could get to the helm, and this told the whole story of Mr. Browne and his ship.

Owen Browne was a good seaman; even the unforgiving Cody admitted it in private. But it was unnatural to the captain that this competence should be possessed by a man without the smallest shred of feeling for the sea. For the first officer had embarked on the discipline of studies that would someday make him master of the *Enterprise* as coldly as a mathematics major taking a side course in accounting. Far more important to him than either his first officer's certificate of his master's certificate was the degree of Master of Business Administration he had received from Harvard University. It was Browne's broad grounding in the computer sciences that had put him ahead of a dozen other brilliant young men who had wanted to be captain of the *Enterprise*. One of them would still make it, because Browne was going to move on. Just as his business training had moved him into the slot he had wanted at sea, his sea training would move him into the slot he wanted ashore. While still in his thirties he would move into the front office of Petromarine, and in these times a young man with his background could go as far in five years with an oil company as he could in twenty-five years with a bank or an insurance company. Then he and Ethel could be close again.

One of the two elevators that ran the two hundred feet from the bridge to the dim tunnel beneath the oil tanks stood in place, its doors open, but Browne didn't want anyone on the decks below to see by the indicator that it had left its place at the top of the ship. He walked slowly down an iron spiral staircase into the control room, where illuminated digits rippled steadily out of a dozen readouts. Tapes whirled and clicked. Browne was a man in a private universe, surrounded by his own winking galaxy. With minute care he studied each trembling needle and winking digit, following its reading back to the condition it indicated. Using only his fingertips, from where he stood he could make up the crew's paychecks, get a diagnosis of spinal meningitis and detailed instructions as to its quarantine and treatment, receive the ship's position from a satellite and override the helmsman with a correction, feed blips off the ship's radar directly into the steering system to avoid collisions automatically. Most importantly, he could move a million barrels of oil aboard or ashore in less time that it used to take stevedores to handle a small freighter's cargo of bananas.

Browne sat down at the loading console, master of enough energy to heat, light and power a good-size city for a year. Beneath the starscape of dials a diagram of the ship's piping system was embossed in aluminum strips. Everywhere in the diagram, lights glowed green, which told him that all the valves were closed. Tomorrow, when he was controlling the unloading of several hundred thousand barrels of oil into Coltry for transshipment in smaller tankers, the board would look different. The punched program he locked into the computer would open and close dozens of huge, oil-pouring valves at precise moments. For hours Owen Browne would remain at the console, monitoring pump speeds and suction pressures, checking to make sure that his computer program was taking oil out of the tanks in certain exact proportions, so that the *American Enterprise* would not break her back on variations in buoyancy along her tremendous length. But he would be only the crude backup system to the machine.

Browne stopped at one more wall panel on his way out of the control room. These dials he watched with even greater care than the others. The needles—thirty of them in ten banks of three—connected to sensors set high in each of the ship's cargo tanks, and recorded concentrations of hydrocarbon gas. They reminded Browne that at least one thing had not changed in oil tankers over sixty years: The ships were still floating bombs. Oddly, the vessel was safest when its tanks were loaded to the tops with oil. Empty tanks, like the Number One Center that the *Enterprise* had pumped out at Rotterdam, were the most dangerous. All the oil could never be drained out; shallow pools remained cupped in the bottom plates, and these pools continuously built up concentrations of hydrocarbon gas. The flash point of hydrocarbon gas was so low that it was considered highly explosive even at temperatures far below zero. For this reason precautions against spark and flame were endemic aboard tankers. No cigarette had ever been lit on deck aboard the *American Enterprise*. No deck activity that might cause a spark was permitted unless the tanks were full and a fresh breeze blowing. Even clothing made of artificial fibers had been forbidden aboard because of the risk of a static spark. Despite all these precautions, the insurance premiums on *Enterprise* amounted to fifty percent of her operating costs.

The panel that Browne now studied was his ship's main defense against hydrocarbon gases. By manipulating the gleaming rows of switches he could operate a series of shunts and fans that forced the safest possible atmosphere into an empty tank. Since Number One had been pumped dry, Browne had warred steadily with its explosive gases. He had drawn the exhaust gases of burned boiler fuel out of the ship's funnel and put them through a filtering system that removed such impurities as sulfur dioxide. This left him with an incombustible gas composed mostly of carbon dioxide and nitrogen, and this is what he blew along special conduits into Number One. Now he had only to retain the mixture and guard against the re-entry of the oxygen into the atmosphere.

The sensors told him that all was well. Mr. Browne left his watch. Descending one more flight of the spiral stairs, he came to the upper bridge deck, two levels below the navigating bridge. The world of supertanker officers being a luxurious one, the first officer's suite shared the deck with only two others, those of the second engineers, Arthur Queene and Peter Case. Both men were ashore; Browne would not be seen. The only other officers still aboard were Captain Cody and Tom Traskins, the chief engineer. Both were quartered on the captain's bridge deck above, and were noted for their habit of keeping to their quarters.

Browne entered his suite through a heavy teakwood door. The beautifully burnished wood was the ship designer's single remembrance of the golden days of steam, when a vessel's woodwork was the chief reflection of its glory. The gesture was treasured by the old officers, Cody and Traskin, and lost on the younger, including Browne. The impressive suite consisted of a large day room—the seagoing equivalent of a living room—the long front of which bore a row of curtained windows looking forward over the weather deck. Behind the day room lay a bedroom not quite as large, with windows that gave out over the sea on the port side. Alongside the bedroom lay Browne's office, windowless but cheerfully painted and lighted. The bathroom would have been the pride of a first-class hotel and there was enough closet space for a family of a half-dozen.

Ethel was seated at the broad writing table under the front windows; Browne watched her in profile. A tall lamp on the table, the only light in the suite, haloed her short, immaculately groomed blond bob. "You leave your watch too much, Owen," was her acknowledgment that he was in the room, but she turned her head not a fraction of an inch from her work.

He took from the pocket of his slicker the small, powerful VHF radio that was the indispensable communications tool of the officers of the huge ship and set it down in the center of a magazine she was clipping. "I'm available for all calls."

"You don't have to do this for me. I know you don't like it."

"I don't do anything I don't like."

"Oh, crap. You don't do anything you *do* like." Still a church-going Queens girl, she pressed her fingertips to her lips.

Owen Browne was eleven years older than his wife, but the span seemed wider. Though he was barely thirty-five, his thinning dark hair was already half gray, and the lines around his pale eyes were beginning to intersect.

Ethel Browne had the blond good looks of the high-school cheerleader she had once been. Her nose was tiny, her breasts were large, and the stylish wire-framed glasses that she was never without made her enormous brown eyes bigger yet. Casual dress did not exist for her; even now, lost in this lonely cathedral of a ship, she wore a starched white dress that would have looked well at a formal garden party. A scarf and jewelry were arranged with care. Her eyes and lips were made up just enough to push her past the point of being an extraordinarily attractive girl; as she sat now, she was a beauty. Browne choked with love.

Now, two years into the life of the ship, Ethel Browne was still the only woman who had sailed in her. Every officer had a suite with a double bed and the right to have his wife aboard, but the wives had needed only brief in-port visits on the *Enterprise* to sense the crushing emptiness of what a six-month stretch would do to them. For Ethel, six months had been only the beginning. Her husband, entitled to a two-month leave after every half-year at sea, had never taken one. He knew that the company was looking for men who were able to deny themselves. His sacrifice could move ahead his promotion ashore by as much as two years.

Before moving aboard the *Enterprise,* Ethel had supposed that a sailor's lonely life was broken by more or less frequent visits to foreign ports. She had not known that supertankers made the sailing life as dreary for the modern seaman as for any who had served under Magellan. The punishing, combined economics of oil and these gigantic ships imposed unbearable penalties on any prolonged stay in port. The *American Enterprise* cost its owners $60,000 a day, including depreciation, and for this reason she was at sea 345 days a year. Even when she was technically in port, she was at sea. Coltry Bay was one of the few ports in the world into whose harbor she could actually bring her full hundred-foot draft, and Coltry was not so much a port as a mouth in the coastline that drank oil. Generally, the ship loaded or discharged at a sea berth—a steel island ten miles from shore—or at a loading buoy, a pipeline left drifting on the surface many miles off the coast. Hence, a visit to an exotically named port invariably meant no more than that the ship anchored for fifteen or twenty hours, and—if the weather was clear—one could catch a glimpse of a smudge of land on the horizon. Generally no one went ashore or came aboard.

Outside of such nonevents, the *American Enterprise* steadily steamed the eleven thousand miles from the Persian Gulf to Northern Europe, with an occasional diversion to North America making an almost indiscernible variance in the routine. In a month's run, Ethel Browne saw all the four seasons insofar as they could be seen at sea. From springtime in Halifax or Coltry, the ship sailed into the fiery summer of the equator and down into the autumn of the South Atlantic; then she rounded the Cape of Good Hope and drove north for the inferno anchorages of Hallul, Abadan or Kharg Island in the Gulf.

When occasionally they steamed through latitudes that allowed it, Ethel borrowed one of the bicycles that the crew used to travel the tremendous reaches of the weather deck, and rode for hours. As she pedaled she ached for the sight of a green and growing thing; squinting her eyes, she would pretend that the towering steel kingposts were the trunks of huge trees.

Her bicycle trips to nowhere always ended the same way: among a horde of bicycling seamen. At first they would be seen only at a considerable distance; then they would pass her singly, waving and muttering greetings, and finally they would be whirling around her, whooping like rodeo cowboys and playing wild games to gain her attention.

Being the only woman on a big ship that sailed for months without shore leave made Ethel the sole subject of intense sexual focus, and she was not unaware of it. Even the quietest and most unlikely men, like the old engineer, Mr. Traskin, sometimes stared at her fixedly, paying no attention to her angry glares. Only her husband seemed unaware of her sexual presence. As boredom increased her needs, his vanished under the pressures of his work. For days now he had strained to melt the coolness his neglect had built up in her.

"I'm going to change myself, Ethel."

The phrase brought to her mind an unfortunate image of a man about to do something with a diaper. "By getting yourself thrown out of the company?"

"I wanted you."

"What about the phone? I could have come to the bridge."

"We couldn't do what I wanted if we were on the bridge."

"And what was that?"

"I wanted to make love to you."

Shocked, she snapped her head around to look at him for the first time. His face was an apoplectic red. *"Physical* love, Owen?"

He nodded quickly, like a man confirming that he had violated a small child left in his care.

Ethel knew that it wasn't sensual desire that had driven her husband down here, but something that offered a different kind of excitement. He was desperate, and women often find desperation stimulating. But now he had frozen in his chair; he had gone as far as he could. Suddenly she felt drunk with opportunity. She nodded, and smiling for the first time in weeks, she took him by the wrists and urged him to his feet. He tried to reach down to turn off the light, a precursor to all their love-making, but she wouldn't let go. "Why can't we do it on the bridge?"

"What?"

"Let's sneak up and do it on the damned *bridge.*"

"We *can't.*"

"It's not church. There's nobody up there, is there?"

"No. But it's the *bridge.*"

"Look, you're *supposed* to be up there."

"Yes, but not . . . not—" Then he started to giggle.

They melted into one another's arms, kissing and feeling and moaning and murmuring. The whole world was about to be saved.

"The chart-room table, Owen. I've dreamed about doing it on that table."

"It's not a virgin, you know."

"You're fooling."

"Hell, no. We lay courses on it all the time." It wasn't much of a joke, but coming from the grim Browne made it seem uproarious. All the way up the two flights of stairs they were barely able to contain their laughter; it leaked out of them in little snorts and shrieks, which only set them off again.

Still, emerging into the long cavern of the bridge, they sobered. The first officer was about to desecrate his awesome ground, and she, a former member of the

Blessed Virgin Sodality who had never known a caress that had not occurred in her marriage bed, was about to sport with her body in a way unacceptable to anyone she had ever respected. Nevertheless the sexual electricity between them was something that neither of them had ever felt before.

Holding hands, they walked into the chart room; it was dimly lit by the glow coming through the open door from the dials of the instruments.

"Leave the door the way it is," Ethel said, kicking away her shoes and stripping off her panty hose.

Dropping his trousers and underwear around his ankles, Browne had to take waddling half-steps to confront Ethel, who had sat down on the edge of the table and leaned back. He hiked himself forward and her thighs slid along his hips.

Dominic Quinn cleared his throat twice before they heard him over their tearing breaths. "I'm awfully sorry," he said from the darkest shadows in the corner of the chart room, "but I'm goin' to need you for other things—and at once."

chapter 5

Colonel Willem Lustgarten was sharing one of the three executive cabins on Mavis A. with Rolfe Zamke. Meteorology predicted no break in the weather, so their departure would be delayed for at least three days.

Lustgarten found Zamke an object worthy of some study. The colonel had not been close to anyone since the early forties, when as a young officer in the elite *Das Reich* division he had commanded companies of Zamkes. The young man was of the type Englishmen used to describe as being "either at your throat or at your feet." He seemed to have not a feeling or scruple to his name, but on this job Lustgarten trusted him more than anyone he had met outside the old Army. In hand-picking Zamke for his adjutant from among fifty others, the colonel had chosen him for the now-forbidden trait of ferocity in much the same way he had picked his key men for the Ardennes offensive. He had told himself that it was because the trait was accompanied so often by unthinking loyalty, but was that really it? The job was essentially bureaucratic, and a better knowledge of paper work, personnel and security routine would have made Zamke more useful to Lustgarten than any martial virtues. It wasn't even that he particularly liked his adjutant. Zamke was bright and interesting enough, but his reptilian blood and lack of imagination generated not even the faintest warmth. On a rare evening out together in Hamburg, Lustgarten had noticed that his blond and good-looking adjutant was carefully avoided by the swarming prostitutes.

Still, the men were close enough during business hours, and were even on a first-name basis on informal occasions. Or when, as now, the colonel had had several long pulls of vodka. "Rolfe, I am afraid I chose you for all the wrong reasons."

"Ah, Willi, I was afraid you would soon discover that a brilliant sense of humor and brittle charm were not enough." Dressed only in socks and underwear, Zamke was seated at the communications desk that was part of each executive cabin. From here an operator could obtain information from the giant transmitters on Level 16. Zamke wore a set of headphones cocked over one ear, and was receiving in code the day's traffic from North Sea Security Headquarters. A mass of disjointed numbers and letters covered a dozen sheets of paper; several pages of German he had already decoded during gaps in the transmission were also strewn across the desk.

"You know, you will only be of real use to me if there is another war."

Zamke smiled. "There will be, sir. There will be. You deserve another."

"You have never killed anybody, have you, Rolfe?"

"No, of course not."

"But you could, young man. It sticks out. You could kill people by the carload."

Lustgarten's tone left Zamke undecided as to whether he had been criticized. He decided to act as though he had been. "Born twenty years too late, then."

"Oh, no. You would have had to wait your turn in that war. There were tens of thousands of men who wanted to come in out of the cold and the Russian rockets and the American bombers. They wanted only to warm their hands around a cheerful oven stuffed full of crackling Jews and Gypsies."

"You should know all about it, Willi."

"But I don't know all about it. I'd rather have been hanged at Nuremberg than have remained alive knowing that I was capable of that."

"I understand that you were very good at killing people; that they could have a tank out of all the decorations they gave you for doing it."

"That was soldier's work, accomplished not against helpless wrecks but against skilled slaughterers, heavily armed and howling for our guts."

"Was it that way at Latigny, too, Colonel?"

"Were you expecting men committed to an advance of forty kilometers a day to care for three hundred bound captives?"

"You might have suggested it."

"A spirited attack, Rolfe. But I am not fooled by what is inside you."

"Nor I by what is in you, Colonel. You emphasize the purity of your nature. You observe my latent bestiality. Yet you have been responsible for deaths by the thousands and I have never killed so much as a chicken. Can it be that we beasts can only be turned loose by you pure souls?"

"My God, Captain. You have the inventiveness of an offended woman. These statements are of a very low order."

"My apologies, then. But I have read this of the death camps, Willi: The commandants would all begin as aloof bureaucrats; they killed according to memos couched in euphemisms and spent as many nights as they could at the opera. But after some months had passed, they would not leave the camp for any reason, and they hand-picked the victims. And in the end they themselves were holding the Lugers that sent the bullets through those poor bastards' necks. Apparently a man is no better than a fox in a henhouse; he cannot stop at killing only what he must."

Lustgarten was sitting on the edge of his bed removing a thicksoled shoe. Without changing his expression, he whirled it by the laces and hurled it ferociously at Zamke. The heel caught the captain above the kidney so hard that the pencil flew out of his hand and the headphones fell off his head. Zamke's familiarity fled, probably for days—which was exactly what Lustgarten had in mind.

"So, Captain, April 17th, 1945 was all that saved me from a rope?"

The young man actually jumped to his feet and stood at attention in his underwear. "Of course not, sir."

Lustgarten let him stand for a while. "I am about as sure of that as you are."

"Yes, sir."

"Tell me, Captain. Would you kill a man at my orders?"

"Forceful defense of the public safety is implicit in the job of a policeman, sir."

"Would you kill a man who was helpless?"

"Not as a result of an illegal order."

"For fun, then, Rolfe?"

"No."

"Of course not. And sir, I am about as sure of that as you are."

Lustgarten dropped his other shoe to the floor. "Sit down, will you. Let's see what you've got so far." Zamke handed him the decoded pages and he lay back on the bed and read them while his assistant picked up his headphones and began to write again.

"There has been a breakout at an IRA detention camp in Belfast."

"I saw, sir. It's not the first one."

"Could be something special about it. They blew up eleven Tommies and at least one of their own in order to pull the job. That's not the way they spend their explosives. Besides, the thing's too heavy for what they seem to have accomplished."

98

"Yes. Only six men turned loose. Still, something could have scared them off before they'd finished what they wanted to do."

"In this business we do not say 'could have.' When you are done receiving, code me some messages for North Sea Security and British Intelligence. I want to know what happened at that camp in all available detail."

"Do you recognize any of those six names? Are there any leaders?"

"None that I have heard of before except one man, George Barton. He was part of a flea-brained scheme to sabotage undersea oil pipe lines by lowering mines from trawlers."

"In the North Sea?"

"No, it was at one of the terminals in South Ireland. Coltry Bay. It was a couple of years ago. All they succeeded in doing was to open up their own hull and kill a couple of thousand fish. By the time the police got to them they were swimming. It was all so amateurish that they never got the sentences they should have."

"Why was he after Irish property?"

"American property. The usual crap about foreign exploitation. But they might have been practicing for us."

"There are no important pipe lines here."

"Don't be dense, Rolfe. An interest in destroying pipe lines is an interest in destroying oil. And oil is all that England has left."

"Oh, my. Poor, poor England." Zamke was recovering a bit.

"Sometimes you sound as though *you* were the one who worked for Uncle Adolf."

"I'm just sentimental. About this Barton. Isn't it likely that he was trying to blow up the first thing that came to hand? That he didn't see any real difference between a pipe line and an outhouse?"

"Maybe, but maybe the man who sent him did."

"Still, it's likely his relationship to oil is casual."

"Actually, very little about the IRA's business is casual. One thing is sure, though; this is a case we've got plenty of time to look into. Ask them to run the records of all the escaped men through the computer and get back to us with all similarities and any points of special interest. The system starts to operate, Rolfe."

As Zamke wrote and coded the messages for the radio shack, he found himself surprised at how anxious he was to have the answers. Men do not survive as well as they do by relying on their primary senses alone, which is why Dominic Quinn's elegantly simple plan began to accumulate resistance even before he had left Coltry Bay.

Captain Cody had taken a grudging liking to Dominic Quinn. From the moment the Irishman had appeared at the captain's door and made a short, courtly introduction of himself and of a man holding a lowered pistol, Cody had recognized Quinn as a man who knew how to get things done. Above all, Cody admired people who made things happen swiftly.

Quinn presented the accomplished fact of a captured, ransomed ship so concisely and without dramatics that Cody felt neither shock nor surprise. A level of potential force was shown, unmistakably, but it was so underplayed that it produced resignation rather than anxiety. The captain had been permitted to wash, dress and even have a cup of coffee. By the time he had been led to the bridge, all the deck and engine-room officers had been assembled there, including those who had been ashore. Only Browne and Mrs. Browne seemed to be nervous. Cody guessed that the others had been brought into the operation as gently as had he himself. Browne, though, had been taken on the bridge, and Ethel and Tom Traskin would have been captured in their rooms. He supposed that Browne's treatment had been less gentle, and explanations brusque or nonexistent.

Quinn let Cody give the orders for the ship to be made ready. The officers were told that each of their captors was well enough acquainted with the routine of an oil tanker to be able to spot disruptive procedures.

Under cold eyes, the officers were then split into

groups. They roused the general-purpose seamen that they needed and ordered them to their posts. The engine spaces were manned, steam raised and power supplied to all areas of the dormant giant. The course was revealed and plotted on the chart. A work party was dispatched to bring an enormous truck onto the weather deck, and it was lashed in place. By the time the order was given to cast off, the truck had been emptied of its cargo of dozens of fifty-pound fiberboard boxes. A swarm of fork-lifts made quick work of transferring the boxes to a corner of the crew's enormous game room on the main deck. A wiry little Irishman took meticulous care in covering the moving cargo with tarpaulins to protect it from the downpour. Cody knew these boxes contained the explosives with which his ship would be sunk if the IRA's demands were disappointed.

Finally the great island of a ship was set in motion. The engines, although under steam, had not yet begun to turn, but the *American Enterprise* was equipped with side thrusters. Powerful pumps directed sideways jets of water from the hull beneath the sea and moved the ship, now freed from its moorings, out into the dark bay with a precision impossible for the ship's twin forty-five-foot screws.

To a man who has made a life of sailing, the departure is the climax, the voyage itself is anticlimactic. Every man on the bridge felt the same deep tremor as the water widened between ship and shore. The vessel so dwarfed even the tallest structure in the town that it almost seemed as though they were slipping away on a safer solidity than the shore itself. Cody was now commanding immeasurably more wealth, power and structure than had Nebuchadnezzar in Babylonia. Standing behind the captain, Dominic Quinn felt that his Kalashnikov assault rifle was as powerless as a broomstraw against the juggernaut under him.

Alongside the helmsman at the operating console, Will James was keeping the bridge movement book. He recorded the exact times and exact details of putting to sea as though this particular departure were a normal, standard company operation.

"Bring up the side ladders," Cody said.

James's hand moved. Out in the night the air-operated ladders retracted into the hull.

"Starboard engine, dead slow."

"Starboard, dead slow." James rang it down on the telegraph.

"Wheel twenty degrees port."

"Port twenty," the helmsman confirmed.

With excruciating slowness the lights on shore began to swing to the stern.

"Two-six-oh," the helmsman called off.

"Quinn, I'll be moving blind. Can I use the horn?"

"No, Captain. You've got the radar."

"That's no help to a man out there in a dory."

"You'll strike no such man on this night, as you well know. And I'd just as soon have only a couple of dozen wondering where we're going. We don't need a couple of thousand. I've got tons of explosives to place before I'm in position to do any bargainin'. I can't sink this thing with a ball-peen hammer."

"Two-six-five."

Since the ship's momentum was an almost insuperable problem, the plunging depths of the bay, the sparseness of anchored shipping at its center and the availability of side thrusters were all necessary for the *American Enterprise* to reach the sea without the help of tugs. Once she started swinging she would shrug off any ordinary attempt at counterhelm. Only by almost phenomenal anticipation with wheel and engines could Cody maneuver his vessel in the relatively narrow bay. In the open sea, moving at her top speed of twenty knots, it would take five miles and twenty-eight minutes to stop her. Captains had tried to make emergency stops of supertankers far smaller than the *Enterprise* by dropping anchors, but they had been torn from the deck like daisies from a lawn.

Cody's problem in clearing harbor was the reverse of that faced by most captains. Usually the problems of shallow water were in the anchorages, requiring the careful following of dredged channels by highly trained harbor pilots. But Coltry Bay was far deeper than most of the seas around the British Isles. With nearly a hundred feet of draft, the *Enterprise* had to thread through these open seas using bottom charts. Some areas were closed to her completely; passing through others, she would clear bottom by as little as three feet.

"Two-seven-oh."

"Both engines slow ahead."

The biggest mobile structure in the world began to gather its awesome momentum, and within half an hour, the first watery mountains began to explode against the block-wide prow. Dominic Quinn felt himself sliding into Irish history.

Zamke rose from his bed in the dark when the communications desk across the cabin began to buzz and blink with piercing lights. Carrying the coding machine to the desk, he switched on a small high-intensity light. Numbers and letters were pouring onto a tape running out of the signals recorder.

Lustgarten got out of bed, too, and pulled a chair alongside his assistant, whose fingers were flying over the keys of the coder like a court stenographer's. Working the coding machine with his left hand and writing shorthand with his right, Zamke filled pages with virtuoso ease.

Only seconds after the recorder stopped printing, he flipped away his pencil and sat gravely studying his shorthand, aware that his commander had to wait for a second translation. Given even this small situational command, he essayed the temporarily lost familiarity. "Willi, it seems that we have an interesting group here. Of the six men who escaped, five are seamen—all with experience on large oil tankers."

"And the sixth?"

"Explosives. Arrested three times on suspicion of murder and sabotage with explosives. They've never made

103

anything important stick, but wherever this man goes, bridges, buildings and automobiles rise into the air."

"Army trained?"

"No. Self-taught, virtually. Some sort of genius at the work, informants say. He's boasted that the East has asked him to come help them blow away some especially tricky targets. A whole chamberful of Italian deputies of the wrong party, for example."

"I want to know how many other prisoners were in the camp, and how many of them were tanker sailors."

"British Intelligence seems to be back up to wartime efficiency. They've already done that for you. There were two hundred and three other men being held. Only two had ever been sailors, and neither had ever set foot on an oil tanker."

"They're probably looking to infiltrate a tanker crew."

"If that's it, we won't be seeing them for months. They're slow planners."

"Slow, but usually good, Rolfe. Interesting idea, going after tankers."

"Where do you think they'll try it? In port or at sea?"

"Depends on how well they can work out their escape. It would be a lot more effective to blow one up at sea. No firefighting help. Much more difficult for salvage. More damage from the oil spill. But there would have to be a way to get themselves off."

"The oil spill. That would be the real point, wouldn't it? If it was one of the big ships, and it happened in just the right place, it would be a real mess. When the *Torrey Canyon* went to pieces off the English coast, it ended up costing millions, didn't it?"

"Yes. And there was a clamor to ban oil-handling operations of any kind off the British coast. They don't need any more of that."

"We should get out an alert."

"Of course. To all tankers now in English and Irish ports, especially the deep-water places like Coltry. Tell them to beware of saboteurs posing as seamen. Have the English send out full descriptions of the men."

Zamke began to scribble a message. "What variations might they try?"

"A hijacking at sea? Boat-to-boat? Not likely. But have them report any small-boat thefts and any unauthorized or unusual ship or boat movement."

"It must be nice to be able to keep us hopping like this."

"Yes, Rolfe. If they had any real imagination, we would be in some difficulty."

Dominic Quinn had moved all the officers with cabins on the middle bridge deck in with those on the upper bridge deck. He had taken Peter Case's suite for himself and Roland O'Driscoll, and the rest of the Irishmen were divided up in the suites formerly occupied by the third engineers, Larsen and Engelberg.

One armed man stood on the bridge at all times, another patrolled the crew quarters and another the engine spaces. One man stayed with The Dropper to help him organize and control the work parties that were to help him place his explosives. Only two men were off station at any one time.

Roland O'Driscoll lay half dozing on the rug with a bolster pillow under his head and a tumbler of Peter Case's whiskey in his hand. He was smiling a bit, which was not like him. The source of his pleasure was Dominic Quinn's fine singing voice, which kept Roland, the older of the O'Driscoll brothers, pleasantly awash in sentimentality. Quinn accompanied himself on Case's expensive accordion.

> *My Johnny's g-o-o-o-ne,*
> *What will I do-o-o-o-o?*
> *My Johnny's g-o-o-o-o-o-ne*
> *To Hi-i-i-i-lo-o-o-o-o-o-o-o.*

He was seated on the big double bed with his back against the headboard. He dearly loved the accordion, the trueness and sweetness of his own voice, the ripple of his fingers on the smooth keys, the great-heartedness of the old songs.

> *My Johnny's g-o-o-o-o-ne*
> *And I'll go too-o-o-o . . .*

To Quinn, Roland O'Driscoll seemed beautiful in the soft lamplight. He wanted to lie next to him on the pillow and hold his hand. Indeed, he knew Roland would let him go that far. They could talk of what they felt at night, and of their cause, and of endless points of philosophy, and of their long, slow childhood together. But if Quinn leaned over to kiss him, Roland would turn his face away and let his friend's mouth linger on his cheek instead. If Quinn laid a questioning hand on his friend's leg or belly, Roland would go sit in a chair or look out a window. Quinn didn't try it much anymore. He had never succeeded in twenty years, and by now he knew he never would.

> *To see them Spa-a-a-a-nish*
> *Gi-i-i-i-rls I kno-o-o-o-w . . .*

Dominic Quinn was a virgin. His only encounters with flesh and the demon were months apart, they took place alone, and his spectral partner was never anyone but Roland O'Driscoll.

"Is there another thing you'd like to hear, Roland?"

"Yes, but I'd only be asleep for it."

Quinn laid the accordion aside. "That's good. There'll be little enough rest between now and the end."

"The end? You say that like it will be the end of breathin'."

"Did I now? Well, I never meant that. I mean for us to be far too busy over the next years to be sleepin' around on the bottom of this chilly sea." He saw O'Driscoll's knuckles go white around the glass. "I'm sorry, Roland. Just a manner of speakin'."

"It ain't you, Dominic. It's that peculiar note in the wind. I can hear them howlin' for me from underneath us—Dad, John, Derek. And the Granddad most of all. It was just this kind of norther, you know."

Quinn knew. He also knew that now his friend would drive himself through it all again. The narrative as heavy and invariable as that of a film seen too many times.

"We never should have been out that day, Dominic. We all told the Granddad so, but he always had this thought that the sea used her storms to test the love of the men who sailed on her. Over a pint he'd swear that we hauled in more fish than any boat our size on the coast because we kept on provin' ourselves to the great, gray mother that fed us. And you know. the way we killed the fish—we'd come home almost awash with their weight when the others could hardly find a herrin'—you could believe him.

"At any rate, there was no stayin' back. Then one day we pushed out into a nasty one. And it got worse every mile out. Then the sea just blew up. It was like we'd been straddled with the salvo of a battleship. The waves went climbin' into the sky sixty and seventy feet up. Out of reflex, we got into life jackets and roped ourselves together, but hell, we were like five cockroaches bein' flushed down a toilet. After a few minutes we heard a sound I don't believe anyone has ever heard twice: the ungodly crack of a boat bein' broken in half over the knee of a wave. For a second we just sat there lookin' at the cabin and bow tumblin' back past us where we sat in the stern. Then the engine bulkhead stove in, and the ocean swallowed our little chip with a gulp you could have heard on Malin Head.

"The first of them didn't die for five hours; the last of them lived for eight. It was as though the sea was tryin' to cram into our hearts all the terrors it had learned in a million years. Roped together in a circle as we were, each watched the other turnin' from a gentle, loved face into an inhuman thing mad with fear, and then finally into a horrid, contorted piece of dead slime that made you scream whenever the waves forced it into your arms.

"We died a thousand times, and then a thousand times more. We froze deeper and stiffer every hour, but there was no numbness to bless us, only a bone-deep pain that felt like it was crackin' the marrow out of us. For all the devil's roar of the sea, we could hear ourselves screechin' above it. We screamed to live, we screamed to die. It's bein' caught between the two that melts your tripes.

"Derek went first. Dad went mad and tore the life jacket off him. Thought he could save himself if he had two jackets. When he came out of it enough to realize what he had done, he raked all the skin off his face with his fingernails and slipped out of his own preserver. Watchin' the white, drowned faces with the open, starin' eyes, risin' and sinkin' and noddin' in front of us was too much for John. He come up with his clasp knife and drove it in under his chin to the hilt.

"For a while longer, the Granddad and I hung there, bayin' like dogs whenever we could steal a breath. Then he pulled himself over to me, pressin' his mouth against my ear and sobbin' for me to kill him. So I put my hand on the back of his neck and pressed his face under the water. He was a strong old man, and he could have broke free like I was a kitten if he wanted. But he never moved after I ducked him down. It was like my touch had been enough to stop his heart.

"I guess it was intended that there be somebody left to carry the fear away. Within the hour the wind and the white water were gone. A blue hole above opened and grew faster and faster until it had pressed those devil's clouds back under the horizon. Next thing I saw was the Granddad risin' up out of the water like it was the Resurrection and the sea was givin' up its dead. Up and up he went. I could see his white, hairless ankles stickin' up out of his drippin' shoes as he cleared the water. Then, one on each side of him, Dad and John rose up—John with the knife still stickin' straight out of his throat, and Dad with a look on his face that the entry into Paradise itself couldn't wipe off. Then I could see that what they were risin' up on was boat hooks. They were gettin' hauled up over the transom of a trawler. The fact that they pulled me out last tells you that I looked just as drowned as the others. When I croaked at them from the end of the hook, they jumped so hard that they lost me overboard again. They thought they were hearin' from the other side, and you know, Dominic, I think they were."

Though Quinn had heard the story before, he was overwhelmed anew by the weight of the telling. "You've been an Irishman too long, Roland. You've had some terrible bad luck. It's healthier just to let it go at that."

"No, I've been saved for somethin', and don't tell me you don't know it, too. You're not exactly a Turk yourself, Quinn."

"Okay, then. I think every Irishman on this ship has been saved for somethin': a free Ireland."

"Dom, I can't go into that water again. I just can't. I know it now."

"Don't be crazy. You took yourself to sea within a month after they picked you up."

"That was on the big tankers. When I was on deck, I'd keep my eyes down on the plates so I wouldn't even have to look at the ocean. When I heard the hiss of a wave or felt a drop of spray, I'd almost faint away. It's why I finally joined up with you and the Army. Not because I was so brave or loved you or Ireland so much, but because I'd rather feel bullets on my skin than the touch of sea water."

Tailor-squatting alongside O'Driscoll, Quinn pulled up his heavy sweater and unbuttoned the dark wool shirt underneath it. A packet of multicolored silk, folded several times, was lying flat against his bare belly. He unfolded the packet with care and suspended it by the corners before the recumbent O'Driscoll. It was a flag, lovingly stitched by hand.

"I've not seen one quite like that before, Commandant. It's pretty."

"Designed it and sewed it up myself."

"And a very nice job it is."

"Thank you." Quinn was pleased. Praise of handiwork is one of the few currencies that has never been debased. "It's for Greater Ireland, Roland."

"Greater Ireland?"

"Yes. The name has to change. We can't have the North feelin' that they've been conquered by somebody; we'd never have a real peace. We'll reshape everything: new name, new flag, new government bodies. In twenty-five years nobody will remember there was ever six separate counties."

"You've changed the colors. And you've got that thing in the middle. Embroidered, isn't it?"

"As a matter of fact, it is. What you see there—in addition to a color scheme that's featurin' orange in a pretty and prominent way—is two hands outstretched toward one another. The one outlined in green is the South; the one in orange is the North."

"Hey, the orange hand has six fingers."

"Aha! You saw it right off, just as you were supposed to. Six fingers, six counties. Symbolic."

"You . . . you don't think it might seem a little . . . freaky?"

"Well, how come so many of the Englishmen's flags are printed all over with unicorns and griffons, which are, for Christ's sake, birds with lion's heads or somethin', and nobody ever calls them freaky?"

"That's a well-taken point, that is. Anyhow, it's an awful handsome flag, Dom. Many a full-fledged country doesn't have one half so nice."

Quinn flapped the flag in an effort to simulate its performance in a stiff breeze. "Someday hearts will fill up when they see this snappin' in the wind. God willin', it's what they'll put over our graves."

"I'd a damn sight rather have that floatin' over me than a hundred fathoms of cold, black ocean."

"You're lettin' that stay too much in your head," Quinn said, carefully refolding the flag along its original creases. "When the time comes, you'll know your duty and do it as well as any of us. If you start to fail, think of this." He took the whiskey glass out of O'Driscoll's clasped hands and pressed the flag in its place.

"Aw, Dominic, I can't be takin' this."

110

"I can't think of anybody I'd rather have hold onto it. And it'll help you remember you're carryin' a whole country in your hands, so to speak. Remember, Roland: that flag could be in a museum, and if they grab you, you can get your picture taken with it. One of them pictures they keep printin' for all time, like the U.S. Marine Corps puttin' up the flag on that Jap island."

"If you say carry it, then carry it I will." Roland pulled up his sweater, unbuttoned his shirt and placed the flag against his body just as his commandant had. Before he could button the shirt again, Quinn had his fingertips resting lightly on O'Driscoll's skin.

"Roland, I still care for you a great deal."

"I know that you do." Roland did not shrink from the hand, but Quinn knew that he could go no further. He took O'Driscoll's whiskey glass and drained it, then lay down on the bolster pillow with his head lightly touching O'Driscoll's, threw an arm across his friend's chest and fell into the unshakable sleep of the righteous.

O'Driscoll dropped off a couple of times, but kept jolting awake when he thought he felt the lap of sea water around his feet.

Chief Engineer Tom Traskin, deep in his sixties, was twenty years older than George Barton, but they both shared the same idea of what constituted desecration. Barton leaned his Kalashnikov AK–47 against a console, placed both his hands on the glass separating him from the whirring, tumbling uproar of the engine room, and shook his head exactly the way Traskin was shaking his. "It's the awfulest thing I ever saw, Mr. Traskin. You'd think there'd be some maritime law against it, wouldn't you?"

"Yes, Barton, but it's all one hundred percent legal. We can be running through a blow just as bad as this one, and we don't have to keep a single goddamned man in the engine room all night long. My so-called engineers tramp in to work here in the morning like a bunch of time-clock-punching ribbon clerks, and go on home—every one of 'em—long before the sun is down."

"But for sure there's someone here in the booth?"

"Not even that. Me and the second engineers have a whole row of alarm lights over our desks and beds. If something went wrong, we might miss it if we were down here poking around in the engines instead of snug asleep or reading in our cabins. Excuse me. Our suites."

"Dear God, even this booth is air-conditioned. Mr. Traskin, I've had chiefs who wouldn't allow an electric fan in the engine room because it kept their skin from tellin' them somethin' was overheatin'. Do you know, there was one of 'em had a stiff knee from a submarine brush in the first war, and it could tell him a bearin' was runnin' hot when he just walked past it?"

"Barton, I guess the ultimate dial will be one over my bed that will tell me that the ship has sunk while I was asleep, and that now I am dead. Then a computer tape will chatter out a final prayer, notify my insurance company and send back my overdue library books."

"At least the sonofabitchin' engines still run the ship."

"Only barely. I've seen tea kettles that were put together better. But what the hell, the write-off on this whole damned ship is ten years—and I served in the engine room of the *Star of Rawalpindi* when she was sixty years old. She had the original engines, and they could have gone on for another sixty years if the hull around 'em hadn't rusted away. But it's the Japs who designed these things—they're the only ones who'd have the nerve. The tolerances are good enough, and the design is as simple as a roller skate, but the idea of two lousy boilers pushing out forty-five thousand horsepower—"

"Two lousy boilers!"

"We're lucky to have that many, Barton. They have four-hundred-and-fifty-thousand-tonners out there with *one*, for Christ's sake."

"How many was it the old *Queens* had?"

"Twenty-four just for the power plant, and another three to run the clothes pressers and heat the tea kettles."

112

"And what the hell is forty-five thousand horsepower for a whale like this? An old four-pipe destroyer delivered twenty-seven thousand."

"Just hydrodynamics. The bigger you build them, the easier they slide through the water."

"Finally they'll build one whose stern you can still see in New York when the bow heaves into sight in Le Havre. It will be powered by an outboard motor. It's obscene, Mr. Traskin. Nobody's takin' care anymore."

"Care? You know how long it took to build this thing from keel plate to launch? *Seven months*. Why, it takes longer than that to build a decent bell buoy."

They stood glaring through the glass, their faces warped with frustration. But the shiny, humming leviathan before them transmitted a strange beauty that their hearts could not deny.

"As a matter of fact, though," Traskin finally said, "those little yellow geniuses have a helluva lot of good ideas."

"Would you walk me around?"

"Sure I would, Barton. Now wait till you see what they did with the condensers. Our own designers could take a couple of hints from 'em there."

In a few minutes they were deep in the engine spaces. Barton had discarded the Kalashnikov for a wad of cotton waste, with which he wiped away spots of oil and grease that marred the brightwork here and there. Soon Traskin had transferred to Barton his deep, secret love for this imperfectly formed child, and they spent a happy two hours making an inventory of steam leaks. It was in neither's mind that this machinery was to be sitting rusting at the bottom of the sea in a little less than twenty-four hours.

chapter 6

One of the soldiers at the hospital room door
examined Benjamin Craddock's military intelligence credentials with excruciating care while the other patted him
down carefully, removing a service pistol, small penknife
and even a pipe-cleaning tool. "Now what the hell's all
this for?" Craddock asked.

"We lost a bunch of men right down the hall there a
few hours ago because they were a little too trusting.
Okay, you can go in." The soldier opened the door for
Craddock and started to follow him inside. The intelligence man placed his hand against the man's chest and
moved him back through the door.

"Sorry, soldier. That clearance gives me command
here, and I'd rather have this discussion alone. Don't
worry, I won't murder him."

"I don't care if you murder him, mister. Just don't do it
on my turn."

Craddock eased the door shut, lit a cigarette and pulled
a chair up alongside the bed. "Cigarette bother you?"

"Jesus and Mary," a strangled voice came through

hands pressed tightly over the face, "my kneecap's in ten million pieces and he asks me if I mind the cigarette. I wouldn't know the difference if you stuffed the hot end in my eye."

"Didn't they give you anything for the pain?"

"A little while they were fixing it. Nothing since. I can't take this, I can't."

Craddock ran his fingertips along the enormous cast on the boy's leg. "It's bad at first because of the swelling inside the plaster."

"Why can't they give me something?" McCarthy removed his hands from his face, which was glistening with tears and sweat.

"I think you know perfectly well why not."

"Because you won't let them."

"That's right."

"But they're *doctors*."

"Probably the same ones who tried to save some of those whom your boys dropped yesterday."

"My boys? Does it look like they were my boys?"

"I'd like this meeting to be a short one for both our sakes, McCarthy. We know perfectly well you've been thick with the Army for months. Now let's get it all out so we can give you a shot and you can grab some sleep." Craddock took a clean, white handkerchief out of his breast pocket and wiped the Irishman's face gently.

"You know I can't tell you anythin'."

"Seems like you already made a little mistake with them. I doubt if one more is going to do much more damage. We'll look after you, help you start somewhere else. You can't stay around here, anyway; you know that."

"They made a mistake with me. I didn't do what they said I did at all."

"Doesn't that make you a little angry? Let's you and me do something to the boys who did this awful thing to you. I mean, think of all you've lost, man. Your mum told me you were a pretty fair football player. You won't be doing any of that anymore."

"My mum never told a policeman anythin'."

116

"Now that you mention it, she didn't. I saw the picture of you in your nice athletic uniform, the shot standing over the stove."

"You're makin' me feel grand."

"And what about the girls? A good-looking young bachelor you may be, but the hard-hearted fluff of today aren't going to want to hop around the dance floor with a crip. Or even take a walk with a chap whose brace is squeaking and who takes twenty minutes to limp a block."

"You bastard."

"*I'm* not the bastard. *I* never blew the knee off you."

"They have to be careful."

"The worst part will be when you're with a bird and take your pants off. They're flighty enough anyway when you're trying to get them down, but when they see that mushy, shapeless thing that used to be a knee, with all that red-and-purple scar tissue, and the muscles all wasted—well, just think of the look on that girl's face, McCarthy. Which will be worse? If she tries to hide the disgust, or if she doesn't?"

McCarthy was crying openly now, like the very young boy that he was. Craddock, however, had often induced the same reaction in grown men. He flipped out his notebook and wet the end of a pencil. This was the most delicate part. He had to slip like a snake through the cracks he had opened. The loyalties of the months in which McCarthy had faced awful dangers with his comrades-in-arms still held, but now the hatred of being maimed was eating away at the kid. Eventually the story could be had, names and all. Craddock was not interested in the names, though; he wanted to identify the event that had brought about the retribution. McCarthy's maiming indicated a failure somewhere. The Movement contained a hundred thousand interlocking pieces, and you never knew which one, being loosened, would detach a thousand others. Sometimes it was the smallest bits that held the microcosm of the much greater whole.

"You say they made a mistake in your sentence. You

know, that could be, and the reason might be that you were accused or judged by somebody who wasn't one of your own boys. You may have been done in by a perfect stranger you don't owe a damn thing to."

McCarthy closed his eyes and rolled his head from side to side. "No, I knew every man in the room except the one."

"Isn't that the man, then? One is all it takes. A man who doesn't know you and trust you like the others, and tells a twisted story that brings you down."

"It was just among ourselves, I'm tellin' you. The other man was a prisoner himself."

Craddock slid off his chair and sat on the edge of the bed. "A prisoner? How do you know? Did they have him tied or cuffed?"

"None of that. It was the way the gorillas were standin' with him, and the look on his face."

"What kind of look?"

"The same kind I was wearin'. Scared out of his wits."

"Did you see him close?"

"Yes, close, but still not that good. He was standin' just half in the light. There were gold buttons . . . stripes . . . uniform."

"Uniform? What uniform was that?"

The boy was obviously sinking toward unconsciousness, so Craddock grabbed him at the angles of the jaws and squeezed until his eyes were fully open. "Tell me about the uniform." He balled up a fist and raised it above the knee in the cast. "I'll do whatever it takes to keep you awake."

"A sailor's uniform," the boy answered weakly.

"You said stripes and buttons. An officer's uniform, then?"

"Yes. An officer."

"Royal Navy?"

"No. A bit different than that."

"How was it different?"

"The cut, and the style of the cap."

"Are you some kind of a uniform expert now?"

118

"I've got an eye for clothes, damn it. All kinds."

"What was it? Russian? American?"

"American, it looked to me."

"What kind of stripes was he wearing? Do you know American naval rank at all? Lieutenant . . . lieutenant commander . . . commander?"

"Hell, mister, I don't know any of that, and how in hell would I remember?"

"What did he look like?"

"Young. Not much older than me. Blond hair."

"I thought he had a cap on."

"Yes, but his hair was long. It came down over his ears like mine."

"Had long hair, did he? That doesn't sound much like an American naval officer to me. Even the Dutch have a few standards left when it comes to the Navy."

"Well, then, maybe he wasn't in the bloody Navy at all, Mr. Wise Man. Maybe he was a merchant officer."

Craddock nodded. "See. I'm teaching you how to be a policeman. That's very good. Did they say anything to him?"

"Not a word."

"Did he say anything?"

"No, nothin' I heard."

"So it all comes down to your vast knowledge of haberdashery." Craddock pressed a button above the bed and almost immediately a sour-looking doctor appeared at the door. "Doctor, you've been neglecting this very important patient. Why don't you give him one of those nice rock-a-bye needles of yours so he'll be all rested up for our next long chat."

"You're a bloody, heartless thug," the doctor said.

"Heartless?" The intelligence man was backing out the door. "Why, even now I'm on my way to the lost-and-found to try to find a little American boy."

In a storm, the older seamen were not comfortable on the *American Enterprise*. There was something unnatural about the way the ship, stretching out of sight in all directions, shrugged off the wildest batterings of the sea. The *Enterprise* did not ride the waves as ships had for five thousand years; the seventeen-hundred-foot length and two-hundred-and-seventy-five-foot beam simply tossed the thousand-ton waves over the ship's back like a bull catching careless matadors. The old-timers braced themselves in vain as they watched building-sized combers riding down upon them; the expected shock never came. Instead, the wave that would have dissipated much of its force lifting the hull rode full fury along the open weather deck, occasionally shattering ten-inch-thick glass high up on the bridge house. As a result, in any sort of blow the deck became as dangerous as the pitching, ice-covered yardarms of a tea clipper trying a winter turning of the Horn. Men who had to venture toward the bow kept to the center of the *Enterprise*'s open deck. Here a partially caged catwalk gave some assurance that a man would not be swept over the side by the first roller coming over the bow. Seamen going forward often noted the time of their departure in a book; if they did not return in a reasonable time, they were searched for. The lucky ones were found caught in the ironwork with severe concussions, cracked skulls or compound fractures of the limbs. Of the less fortunate, only a boot or glove would be found, signaling the spot where its owner had tried to wedge a hand- or foothold into an angle of steel.

Captain Cody viewed a terrible dawn from the vast bridge. Pushing north to round Scotland into the North Sea, the ship was sailing at the ragged edge of the great storm. To the east, the blow was in full rage and growing worse. To the west, bright gray chunks of sky still opened and closed among the muddy billows of storm clouds.

Cody watched with undiminished wonder as the waves thundered along the acres of red-painted deck. The kingposts forward did not even shudder against the sky. Owen Browne stood alongside Cody, who sat in one of the high, swiveling captain's chairs more than a hundred feet away from the helmsman at the center of the bridge. Father

120

Costello, his automatic slung behind his back, stood half-way between the helm and the officers.

While appearing properly grim to Owen Browne, Jim Sam Cody was in fact in a state approaching euphoria. Not since the early forties had he known the surge of almost sensual excitement felt by men before the approach of battle. He remembered the majesty of the United States task force wheeling across Leyte Gulf to meet the daring sortie of Admiral Kurita, and his soles again felt the shock of the dreadnought *Yamato*'s eighteen-inch salvos shaking his doomed light carrier. He recalled the cold sea and the torn flesh, tasted oil and saw blood. He had thoroughly enjoyed it all.

As the captain started to speak to Browne, the first officer crouched and pointed to a speck in the center of a momentary clearing in the thickest clouds. "What in holy hell is that?"

The speck grew bigger, dropping down almost to the wavetops. Soon it became recognizable as a large, propeller-driven four-engine flying boat, which, though hindered by the wind, proceeded to fly in a wide circle around the *Enterprise*.

Browne clapped his forehead in wonder while Cody shouted with laughter. Costello unslung his assault rifle, ran the bolt and hurried to the officers. "What's the plane?" he shouted. "How'd he find us?"

"That plane," answered Cody, "is a Short Sunderland that is every day of thirty-five years old, and I didn't know there was a one left flying. He found us because we are dozens of hours off schedule, hundreds of miles off course and in the center of the worst weather in five years. In perfect weather, given our exact course, speed and timing, he'd probably have missed us completely. What he wants is to see whether we're polluting the waters—leaking or releasing oil in any way. That's one of the planes sent out by IMAPO, the Intergovernmental Maritime Anti-Pollution Organization. They've got some of their own patrols now, even on damn little funding."

"But why is he flying in this weather? There's no visibility you can depend on. A plane can hardly stay in the air."

"Because IMAPO is a bureaucracy, Costello," the captain said. "The weather report, I imagine, won't be official until it clears through channels, which will be about eight days from now."

Browne pressed a button on an intercom panel. "Radio. Any contact with a plane overhead?"

The voice of a radioman came back. "No contact, Mr. Browne."

Eamon O'Driscoll's voice broke in. "Browne, who's up there with you?"

Costello leaned into the speaker. "It's me, Eamon. Don't worry about the plane. Just snoopin' for oil spills.

"What if he radios down, Father?"

"Then we'll wake Quinn. Meanwhile, it's like Dominic said. No transmissions."

The plane leveled out of its bank and began a climb to the east that quickly took it out of sight.

"He's sending a position report on us, Mr. Browne," the radioman said. "But no direct contact."

"Okay, Franks. Thank you."

"Why the report, Browne?"

"Routine. So other planes can pick us up later."

"That's mad. In a few hours we'll be in the heart of that madhouse. Jesus himself couldn't find us."

"If you'll put your comments in writing and file them in octuplicate with IMAPO, I'm sure they'll take them under consideration."

Costello snorted and began the long stroll toward the helmsman to recheck the course.

The officers waited until he was out of earshot. "Owen, if you were an old, experienced terrorist organization and you kidnapped a ship for ransom, when would you let the authorities know what you were up to?"

"The very moment I hit the open sea. The people ashore might have already discovered that something was fishy and begun to take countermeasures. The more the ultimatum takes the shore by surprise, the more effective the demand. The most successful operations of this kind have been the ones where the authorities had the shortest time to react. Of course the Irish did say that the blowup would have the greatest impact if they did it in the North Sea."

"Yes, but how much better for them if they announced that they were setting off the charges the moment they reached a preannounced position. Do you see the kind of time pressure that would create? Why add negotiating time to the operation after they're in position, when it's so much more to their advantage to begin negotiating before they reach the spot?"

"So what do you think it means?"

"I don't think they're doing this for ransom."

"What, then?"

"I think they mean to blow up this ship in the North Sea without asking for ransom or prisoners or anything else."

"They couldn't. Not in this storm. Nobody would get off—not us, not them."

"I've got that man Quinn sized up, Owen. He'd do it. Believe me."

"But why? What's destroying an American ship going to get him? He could have scuttled her in Coltry if it was deep water he was looking for."

"There's the oil. It would create a lot more of a problem for Britain in the North Sea."

"They've dealt with big spills before. Not the size that this one would be, maybe, but they could surely handle it. It just doesn't seem worth the trouble."

"Agreed. There's something missing—something that will make whatever it is Quinn is doing worth all our lives."

"What you're getting at is that we're taking it much too calmly."

"I'm sure that's just the way they've planned it. As long as we think it's just a little cash transaction, we'll think of it as an exciting vacation and sail their damned ship for them as if we were a litter of kittens."

123

"We've got to get the ship away from them, then."

"I don't think we'll be able to do that. They've been shooting people for a long time, and they're extremely good at it. We'd just get ourselves killed."

"Maybe they need us too much for that."

"Maybe not. Most of them know their way around big tankers pretty well. I've chatted with them every chance I've had. They were picked for this, I'm sure."

"Which would make crippling the *Enterprise* pretty tough, too. They know everything we're supposed to be doing. They'd probably notice any monkeying with the routine."

"Basically true. We'll have to be careful and only fool with things not likely to have been on smaller tankers."

"We'd better get some ideas soon, Captain. Evaporators?"

"No. The damage takes too long to show up."

"Alternators, maybe. It wouldn't interfere with the propulsion, but it would take out everything we need to navigate."

"Tom Traskin says the man they call Barton—he seems like a sharp one—made him point out the emergency diesel alternator almost the first thing. They'd have all the power they needed right back on in a couple of minutes."

Browne forced a laugh. "We can hardly keep this big tub moving when we want to, and now we can't think of a way to stop it."

"Maybe we're trying for something too big. That automated engine room has all those sensors. Maybe if we could just trigger one . . . Some of them shut down the boilers automatically."

"What would be the first thing you'd do if the boilers shut down now?"

"Uh-huh. Check the sensors to see if one of them was malfunctioning. And they'd do the same thing."

"So that's no good. Besides, what would they do to us if we stopped the ship here instead of where they want us to? They might kill us on the spot. Or blow up the ship and the oil anyway, which would probably amount to the same thing."

"I don't think so, Owen. The care they took laying this course tells us they want to get to a particular spot."

"More particular than just the North Sea?"

"Yes. They've got some sort of rendezvous at the end of this course that we don't know about yet."

"With whom?"

The captain shrugged. "We don't have to know. It's my guess that if we can stop them before we're much deeper into the storm, they'll call the whole thing off. It won't be worth the cost anymore. By IRA standards, this job isn't a serious one yet—a parking-ticket crime. As far as I can tell, nobody's been hurt. The way Irish amnesties fly around, they'd get a little time in the slammer and live to fight a lot more days."

Cody was quiet for several minutes before he spoke again. "Owen, we've got to ground her."

"In waves like this? In a ship that doesn't ride? She might break up."

"She could. I suppose she would. But I think it's the best we can do."

"They're watching the course too closely." They both glanced toward the helm, where Costello was in the act of checking the compass over the helmsman's shoulder.

"We won't change the course. There's another way, and it's damned likely to get us killed. Interested?"

"Go on, sir."

"There are spots on this course where we've only got two or three feet of water under our keel. What if we brought the head down by those two or three feet and drove her full tilt into the mud? It would take a lot of hours to pump out enough oil to tighten her for a try at backing off."

"The only way to bring that bow down is to let in an awful lot of sea water."

"Yes, Owen. We've got to open the hull. Not all of it—just enough."

"We need explosives and someone who knows how to set them."

"No, we don't. We're carrying an explosive as powerful as anything they brought aboard on that truck, and it's in exactly the right place."

"My God. Number One. The bow tank. It's empty."

"That's right. And if we've got the technology to keep that tank safe from explosive gases——"

"Then we can also turn it into a bomb."

"The Irish probably don't understand half of what you do in that control room. Next time you're in there, start changing the atmosphere in Number One back to oxygen. Cut the flue gases. Use the blowers any way you have to to speed things up."

"They don't let me in the room alone."

"Then don't move any setting too much all at once. Get at the controls every couple of hours. They'll think it's standard procedure. Adjust the atmosphere dials on the other tanks, too. If they ask, tell them it's some kind of viscosity adjustment."

"How long have we got, sir?"

"Let's check the chart."

Cody slipped off the chair and lumbered stiffly and unhurriedly toward the chart room behind the helm. "Having a look at the chart," he barked at Costello. The ex-priest came to the doorway of the room and watched the captain fiddle with dividers and pencil under the brilliant light of the chart table.

"Costello," Cody said, "get us the heading like a good fellow."

Costello started to call a question to the helmsman, but, as Cody thought he would, decided to avoid any chance of misdirection by checking the compass himself. "Heading three-fiver-eight," he shouted back. As Cody also expected, he did not bother returning to the chart room, even when Browne strolled in to join his captain.

Cody dropped his voice to just below what Costello could hear if he drifted back toward them. "We're right here, just clearing Ireland and getting ready to come north-northeast for the tip of Scotland. Right along here, just off Cape Wrath, the water shoals down to about ninety-five feet, with plenty of wrinkles where it's less than that. If we blow the tank right about here"—he made a light mark on the chart—"that bow will be down three feet and well into a sandbank in the half hour or so it will take us to lose way."

"Looks like we have about eight hours to get the tank ready."

"Can you get it done by then?"

"Yes, sir, I think so." Browne lit a cigarette with a disposable butane lighter. "We'll have to set it off manually." He flipped the lighter in his palm. "This will be just the thing, don't you think?"

"Yes, I can just tape the switch open and drop it through one of the manholes."

"You? No, they know where you are all the time. They're a little more careless with me and the others. I'll do it."

"This is not for a married man."

"Don't be so considerate, Captain. Knowing the kind of marriage that I have . . ."

"Hell. Growing pains."

"Oh, I mean to come back. What kind of damage do you think that tank will do?"

"Well, it could interfere with your plan to come back. Number One's our smallest tank, but the explosion should be a good one. It will take out the collision bulkhead, break the frames in the forepeak and open the bottom forward of the alleyway under the tanks."

"Right. The alleyway doesn't extend under Number One. The blast will get at the bottom nicely. Will it rupture Center Number Two? Or the Number Two wing tanks?"

"Possibly, but that's not a big problem. The watertight doors behind Number Two will contain the sea water forward where we want it."

"What about the boom going straight up through the

weatherdeck plates, where the man who's dropped the lighter will be standing?"

"Your chances are a lot less than fifty-fifty, Owen. I've seen quite a few supers that have blown tanks, and the deck plates were mostly gone. And even if they stay put, the shock would likely break your legs, and maybe your back, too."

"Jesus." Browne's face was as white as his cap.

Cody held out his hand. "Give me the lighter."

Browne shook his head. "I go or nobody goes."

"Maybe it should be nobody. We could be wrong."

"Yes, we could be."

"Maybe we could attract attention. Get help."

The first officer waved a hand at the rain drumming on the skylight. "In this?"

"That IMAPO plane found us."

"A chance in a thousand."

"They've got our position now. They could check back."

"What would it get us?"

"Never underestimate a bureaucrat's ability to cause trouble. I'll have Tom Traskin pump some bunker oil overside. That will give them a nice big slick to find and report."

"Okay, Captain."

"Will you still do it if it looks like we must? I've got to know."

"Oh, I'll do it. It's a chance to move up faster—one way or the other."

Having been relieved by his brother of duty in the radio room, Eamon O'Driscoll came down to the vast crew's game room to join Punchy Devlin, who was on guard duty, and The Dropper, who was supposed to be asleep.

Outside of the engine area and tanks, the game room was the largest enclosed space on the ship. It spanned the two-hundred-and-seventy-five-foot beam of the *Enterprise*, and the hundred-and-fifty-foot depth of the super-

128

structure—a deck to itself. Large windows ran all across the stern, giving a magnificent view of the ship's wake. On the rare days when the temperature was right, these windows were propped open to bring the outdoors inside and make a promenade as grand as any on the old *Queens*. The other bulkheads contained portholes for greater strength against pounding seas.

At the room's center was a swimming pool, now covered by a sliding hardwood floor and used as a soccer field. Scattered about were Ping-Pong tables, card, chess and checker tables, exercise machines, wrestling mats, a collapsible boxing ring, basketball hoops, a handball court, sun lamps and a small wooden sauna. Behind a curtain was a gigantic movie screen.

The Irishmen had never seen anything like the game room. They took to spending every off moment in it, and ordered all the crewmen who were not officers to remain there while off duty. At the moment twenty seamen, on the whole cheerful, sat reading, dozing, talking and gaming in a group under the stern windows.

Devlin and The Dropper sat in reclining deck chairs facing the group. The hairless Devlin, hands closed on the Kalashnikov despite the amiability of the men he was guarding, looked more cheerful than Eamon O'Driscoll had ever seen him. Lying with his eyes half closed, The Dropper also seemed unnaturally contented. He was wearing an electrician's utility belt, still loaded with tools, and his jacket pockets bulged with hardware and odds and ends of wire. His hands were freshly abraded and scratched, and streaks of dirt ran across his face and neck. He shifted his weight gingerly, as though his back hurt him.

Eamon saw that the vast pile of boxed explosives once stacked in a corner of this room were gone. "That was fast work, Dropper. Everything in place, is it?"

"In place, yes. Set, no. I had a dozen of these ship monkeys help me trot it down the lift to where I want it."

"And where's that?"

"A beautiful spot. It's as though the boys that built this

ship wanted to make it easy to blow. No crawlin' though the bilges and over the frames for the old Dropper. They've got this lovely alleyway that runs under the tanks from Number Two all the way back to the engine room. Well-lit, well-aired, a mile wide, and full of fine places where the tanks and hull come together for one charge."

"What's the alleyway doin' under there anyways, Dropper?"

"There's all kinds of pump plumbin' runnin' up out of it. I suppose pumps at the bottom of the tanks make it a lot easier to clean 'em."

"Is it goin' to be a big job settin' the charges?"

"Big enough. The bow tank is empty, but that leaves nineteen more, each divided into a center tank and two wings. That's at least fifty-seven charges to undress, pack and wire. A mile of walkin' and a mile of wire."

"So why are you lyin' here on your ass?"

" 'Cause I'm made out of meat, not iron, and I'll be needin' your brother for help. I can't trust anybody in the crew for the wirin', and Roland's got the mechanical bent I need." He picked a huge blueprint of the ship's hull from beneath the recliner, rolled it open almost to the full span of his arms, and with his throat gave an uncanny imitation of the sound of rushing water.

Devlin spoke so rarely that the other two almost jumped at the sound of his voice. "Jesus, I hate to have us drown this beautiful place."

chapter 7

Cullenbine's quarters on Mavis A. included a plush conference room. Even with himself, Magnus, Lustgarten and Zamke around the long table, three-quarters of the chairs were empty.

Lustgarten stood at the head of the table, a manila folder and several sheets of paper in front of him. "My friends, I have asked for this meeting because suddenly this platform may be in considerable danger."

Since no man at the table could truly believe his statement—including, down deep, Lustgarten himself—there was no sign of tension at this announcement. Magnus, wearing a turtleneck sweater and his old Navy bathrobe, welcomed the suggestion of an emergency. He had become a hopeless lover of action during the war. "Something on the wireless, is it, Lustgarten?"

"Several things. No single one of them of great concern, but looking like trouble when they're taken all together."

"May we have the messages in the sequence you received them, Colonel?" Cullenbine asked.

"First we had a routine news scan from North Sea Security which told of a detention-camp breakout by six IRA terrorists. It was engineered from the outside, and accomplished with great risk and heavy loss of life to the guards. The attackers lost at least one of their own, as well. The news was only of interest to me because one of the men had been involved in seaborne sabotage of oil fields, though in a minor way. However, we ran a standard computer check on the escaped men and found that five of them were seamen—oil tanker men, to be specific. The sixth was an explosives expert. The freed men were virtually the only seamen among hundreds of prisoners in the camp, and certainly the only ones with tanker experience.

"Now, supposing that a sea operation might be planned, perhaps against North Sea oil, we put in a general check on all oil shipping—that is, tankers at sea or in port in the British Isles or North Sea area. Nothing seemed to be out of place. All shipping was where it was supposed to be, according to communications from either the ships themselves or from their home offices."

Zamke had taped several Admiralty charts to a large sheet of cardboard, and he propped this up against a lamp on the table. Blue pins dotted the area along the west coast of Ireland, and around Scotland near the spot where Mavis A. stood in the North Sea.

"These pins," Zamke explained, "represent all the ships we knew to be at sea in the area that concerned us. Until a few hours ago, we thought this was the complete picture. As you can see, the storm has held traffic down considerably. We count seventeen vessels strung out between southwest Ireland and the mouth of the North Sea."

Lustgarten picked a sheet of paper off the table and waved it. "This came in from British Intelligence in Ireland. It looked like a standard IRA punishment thing; they blew the kneecap off a man who was nobody special. But the man saw something in the room where he was shot; the Irish had a prisoner who seemed to be an American, and he looked to be a merchant-ship officer."

"That's why the information was put through to North Sea Security?"

"Yes, Mr. Cullenbine. Every man and piece of machinery that floats on this sea is our concern."

"You put out a tracer on the man?"

"Not an easy thing to do. Seamen in port do not leave word of their destinations, and there are a great many ports in the Isles. Nonetheless, we checked every ship in harbor and—whenever possible—its owner."

"The information you got couldn't be conclusive enough for any action," Magnus said. "There'd be dozens of men unaccounted for."

"Yes, it was a long shot. But we did come up with a startling piece of information. When the Petromarine Corporation attempted to contact their *American Enterprise*, which should have been in Coltry Bay until tomorrow, the ship was gone. Slipped out into the storm. Cast off without help. Left no word with anyone."

"She's the biggest ship in the world," Cullenbine said. "Somebody must have seen her go."

"If somebody did, we haven't been able to find him yet."

"Maybe the captain saw some break in the weather, or decided to pull out without a lot of shore traffic to complicate things."

"A possibility. But she was due to do some unloading tomorrow, and so far all attempts to raise the *Enterprise* by radio have been fruitless."

"Interference from the storm? Radio equipment damage?"

"The chances of those are so slight that we can forget them, I believe."

"So what might we have here, Colonel Lustgarten?"

"In order of likelihood, Admiral Magnus: first, an operational deviation or mechanical accident that will seem painfully ordinary and expectable when they tell us about it. Second, a terrorist kidnapping. The world's largest tanker—loaded almost to full capacity, I'm told—would be a very gaudy thing to hold for ransom. And lastly, a plan to bring the *Enterprise* into collision with an oil plat-form, with Mavis A. being the prime choice."

Again, there was no reaction from the Englishmen. Cullenbine was pleased to be able to show that his side could be even cooler than the Germans. "You've made a rather large jump there, haven't you, Lustgarten?"

"A jump, yes, but maybe not so large. An IMAPO patrol plane has found our lost leviathan. She was at the edge of the storm and steaming at full speed north, not west toward Newfoundland, her next destination."

"Was there positive identification?" Cullenbine asked.

"There's only one ship like the *American Enterprise*. The plane couldn't have been wrong."

"Did he make radio contact?"

"I'm afraid he didn't bother. He saw no reason to be-lieve that she wasn't exactly where she was supposed to be."

"What do you propose?" said Magnus.

"I'd like your permission to call the Royal Navy and Air Force into a search for the *Enterprise*."

"And if they find her?"

"Shadow her. And if she does not give a satisfactory response to inquiries and continues toward possible col-lision targets in the North Sea . . . sink her."

Suddenly Lustgarten had the full attention of all the men around the table.

Anger crept into Magnus' voice. "Colonel, here we would rather think first and kill later. It's an old habit with us."

A hard smile fixed itself on Lustgarten's face. "Well, now, there it is. The chance you waited for. You've put the brutal, unthinking, unfeeling German in his place."

"Words alone have never been enough to do that, Lust-garten. Now, out of idle curiosity, what about the lives of the crew on that ship?"

Lustgarten was taken more aback than he showed, for the truth was that he had not thought about the American crew. He had not even anticipated Magnus's reaction to

134

his suggestion. Nor, he knew, had Zamke. God, was he so much like his aide?

"We would warn them first, of course. Give them time to get clear."

There was an unpleasant growl from Cullenbine, who jerked his thumb at a porthole. "In this? It would be like telling them you won't kill them if they'll commit suicide."

Angry, Lustgarten brought out his favorite defense weapon and counterattacked. "Magnus, you were an admiral. You were in action for five years. Did you ever send men to their deaths?"

"Many times."

"Did you ever send men to their death mistakenly?"

This answer came slower. "Many times."

"You are charged with protecting the life of your country, as you would like it to remain, no less now than you were then."

"But this is not war."

"Then what is it, sir?"

"I could not give such an order in any case. I am no longer in the military."

"I'm sure you are aware of your importance. Let's not make any pretenses. You know perfectly well that your country would fling itself against the Russian Navy itself if you said that they were about to keep you from that oil."

"He's right about that," Cullenbine said. "They would sink her on your word."

"I think this may be a meaningless point. If the *Enterprise* turns into the storm, which she may already have done, it might be that nobody will be able to find her."

Zamke broke in. "Mr. Cullenbine, if she is not found, wouldn't that be evidence that she has turned into the storm and is moving east toward us?"

"It may only mean that the storm has spread west and swallowed her up. Or that they have overlooked her. What's your point, anyway? If they can't find her, they certainly can't sink her."

"The point," Lustgarten said, "is that we could begin to take defensive measures."

"We have no defenses. There's not a military weapon on this rig. Besides, you need torpedoes or heavy shells to stop a ship that size."

"I meant the word passively."

"We sure as hell can't maneuver out of her way," Cullenbine said.

"We must accept that we will be struck. All we can do is minimize the damage. We must shut down the wells at once."

"That's simply out of the question," Magnus snapped. "Good God, do you know what that would cost us?"

Cullenbine pounded both his big fists on the table like a child in a temper tantrum. "Do you know what you're saying? You know it isn't a matter of just turning a faucet."

"I thought that was exactly what you did on a well that was already producing."

Cullenbine turned a fiery red. "We've got the Christmas-tree valves at the top of the shaft, not at the goddamned bottom. We needed all the space we could get down there. Besides, we had to figure that if there was going to be any trouble it was going to be with flooding, so we wanted the shut-offs above the water. If that ship hits us, it will shear away the pipes well below those Christmas trees."

"But there must be things you can do."

"Sure there are, but I'll have to manage it with what we've got aboard. It'll be all acetylene torches and mud and the goddamnedest mess ever made."

"How long would it take?"

"For all three legs? Six, eight, twelve hours—I don't know. We'd be writing the book, not going by it."

Lustgarten leaned toward Magnus. "I tell you that you must order Mr. Cullenbine to begin capping those wells at once."

"If I give that order, I must do the same with every well in this sea. They might pick any of our platforms. Or mistake one of the others for this one."

"No," Cullenbine said, "if it's going to be tried, this

136

would be the target. And we stand alone in the Mavis Field. If she comes after us, she'll get us without a mistake." He thought for a moment. "I think we should shut down."

Magnus waved a finger. "Tell me what we'd lose in a shutdown. Time, oil and money."

Cullenbine picked up a circular slide rule, reached for a pad and pencil, and calculated for perhaps ten minutes. Finally he ripped off a page and shook his head at the figures.

"The problem isn't really getting it all shut down," he said. "That's mostly tearing things apart. Where we run into trouble is putting the job back together again. A lot of the pipe we'll be cutting up was custom-made for Mavis, some of it in the United States. We'd probably have to crank up production again. Before we could do that we'd have to get the authorization and funding from BNOC—and just getting those guys together to talk about it could take a week. The steel plant would have to work us into their casting schedule, and that could take another week. There's the actual mill work, and then there'd be the shipping. This stuff is too big and heavy to ship by air in anything but the largest Air Force troop carriers, and they won't lend them out commercially; we've tried before. That means rail from Pittsburgh to New York and a slow boat across the Atlantic. The equipment would have to be transferred to lighters in Scotland—between longshoremen's strikes—and then towed slowly and carefully —allowing delays for bad weather—into the North Sea. To bring the equipment aboard we'd have to cut through the main deck and open up the tops of the legs again. We didn't figure on having to put anything major down into them after the main equipment was in place. I suppose we could spare ourselves some of that job by lowering the stuff down in pieces and doing the welding below, but it probably wouldn't save a helluva lot, and the work wouldn't be as reliable. Then we'd have to get the flow going smoothly again."

"The figures, please, the figures."

Cullenbine said, "As near as I can work it out, Mavis A. would be through pumping oil for between six and seven weeks. We'd lose about one-and-a-quarter million barrels of production. The repair work would cost about two million pounds, and overtime could drive that a lot higher. We'd be lucky to get the whole job done with a loss of ten million pounds, counting the present value of the oil."

Magnus walked a slow turn around the table, shaking his head. "No, no, no, no. No. There is entirely too much supposing in this, and that cost is unbearable. If we were wrong in shutting down—and nine chances in ten we'd be wrong—it would destroy all of us."

Everyone in the room was a brave man who would have stood up unflinchingly to gunfire, but the thought of a career in danger was something else. All hope of an immediate move died in that moment.

Lustgarten said, "Perhaps it would be wise to wait for positive word that the ship has turned east."

"It will certainly be a few hours before we hear," said Cullenbine.

Zamke nodded. "Yes, we should have more concrete evidence to act on. We will ask the Navy and Air Force for help. If they can't make visual contact, they can try with radar."

Noel Cullenbine knew that he could get a job anyplace in the world where an oil derrick stood. "What the hell is radar gonna tell you that's positive? You said yourself that there's a whole bunch of ships milling around in that storm. How can you tell them apart? Their captains will turn any way they have to in order to ease off the pounding. You'll never get them untangled."

"We can ask for position reports from all shipping."

"So then you'll know that some blips are *not* from the *Enterprise*—if they get a blip at all in a sea like this."

"We must shut down, Admiral," Lustgarten said.

"Admiral Magnus," said Cullenbine, "we're sitting on a high-pressure field of unbelievable size. If that oil starts pouring into the ocean, half the people on this planet

138

might have to start looking for someplace to live. Like Mars."

"They'd hang us awfully fast for that kind of a blowout," Magnus said. "Just for having been here. I suppose we should establish a point at which we begin to shut down."

Lustgarten agreed. "Yes. After we get visual evidence that the ship has turned this way. We can't wait for more than that."

"All right," said Magnus. "Alert the military and request sighting reports from anyone who might come across the *Enterprise*. If she turns this way, we shut down."

"There's more to it than that," Cullenbine said. "What about the men? The rescue boats are gone, and we don't have survival capsules. There are only some rubber rafts scattered around for 'man overboard' situations."

"There's no need to worry about it."

"Why not, Admiral?"

"Because nothing is going to happen." Magnus nodded a goodnight to the men, walked to the elevator and disappeared behind its closing door.

"I'll get the men ready to move fast," Cullenbine said.

"Will you tell them what's going on?" Zamke asked.

"I think not. Discipline isn't good to begin with, and all these months cooped up haven't helped things much. We want them available to work on the shutdown, not busy building rafts and fighting over the ones we've got. I'll tell them that there's some technical problem—that the pressure has built up in some way and they've got to be ready to stop blowouts, or some such. Make it plausible."

"Is that fair? Maybe they *should* be working on ways to save their skins. Nobody else is giving it much thought."

"There's no way to go backward on this. The shutdown must come before we lose them. And let's look at it squarely: If Mavis A. goes over in this sea, the only life raft worth anything will be what's left standing above the water—and that will be damned little, I'm afraid."

Lustgarten wondered how the clear purpose he had felt when he entered the room twenty minutes before had dissipated so quickly in confusion and compromise. He felt infected by it. Five years ago he would have had the personal force to override Magnus's objections in the face of any consequences. He had the feeling that Zamke, young as he was, could have done it. Why hadn't he turned him loose? Perhaps, he thought, a feeble hand fears a sharp tool.

Noel Cullenbine had spent the last dozen years of his life bringing order out of the work of wild, strong men, most of them dangerously drunk or murderously bored. Being able to handle them one at a time with his fists was important, but being able to control them as an effective group when they were out of sight was indispensable. He exerted much of his control via two elaborate games, one played with liquor, the other with women. These contests provided diversion and contact, and they kept his relationship with the crew on the requisite adversary basis.

Liquor was forbidden aboard Mavis A., but this was a standing joke. Every supply lighter that arrived carried almost as much whiskey as it did pipe and cable. When Cullenbine uncovered a cache, he would make a great show of forcing the malefactor, if caught red-handed, to march it across the main deck and dump it into the sea. The chorus of threats and curses that always accompanied this ceremony came only from men hidden among the tools and ironwork. The dumping had its usefulness in holding down the cases of roaring, inoperable drunkenness, since this led inexorably to the discovery of too much liquor. The worthiness of Cullenbine as an opponent gave the game of procuring and hiding the whiskey an unusual measure of risk and excitement. It was universally known that the rig's half-dozen hardsuit divers drove themselves to exhaustion trying to recover the precious bottles from the sea bottom at the end of their working dives. Cullenbine pretended not to know, since the amount rescued was minuscule and the enjoyment great, but he took malicious joy in stone-facedly phoning a complicated and strenuous extra operation down to a diver who he knew had ranged a hundred yards afield in his search. No amount of effort could hide the consternation on the faces of the diver's tenders. They knew their man would come up rubber-legged, glassy-eyed and ready for nothing but twelve hours in bed. Yet the game went on.

Then there were the women. Usually they were the toughest, nastiest whores that the slums of Glasgow could breed. They had to be in order to endure the round-the-clock demands of six hundred hard and lonely men. There had been one girl who had been forced to give herself up for medical attention. The doctor had been astonished to find her vagina so laccrated and bleeding that he had to order emergency helicopter evacuation to a hospital. The cause of her injuries had not been brutality, but simple wear. As overuse made her performance more and more painful and reluctant, the desperate men had wildly bid up the price of the act. One tool-pusher had given her two hundred pounds for a single act, and her greed had been so great that she had ignored her pain until she had finally fainted and slipped into shock.

Although he knew where every screwdriver on Mavis A. was at a given moment, Cullenbine never could discover exactly how many women were aboard. He estimated a constant number of between two and five. The men had shown such ingenuity in smuggling them onto the rig that it bordered on genius. Women had arrived in pieces of pipe swung up by cranes, in dummy oxygen cylinders, in sea bags slung over shoulders, in helicopters, and on at least one occasion, in a canoe.

The hiding places found for the girls were every bit as ingenious. There was hardly a storeroom or toolroom aboard that hadn't had a false wall built into it, behind which operated a cozy, sometimes even luxurious brothel. At one time the welders, working at night and at great risk to their lives, had managed to hang an entire apartment beneath the main deck. When Cullenbine discovered it after five happy months of operation, he had found it heated for winter, air-conditioned for summer and equipped with a television set, a propane stove and running water—not to mention a French provincial bed bearing a mattress that had disappeared from his own cabin. He also found evidence of an attempt at constructing a chamber beneath the seafloor at the bottom of Blueleg.

The discovery of a woman was only serious if she had been aboard for some months. A girl caught tucked in a sleeping bag tied to a helicopter skid would be sent right back the way she came, and there would be only laughter and a few groans. Catching a girl after a few days would bring on some cursing and sullen muttering. But sending off the long-term girls would cause breakdowns, wild rages and even vicious physical attack. For this special, lonely breed of men felt a compelling need to fall deeply, irretrievably in love with any regular object of their affections. Cullenbine suspected that a lot of nasty knife work was the result of these impossible romances.

But now, with the sudden threat to the rig, he had to dig the hidden women out. For one thing, he didn't want them dead, trapped in some rathole when the whole business went over. For another, he didn't want the men leaving critical work to save them or—God help him—make love to them.

The inactivity forced by the storm made all the jobs facing Cullenbine more difficult. The men would be drunk, lethargic and reluctant to return to their cold, bone-tiring work. Also, their swarming presence on every deck would make the search for the women very hard; when they saw he was getting warm they would come up with a thousand reasons for his presence elsewhere.

But one thing at a time. He would have to be in a hundred places at once to prepare for the shutdown. It was desperately important that he pound a new sense of discipline into his men. Were there any shortcuts? He had lashed out at them so many times that—among the veterans at least—he had lost some of his ability to shock. But he'd find a way; he always did.

Cullenbine stopped by his cabin and got into his heaviest clothes: laced leather boots that ran to the knee, a cable-knit sweater high up around his throat; a thigh-length coat of canvas so thick that the arms could hardly be bent at the elbow; and trousers of the same material. He topped off this outfit with a hard hat buckled tightly under the chin, and a pair of thick-fingered safety gloves through which ran tendrils of steel. Now he was protected against the draining cold and damp that prevailed deep in the rig's legs, but more importantly he was formidably armored for violence. He opened the signals box next to his cabin door and turned down the orange handle that sounded the general alarm.

In the interest of normalizing the atmosphere aboard the *American Enterprise,* Quinn had decreed that the ship's officers take their meals with full decorum, despite the presence of an IRA man. As always, these meals were served in the sumptuous officers' wardroom on the lower bridge deck.

Petromarine tried to compensate its crews for the boredom of the interminable trips by making all the creature comforts exquisite. As a consequence, the men aboard concerned with food were present in numbers and quality disproportionate to the operating crew. There were two first chefs, each with a different list of specialties. The menu was almost absurdly varied, sometimes to the chagrin of the men. An entrée that would be the talk of the wardroom might not appear again for three months. All pleas for an unscheduled repeat, including requests from the captain, fell upon stony hearts as the chefs showed their versatility; they stuck to the menus they had planned months ahead as though they were programmed into the ship's computers.

The four mess stewards, after the senior officers the oldest men on the ship, were all Filipinos who had behind them long experience in the United States Navy. They brought such grace and dignity to their work that many of the crew felt that this service was what they would miss most on a lowlier ship.

The Dropper, whose total knowledge of foreign languages ran to a couple of hundred words in Gaelic and the essential whorehouse terms in Arabic, was intimidated by the menu card and just pointed to a line at random when the steward asked for his choice. When he tried to hide his discomfiture behind a noisy check of the action of the assault rifle lying alongside his chair, he drew angry stares from Captain Cody, Owen Browne, Ethel Browne and Tom Traskin, his fellow diners.

"Sorry for that," The Dropper muttered, burning inside.

"I see you've come to the table filthy," Browne said. "You might at least show us the courtesy of washing yourself before the meal."

"Most of it is shavings from electrical wire insulation. It gets on your clothes and hair. It would be hard to get it off without a shower."

"You mean you've taken over the entire ship except for the showers?"

"I mean that I have much to do. I didn't have the time."

Captain Cody was as amazed as The Dropper at the mildness of the response to Browne's attack. But the first officer could do that to you. When a man has gone through his entire life without making a significant mistake, it leaks into his voice, and there is an I-am-right in the tone that delivers devastating power. Cody himself had fought against it many times. Still, the Irishman should not be excited further. He spoke to The Dropper in a soft voice. "Will you use all the explosives you brought in the truck, Mr. . . . ."

"Mullins. My name is Molaise Mullins. And your answer is yes. Every ounce of it."

"I suppose you need it to sink a ship this size."

"Not just sink her. I could carry enough stuff in my pockets to do that."

"Not just sink her? But what more is there to do?"

"Shit," The Dropper said when he realized he had said more than he'd meant to. "Well, Captain, you know, if it came to havin' to put her down, we'd want her to come apart enough where she couldn't be salvaged. And we'd want all the oil out of her."

Browne jumped back in. "I'd like to ask you to watch your mouth while my wife is here. I suppose there's nothing I can do about your dirty trade and politics, although you might try keeping them to yourself, too."

Ethel recognized the sting of that tone so well she reacted as though she had been its target. "For God's sake, Owen, will you let the poor man eat his dinner? It's nothing but good manners, isn't it?"

This vehement and unexpected attack on his flank sent Browne into a shocked, silent sulk.

The Dropper's heart opened to Ethel. For the first time he looked at her directly. In all, he was a good-looking man. He had large, delicately blue eyes and good facial bones that made up for the coarseness of his features. His hair was thick, with sandy curls of the kind often seen in miniatures of young Victorian children, and he was used to success with the ladies. In another place, he would have taken the time to fall in love with her. She had the look of his sisters as children, lifted laughing and dripping from the kitchen washtub by his mother, their skins glowing rosy-red from the scrub brush. The neatness of her simple blue dress and smooth, golden hair—even the precision with which she ate her food—excited him. He was enchanted with the exquisite white sweep of her neck. Could she be had? Was there time?

The Dropper was one of the blessed few who make a vassal of time. No matter what the press of events, he could change his routine to create small, hidden alcoves of minutes. "Thank you much, ma'am. I'm but a rough man on a hard job, like they say. It pleases me that you allow for my poor manners." Not bad for a Bogside kid, he told himself.

"Ours have not been any better," Ethel said.

Browne flung his napkin on the table and stood. "Do I have to listen to any more of this?"

Now The Dropper had him. He motioned Browne to be seated again with a wave of his fork. "You'll stay at this table, seated or standing as you please, until I've finished this meal. And you can see that I have only just begun."

There was the distinct edge of a smile on Ethel's face as her husband dropped back into his chair, and both Browne and The Dropper noticed it. She had changed sides. The gunman was groping for a way to increase his lead when Browne did it for him.

"Ethel, you'll not leave our rooms for any reason whatever after this, and you will lock the door. Will that be all right with you, Mullins?"

"Uh-huh. And is it all right with her?"

"It doesn't make any difference." Ethel looked straight at The Dropper as she said this.

"Don't you think it was a great mistake to take up this life so young, Mrs. Browne?" The Dropper pushed his advantage.

"It's a mistake I'll fix as soon as we touch shore again."

"What is that supposed to mean, Ethel?"

"That I'm leaving this ship for good."

"It doesn't matter to you that you'd be with me just a few weeks a year?"

"That I think, might be the whole point."

Cody spoke without looking up from his food. "Perhaps if I put this on the public-address system, the whole ship could enjoy it."

"Captain," The Dropper said, "these young people are finally sayin' things they should have said long ago. Please don't be gettin' in their way."

"You're not helping things, Mullins," Traskin said.

"It could be that I'm helpin' things a good deal, Mr. Engineer."

Soon Ethel and The Dropper proceeded to a profound comparison of the year-round weather systems of northeast Ireland and eastern New York State. Their

146

babble grew increasingly bold and cheerful, infuriating Browne, but its impact fell hardest on the old hands, Cody and Traskin. They heard a new meance creeping closer with every word. The meal was a long one.

Granby Wheelis was almost too old to be flying Piper Cubs on a Sunday afternoon, but here he was in an ancient four-engine flying boat in wild winds, at the fringe of the worst storm in his memory. What's more, the dirty-gray daylight was failing fast and the ceiling was coming down like a stone. The rate-of-climb indicator showed that the plane was leaping and plummeting as much as a hundred feet every few seconds. Still, Wheelis kept the Sunderland so close to the wave-tops that Miles Ames, his terrified copilot, swore to himself that there was more seaspray than rain drenching the hull.

"Granny, we can't hold any kind of course in this stuff. Let's give it up and go home while we've still got some light and petrol. We're liable to have to go clear to France to find water smooth enough to land on."

"For a good violation report, it's worth it, Ames."

"But she wasn't violating. We went around her several times in light a lot better than this, and there was nothing.

"I'll make you any wager you wish that there's something now. Headquarters believes that this weather will be a great temptation to our good tanker captain. He could dump ten thousand gallons of sludge in cleaning a tank, and IMAPO would never be able to trace the slick back to him. They're hot to catch him in the act, give him a fine and a lesson that will serve as a useful reminder in future."

"They said something about the Navy and Air Force looking, too."

"About time we got their help. We should have it full-time anyway. Oil pollution is more dangerous to the life of our people than any foreign military threat, I assure you. Not that those service nits will be able to find anything—they're accustomed to flying only when the sky is blue."

"At least they've got some real airplanes. This bloody antique should be in the Imperial War Museum."

"With a budget like ours, we're lucky they don't send us up hanging onto kites. The simple truth, Ames, it that they do not wish IMAPO to prevail. The oil and shipping companies want to kill everything in the oceans with their miserable black poison; then no one will care about dumping or spillage anymore, and they'll be left alone."

"That's a little strong, Granny."

"It is not. Now look sharp, Ames. The light and ceiling are almost gone."

Prior to this year, the last time Granby Wheelis had touched a throttle was in the cockpit of a Lancaster bomber in 1945. His offer to fly patrols for IMAPO was taken as a joke until he applied the pressure of his credentials as a world figure in the ecology movement. Over the past fifteen years, hardly an outdoors periodical in Europe or North America had gone to press without mention of, or an article by, G. R. C. Wheelis. He was continually deploring the slow disappearance of the sea otter, the blue whale and the unmarred beach. A call from certain government ministries had gotten him checked out on the Sunderland and given him a generous daily search area all to himself. Independently comfortable, he turned his meager salary back to IMAPO and hoped for that *big* violation. All the tanker captains in the North Atlantic loathed him.

Ames, a workaday pilot just doing a job, thought Wheelis was a bit around the bend. If not for the extra pay due for this second search of the day, he would never have dreamed of being out in such muck. He didn't like the look of the oil pressure on number three, and spent as much time watching the gauge as he did eying the wild ocean skimming just below.

Wheelis felt as if he were flying over the Alps. Snow-capped peaks and wide, rolling valleys passed under the wing. Fighting the hypnotic effect of the unchanging wave patterns, he closed his eyes for a moment and shook his head hard. When he looked again, the sea had changed; a

148

broad, smooth, gently rolling highway cut through the watery uproar. He held his breath, making sure that the glassy swath continued. It did. "A slick, Ames. An oil slick, and a damned big one."

Ames craned to peer over the nose. Even he couldn't keep a laugh out of his voice. "Talk about flyshit in pepper. You'd better pour it on, Granny. There's not more than ten minutes of visibility." The copilot took it on himself to advance the power settings, and the airspeed crept up a few knots.

They followed the slick for several minutes without speaking. After a while Wheelis became aware that he was holding the plane in a gentle bank. "She's made a turn to the east. We've gone from a steady three-five-five or so to zero-two-zero and still swinging."

"Shall we turn on the landing lights? Perhaps they'll see us and give us a lamp."

"While they're pumping out oil like that? Not bloody likely. But turn them on, anyway. Might put a little fear into them to see us coming."

Ames hit the light toggle and the slick wave-tops took on a ghostly shimmer.

The gyro horizon still showed the right wing faintly lowered, and the compass continued to move toward the east.

"Heading zero-eight-zero now, Ames. She's too close in to be doubling back down the coast. She's rounding, no doubt— Oh, *Christ*."

A monstrous blackness thinly starred with lights was rushing at the lumbering Sunderland. Wheelis rammed the propellers into flat pitch and drove the throttles to the firewall. At barely a hundred feet of altitude he was flying dead at the huge ship's stern, with a hundred feet of funnel and bridge house still to clear. With no way to climb fast enough, he tried to pivot on a wing tip, dropping the wheel hard right and stamping in full rudder. He felt the waves' hungry reach for the lowered tip, trying to pull them into a final, sickening cartwheel. The nose mushed into a nightmarishly slow turn. In the landing light's glare,

Wheelis was able to read the name on the ship's stern with astonishing clarity: "*American Enterprise.*" The twenty-foot letters seemed about to float into the cockpit. Sighting along the left wing, which was pointing almost straight up into the sky, he saw the rotating dish of the ship's radar spin away to allow the Sunderland's tip-float to pass by. Suddenly there was only empty night and a wildly tilted sea in the windshield. The twenty-knot forward motion of the *Enterprise* had given them the inches they needed.

Wheelis fought the desire to bring the wing tip level and away from the sucking sea; he shallowed the bank only a little and allowed the howling engines to pull him around in an incredibly tight turn. He wasn't going to lose this clear and flagrant violator so easily.

Ames was astonished at the old man's miraculously intact flying skills. He had heard stories about the old Lancaster pilots performing aerobatic maneuvers far beyond the bomber's red-lines when the night fighters were barreling in, but this was the first hint that it was more than two-burning-and-two-turning talk inside a cozy pub.

Somehow Wheelis completed the turn without losing sight of the fast-dimming mass of the ship, and set up the tightest circle he could above her.

"Get back on the radio, Ames. First, a call to IMAPO. We have positive identification of the *American Enterprise* on a heading of zero-eight-five. We also have a positive dumping violation in the very heavy range."

Ames unbuckled and began to make his way aft, bracing himself against bumpy air and the steep bank. "The cheap bastards should either give us a radioman on every patrol or else some equipment we can operate from the cockpit."

As Ames sent his message, Wheelis watched the ship fade until only her scattered lights indicated her location.

"Okay, IMAPO knows all about it," Ames said to Wheelis over the intercom.

"Good. Now raise the ship and tell them we've got

them squarely, and that we're not leaving here until that slick stops."

"Come off it, Granny. I can't see number four engine out the port here."

"*Get* them."

Three minutes later Ames was sliding back into his seat. "Now shove this thing out of here while we're still wearing our wings."

"You got them?"

"Yes, I did."

"And what did they say?"

"One word. 'Understood.' "

"Playing it upper lip, are they?" He brought the Sunderland's wings nearly level and commenced a full-power climbing turn to the south. The ship's lights began to slip behind. "Very well, my friends," he said to the unseen crewmen below, "but I can promise you that this little visit of ours will cause a great deal of trouble for you down there."

chapter 8

Ethel Browne was only faintly aware that something was going on. She had heard one of the Irishmen shouting and swearing in the corridor outside her locked door, and had looked out her windows and seen the lights of a circling airplane. But she didn't let the incident excite her. Whether the plane represented rescuers or another move by the plotters, it was all the same. If it was going to affect her, someone would come and make it clear.

Though it was hours before she usually went to sleep, she was already dressed for bed; Owen would be off his watch in an hour, and she wanted to be asleep before he arrived. She wore the slightly oversized men's pajamas she felt most comfortable in, and a long white terry-cloth robe.

Having decided to avoid her husband, she had taken triple the prescribed dosage of his sleeping pills. She had decided to stay up for a while, because her rare experiences with barbiturates had taught her that heavy doses often brought on nausea. Now she sat in a wooden chair close to the bathroom; if she could keep the pills down for fifteen minutes, she could go to bed.

Her head grew light and there was a ringing in her ears. Grasping the sides of the chair tightly, she concentrated her gaze on the carpet pattern. Soon she became aware that a pair of shoes was standing just within the narrow cone of her vision. They were dripping, thickly laced, ankle-high work shoes, into which were tucked the legs of a boiler suit. She raised her eyes and saw the smiling Dropper.

He twirled a ring of keys around his index finger. "Master keys. I can open any lock on the ship."

The panic that she might normally have felt was completely obliterated by the sedative.

"Are you drunk, Mrs. Browne? You don't look right."

"I just took some medicine. It's making me a little weak."

"You should lay yourself down. Come, I'll help you to bed."

She clung more tightly to the chair. "I'm better off sitting up, for now."

"I'm not scaring you, am I?"

"I don't think so. You're the only one who speaks to me as if I were a person, not just a piece of ship's gear."

"My name is Molaise. A good old Irish saint's handle. Why don't you call me that? Or call me Dropper, like the other boys."

"Dropper?"

"It means I like to drop things. Break 'em. Buildings, monuments, armored cars, bank vaults."

"Monuments? Why do you want to smash monuments?"

"Just an indulgence. A hobby, almost. What I do on my day off, you might say. Remember the Nelson monument in Dublin? You must have heard that it was dropped."

She was becoming dull and giddy.

"*I* done that one," he went on. "All alone. Took me weeks, walkin' around it like I was a tourist, and all the while cuttin' here and there with a little masonry drill, and packin' in the C-4 and caps. Went down in the neatest sort of pile, with a noise not much louder than a pistol shot. Nobody hurt, except in the pride. What a sad, lovely look the Englishmen's faces had when they came to see the wreckage. Couldn't tear myself away for days."

She thought she should keep his attention diverted. "What else do you . . . drop?"

"Lately it's ships. If you felt a bit better I could take you below to show the fine job I'm doin' all along the hull. A good many technical advances, and a lot of them Molaise Mullins originals."

Her voice seemed to grow thicker. "You know they're going to pay the money. All that work's going to be for nothing."

The Dropper knelt in front of Ethel's chair, unzippered his wet work jacket and began to slide out of it. "Mrs. Browne, I'm goin' to be very direct with you. You are a very desirable woman to me. Beautiful in the face, very neat and finely made. Also intelligent and quiet. With, I think, a strong, brave heart." He stripped off his khaki turtleneck sweater, throwing it behind him. "I would not have made the approach to a woman like you, exceptin' I saw how unhappy you are with that husband."

When he undid the belt of her robe and laid it open, she crossed her hands over the lap of her pajamas. "My husband and I are in love."

"What in hell has that ever had to do with bein' happy? Can I call you by your first name?"

"It's Ethel."

"You would be a great prize for me, Ethel. I never had anythin' of any value before. My friends would respect you. You're the type of woman that a rough man can treasure and a fine man can't." He moved his hands up under the sides of her pajama top, hooked his fingers in the waist of the pants and drew them out from under her.

She thought about screaming and running, but the drug had too firm a hold on her.

"Good . . . good God, you sound like you're talking about getting married."

"I am, if you like." With a hand on each of her thighs, he brought her legs apart. Moving forward on his knees, he brought his lips between the legs so they could no longer close.

"My husband." It was getting harder to stay awake.

"He'll be dead. Right along with everybody else in the crew."

Her mind tried to fight clear. "They'll pay your ransom, I know they will."

"Nobody's goin' to ask for any ransom. This ship is goin' down. That's the way the plan is."

"You couldn't. You couldn't drown us all. You're not that kind of men."

"It wasn't planned that way, honest. In any ordinary blow, you'd have been off in your own boats. But we didn't count on the weather bein' this bad."

"What about you? How will you get off?"

"Our chances aren't so great, either. Rubber rafts and a lot of luck, I guess. Quinn's been pretty close about it. But you can come with me, Ethel." He worked at his lower clothing, revealing thighs as white as a baby's. Dimly she saw his hand check something on the belt that had fallen around his knees. A sheath knife. Did she have a choice? No. Adrenaline tried to fight against the barbiturate. She opened her legs deliberately and drew him forward by the hips. He slid into her smoothly. Deep inside her, he did not move. His face was so close that her eyes could not focus on his. She wondered whether he would kiss her. Her body prickled, feeling the thickness of a man who was not her husband. Why did he stay so still? He held her by the neck.

"Then you'll come with me, Ethel?"

With her consciousness slipping steadily, she managed to nod.

"That's marvelous, my darlin'. I didn't mean to be unmannerly waitin' around like that, but I wasn't wantin' to make love to somebody I was goin' to have to kill."

156

He began to rock, sliding inside her.

She lay back. Why was it so different from Owen? It was better, wasn't it? Just before her eyes went shut, she looked at The Dropper's coarse, strong face in the lamplight and on it saw more tenderness than she had ever observed on the face of her husband. She crossed her calves over his buttocks and drew him to her tighter. A long tremor shot through her, and then the nausea rose again. She threw up on The Dropper and fell unconscious in his arms.

Sadie Buck and Gail McCormick lived strictly by their old wind-up alarm clock. Not seeing the sun or stars for days at a time, they had to. The two tiny girls—Gail as fair as a summer cloud and Sadie as dark as a Spaniard—had been picked as much for their youth and strength as for their bravura good looks. They needed all the stamina that their nineteen-year-old bodies possessed, for they had been serving sixty men a day between them for more than five months, and their ten-by-eight chamber beneath the seafloor in Redleg would have been condemned by any penal reform commission on earth.

The steel box stood barely five feet high, so that even these small girls could never quite stand upright. The primitive ventilation system couldn't control the excessive heat and humidity, and the electric lighting was held to a minimum in an effort to control the temperature. When the girls were in action together—which was almost always—the sight seemed to come from some peculiar chamber of hell.

Each bed had been built four feet wide, to accommodate romantic acrobatics, so there was barely two feet of space between them. The naked bodies that writhed and panted in the feeble yellow light glistened with perspiration as if they had been oiled. Not so much as a blanket for privacy separated the beds, but in the platform's world of communal property the men were content to concentrate on what was momentarily theirs alone. Despite the fact that bodies often touched accidentally in the course of various thrashings, group activities never occurred, even though the girls had thoughtfully established a rate for it.

The last two customers were finished and gone within five minutes after they had dropped through the overhead hatch; the oppressive climate had been too much for them to take advantage of the twenty-minute limit. Now they would be making their way up through the great tangle of loose piping and tools that had been artfully scattered to hide the two-and-a-half-foot circular opening leading to the space below.

Neither of the girls moved to touch the button alongside the hatch. This was attached to a small light bulb recessed in the lid, which, when lit, was a signal for the next man to come forward.

Their vitality had dropped sharply over the past week, along with their spirits. They sat naked on the edge of one bed, their thin arms wrapped about each other for comfort. Miserably, they watched the rivulets of condensation run down the wall to feed the reeking, suffocating spread of mildew. It had been three weeks since the men had been able to sneak a steam hose down during the night for a cleaning. The chemical toilet was perilously full, and there was not enough water in the hanging plastic bags to cat-wash a sedentary Aberdeen housewife, much less two hard-driven whores in a steaming hole in the ground.

"Sadie, what in hell have we done? Look at this place. Look at us."

Gail McCormick felt the same way, but she tried to cheer her friend. "Ah, hell, dearie, there's nothing changed. It's been the same stinking pit since we got here, and it's never got us down yet."

"I never felt like this before. It's not just that I'm tired; I'm scared. I dreamed last night that this place was full of ice-cold water, and that there was a bloaty, naked, drowned man floating over me. I tried to get a dress on so God would take me in, but I was too cold to move. When I woke up I was shivering so hard I could hear my knees

158

knock together. And it's hot enough to melt your ass down here."

"It's the lack of proper exercise that's getting us morbid, Gail. I'm going to tell Randy Martin that he's got to get us out of here for a run tomorrow night, come what may. That'll be a real laugh, won't it, dearie?"

The thought of it cheered them both for a moment. They loved it when the crewmen bundled them up in bulky bad-weather gear and smuggled them onto the elevator inside Redleg. Somewhere near the top, the elevator would halt and they would leave it for a narrow catwalk that took them through a metal door and into a tunnel. This brought them out into the jungle of steel trusswork that ran under the main deck between the three legs. On some nights the moon would splinter into a billion diamonds on the water far below, and then the girls, lithe, brave and nimble as monkeys, would race madly across darkened girders, climb squealing through the latticework of braces and turnbuckled cables, and swing hand over hand along electrical pipes, often with nothing beneath their rib-soled work shoes but the North Sea.

At first the half-dozen men who had accompanied them would be nervously on watch, making a great show of light signals and trying to quiet the laughter that seemed to come from birds flying in the dark framework. Then the younger ones would take off after the girls in a game of tag so perilous that no one on the rig would have undertaken it as part of his work for any amount of money. Next, growling, shamefaced and tentative, the older men would slip out, and after a few minutes, all caution would be abandoned and they would tear about the rig screaming with laughter. The girls would separate to remote cages of braces and call tauntingly to the men, who would scramble after them like howling wolves. Finally, when their breaths were reduced to long, asthmatic wheezes, they would drag themselves back to the small open platform in front of the door. Here they would sit, their backs against the concrete leg, and smoke a last cigarette before the girls had to return to prison.

Most of the giggling small talk concerned the miracle of their not being discovered by the all-seeing Cullenbine, but it was here, too, that romance bloomed. The men would fight with words, or fists, or even draw lots to be on the party that accompanied the girls, for this was their only chance to display their wit, courage and charm in exchange for feminine admiration. The opportunity was not without economic peril; discovery by Cullenbine would bring automatic dismissal and a probable blacklisting on all the other rigs.

Against all the odds, Randy Martin, a piefaced, cheerful toolpusher, and Bairn Harrison, a scarecrow-thin mud engineer, had won the hearts of the girls.

Gail renewed the friction tape that held the curling photograph of Bairn Harrison to the piece of dark wall by her bed. The long face smiled out timidly from the gallery of bedizened rock stars taped around it.

"Gail, is it proper to keep your man's picture looking down on your customers?"

"Bairn likes to see it there when he comes in. Lets him know I'm thinking about him no matter what's happening."

"I keep Randy's picture in my money bag. All the things I hold dear in one place, you see." She pulled a bulging pillowcase from under her bed, untied the electric wire that held it closed and pawed inside among tightly packed bank notes. "Well, I can't find it right off, but it's in there somewhere." Over eighty thousand English pounds were in the pillowcase. Gail had one under her bed just like it.

"Seems a shame that our boys have to wait their turn just like everyone else, Sade."

Sadie emptied a shoebox of bank notes—the day's take—into the pillowcase. "There's not many laws for us, but that's one we don't dare break."

"Why couldn't they just come down and sleep with us after we're done? Wouldn't have to touch one another in a sex way at all. They could have that in turns just like everybody else."

160

"And I suppose we could invite a committee of the other men to sit about and make sure of that. Hah."

They giggled together, and then grew sad again.

"I can't stay here anymore, Sade. Are you with me?"

"Sure. I'll ask the boys to get us off on the next lighter. They can start looking for some new girls right now."

Gail looked as if she might cry. "The new girls. Do you think *our* boys will stay with them?"

"Hard to say, dearie. Men aren't constant."

"Maybe they'd come with us. We could take care of them just fine."

"Ah, you know these oil boys. They'd be missing the mashed fingers and punch-ups. Still, we could ask them."

They looked at each other bleakly. Their skins were worm-white and their muscles slack from lack of use. Their long hair, not properly washed since they came aboard, was a greasy, odoriferous tangle, and the eyes beneath their prematurely lined foreheads were as large and feverish as those of starving children.

Sadie gave the light button a series of three fast pushes. "I'm ending it for today. Let's have some rest." She took a handful of forty-five-rpm records out of a net bag and put them on a battery-powered phonograph. A dark, slow-rock beat accompanied the tale of a young girl dying of an overdose while her lover rushed vainly to her side on his motorcycle.

Gail took a bottle of wine from under the corner of her mattress and filled two dirty water glasses to the top while Sadie set a pair of candles on each of the low lockers at the ends of the beds.

"Sade, the men said we shouldn't light the candles down here. They use up too much air."

Sadie lit the candles and switched off the overhead bulbs. "By now we can live on a thimbleful of air a day."

Lying wet and naked on their beds, sipping their wine in the candles' glow, they felt the thrum of the drill string that plunged deep into the earth alongside them.

"Christ," Sadie said. "It's like we're dead and they brought the candles inside the coffin."

Owen Browne came off his watch in a mood so black that he wasn't sure he was not on his way to murder his wife. Stamping down the corridor, his fists knotted, he muttered loudly to himself. Like all emotionally immature people, his mind was not on a teeter-totter, allowing one feeling to sink as its opposite rose; within him, love and hate waxed together in a perpetual purgatory.

When he turned the key in the lock, the door would not open. He turned the key back and was able to work the knob. Who had unlocked the door after he had left? Ethel, deliberately disobeying him? It would have been like her, given her present mood. Or was it Mullins, who had asked for the master keys? Browne had assumed he wanted them for his work with explosives.

He charged into the room. Nothing seemed wrong: just two chairs out of place, one overturned. Ethel was in bed, the covers drawn up to her neck. He stood beside her, trembling with love and rage over the pale, beautiful face. He saw that she had not moved a hair since she had gone to bed. The only impression in the pillow was the one where her head now rested. The sheet and blanket were drawn up so smoothly and tucked beneath the mattress so tightly that he didn't know how she had managed to get underneath the covers.

He noticed a sour smell in the room, and he traced it to the wadded-up pajamas lying near his feet. Shaking them out, he saw that the top had been spewed with vomit; the pants had apparently been used to wipe up. Gently he lifted the covers off his wife. She was naked. Her skin was damp and unnaturally cool beneath his hand. The nearly white pubic hair was matted, plastered to her belly and thighs. Lust overwhelmed him; he shook it away. Should he wake her? She might have been sick for most of his watch and just now fallen asleep. Or perhaps this wasn't a healthy sleep at all, but a coma. He brought his ear close to her face. The breathing didn't seem right; it was too slow and shallow. Nothing happened when he shook her shoulder. Panic touched him and he shook her roughly.

"Ethel. Ethel. Damn it. *Ethel*." Her eyes opened, but the irises rolled up into her head. Sharply repeated slaps brought her half awake. "What happened? You scared me."

The first words she tried came out a blurred garble.

"Is it whiskey?" There was disgust in his voice.

She tried to sit up and embrace him, but he pushed her back. "Have you filled yourself up with whiskey?"

She shook her head slowly and waved shakily at the nightstand.

Opening the drawer, Browne saw the pills. He grabbed the bottle and poured them out in his hand. There were too many left for her to have taken an overdose. "How many?"

Her voice was cracked and low. "Six."

He became the parent, the man in command for a moment. "My God, Ethel, these are very strong. Three would put away a full-grown man. They could have killed a girl your size. Or was that what you wanted?"

When she groped to hold his hand, he tried to pull it away, but the desperation in her grip made him stop. Before he knew what he was doing, he was kissing her—first on the forehead, then on the eyes and lips. The very foulness of her breath excited him; his cool princess was now a malodorous animal.

He put his hand on her breast, then moved it down to her pubic mound in what was, for him, a terrifyingly bold move. Her hands came up to his face, pushing him away and her rejection was unbearable. He felt like a fiend attacking this sick, weak little girl, and simultaneously loathed her for deflecting his lust.

She saw all this in the twisted face above her. "Wait. Wait. Owen. I have to tell you something. I know something. Why aren't you listen—"

He couldn't bear to have her reading his disappointment. Sliding off the bed, he backed away. "It's all right, Ethel. That was a terrible thing for a man to do to an ill woman. I should have been getting something to help you. Instead, I was pawing at you like a wild baboon."

"No . . . no. Listen, Owen. Will you . . . listen to me."

He fled to the bathroom, shame burning through him. "Those pills are hard on your stomach. Maybe something to coat the inside of you." He had to drown the pitying sound of her voice. He rummaged noisily in the medicine cabinet, purposely clinking bottles and dropping spoons. "We managed to get ourselves spotted. Engelberg leaked some bunker oil overside and IMAPO spotted us. Can you believe it? Even in this weather they hound us. Quinn wasn't mad at all. Said he understood and laughed it off. The government will know where we are now. That's good for us, because Cody and I—" His babble stopped; something on the far side of the toilet had caught his eye. He scooped up a turtlenecked military sweater. An attempt had been made to wipe up the vomit with this too, and there were dirty tissues floating in the toilet.

Then Browne placed the sweater precisely; at dinner Mullins had tucked his napkin up under this very turtleneck. He dropped the sweater and sat down weakly on the toilet.

What had happened: Had Ethel unlocked the door to admit Mullins to a knock, or to a prearranged assignation? Or had the man let himself in and confronted her? Her reaction? Lust? Terror? Did she come immediately into his arms or pretend to struggle, and finally give herself to him with barely concealed eagerness? Or did she fight? He snorted at his hope. She had been tucked neatly into bed without a mark on her. When had she taken the pills? Afterward? Remorse? Or to make it seem so in case he found out?

She appeared at the doorway, staggering. "You've got to hear me. Please don't be angry, Owen."

Did she know that he was on to her? Would she deny it all? He mustn't give her the chance. He forced her flat on the floor, turned her on her back, stuck his fingers roughly into her body, twisted and withdrew. He stared at them, trying not to believe what he saw. "You've been with a man. I've got part of another man on my hand here, haven't I?"

She gave a stiff nod.

"Did he make you do it?"

She could have said yes; it was half true. But she felt herself shaking her head. She had thought she might enjoy seeing his pain, but it hurt her when he winced.

"It was Mullins, wasn't it?"

When she tried to speak, he pressed his hand over her mouth. "Don't say it. Keep your rotten secret."

Somehow she rolled away from him and wobbled to her feet, but before she could speak he began to beat her. She moved along the wall, covering her face with her arms. The beating was ineffective; Owen Browne was one of those robust-looking men who are born without a shred of athletic ability. His blows were weak-wristed, washerwoman slaps thrown without force, and glancing off her shoulders and elbows. His lack of grace had often annoyed her; now, seeing his physical incompetence, she felt only contempt. A glancing slap against her nose made her eyes water.

"You don't even know how to beat a woman, you sonofabitch."

It was the first swear word Browne had ever heard her use. She had to be punished. He looked for something to beat her with. Snatching a magazine off the desk, he rolled it into a tube and began to strike.

Suddenly Ethel dropped her arms and began to laugh at him. It was a deep, bitter, sobbing laugh that at once chilled and mocked. His ridiculous weapon was scarcely reddening her skin. When he swiped at her face she ducked away easily or, even worse, took the insignificant blow with more laughter. His cheek began to twitch and his breath came in gasps.

"Owen, if you knew how ashamed it's making me to be married to a thing like you."

He threw the magazine aside, wanting to drop weeping at her feet. He couldn't bear the thought of losing her.

Cupping her breasts, she took a step forward and thrust them into his face. "*Boo*." The gesture sent him flinching backward.

"That scares the shit out of you, doesn't it?"

Browne retrieved his fallen cap, set it slowly on his head, retreated to the door and let himself out. By now, his face was once more emotionless.

As soon as her mind began to clear, Ethel called the bridge on the intercom. When one of the Irishmen answered, she asked for the captain and was told that he was in his quarters. In the seconds it took her to break the bridge connection and ring Cody's suite, she began to sob uncontrollably. She slammed down the receiver. The room began to shimmer and fade, and she barely made the bed, falling into its center like a sack of meal. Just before she passed out, a thought she'd never in her life entertained before popped into her mind: *"Fuck them."*

chapter 9

The general alarm was still clattering as Cullenbine had the men off duty drawn up in the huge cavern that doubled as a mess hall and a gymnasium on Mavis A.

The folding tables were stacked against the wall behind him and each man stood on a number painted on the floor between the markings for various games. By sighting down the ranks, Cullenbine was able to determine who was missing by checking the number against the list of names he carried on a clipboard. Aside from the sick-bay list and those on watch, only two were missing.

"McArdle. MacCrummon," roared Cullenbine.

"Not feeling well, Mr. Cullenbine. Neither one of them," said Fred Morrison, one of the tight little band of Scots that had given Cullenbine trouble from the day they had arrived on board three months ago. All five of them worked well enough when they were at their posts, but there were sudden and unexplained absences when one or two were not available for duty and seemed to have vanished from the rig. Their explanations were arrogant, intentionally flimsy, and almost always delivered loudly and within the hearing of the other men. This response threatened to have a disastrous effect on the discipline that Cullenbine had to keep. For this reason he had once had to administer a brutal beating to this same Fred Morrison. While it made its point, it wasn't enough; Fred Morrison was tough but he provided no real challenge to Cullenbine. The Scots leader, Tiny McArdle, did, and he had quickly established himself as a fighter second to none in the crew or to any of Cullenbine's foremen. He could have fired all of them at the last crew change, but they were in thick with the union stewards, and he didn't need any more labor problems. Besides, it would have been admitting that he couldn't handle a man like McArdle. At times, handling a McArdle was worth all the talk on earth, and Cullenbine had a warm feeling that this was one of the times.

Morrison's half-jeering explanation of his friend's absence brought an ugly ripple of laughter and mock sympathy from the ranks. Several of the bolder men stepped off their numbers, lit cigarettes and began talking. In another minute they might be lost to him as workers. If he turned them out to their jobs, only those within his sight would work hard.

Cullenbine signaled a foreman to kill the alarm. With the bell quiet, his voice dominated the room. "Morrison, the way your pals McArdle and MacCrummon are always missing together makes me think that they stick it up each other's ass. Any truth to that?"

In an environment where homosexuality often infected men who thought themselves immune, these were deadly words. All conversation stopped.

"Why don't you ask Tiny yourself?" growled Morrison.

"I mean to. Go get them. If they're stuck together, roll them on a fork-lift and drive them here."

"Do it yourself."

Cullenbine caught him by the testicles. "I see you're not wearing a safety cup, Morrison. That's against good working procedure. You could get hurt real bad. In the

168

next thirty seconds you have three choices: your two nuts or Tiny McArdle."

Turning pale, Morrison said, "He's really sick, Cullenbine. Haven't you got a heart?"

The answer startled Cullenbine. The Morrison he knew would be running after McArdle to come up and drink blood. What the hell was wrong? Morrison wasn't afraid and McArdle wasn't sick. He could run a hundred-yard dash on two broken legs.

Cullenbine kept his momentum. He dug his fingers into Morrison and twisted, keeping the moaning man from falling by catching the front of his jacket. "Going soon?"

Morrison limped across the hall and disappeared down the stairway that led to the crew's quarters on the deck below. Holding the silent men with his eyes, Cullenbine wondered what would happen if McArdle refused to come up. If he had to go down after him, the battle would take place below, and he would waste a lot of time and perhaps get himself maimed and unable to supervise. If he were McArdle, that's what he'd do: stay in the room and maybe rig an ambush just inside the door. Down there MacCrummon could help, too; he was slow and clumsy, but dangerous at close quarters. This thing's going to blow up on me, Cullenbine thought.

Then McArdle came up the stairs to a muted murmur of encouragement from the crew. MacCrummon wasn't with him. Why not? Even if they weren't planning to jump him together, the threat of it could count in a close fight where you needed both eyes on your target.

McArdle had not neglected to prepare. He too wore steel-woven safety gloves, steel-capped shoes and hard hat.

Cullenbine read the murder in his look—but there was something else there, too. McArdle didn't want to be here. "Did you come up for more Vaseline, McArdle?"

"Forty-pounders," McArdle said.

There were gasps and some low whistles. A challenge to fight with the huge forty-pound wrenches was usually a challenge to the death. A refusal to accept meant a trip off on the next helicopter for anyone, including Cullenbine.

"Morrison," Cullenbine said, "you're a good errand boy. Bring us a couple of nice, rusty forty-pounders."

"What could make me happier?" Morrison said, and sprinted for the elevator.

"While we're waiting around, Tiny, I'll tell the boys what we're going to be doing after I've put you in the hospital for a couple of years." The distance to the rear ranks would have required most men to use a bull horn, but Cullenbine made himself heard easily. "The geology boys say there's some kind of big pressure trouble down in the formations. I don't know what the hell they're talking about. It's all mumbo-jumbo to me." This didn't sound right to them, he could see. They knew there wasn't anything about the oil business that he didn't understand. "Anyway, we've got to get everything ready to be capped. All three legs. And they want it done at the bottom, near the sea bed."

There was a rush of groans and curses. Cullenbine saw that McArdle's eyes had gone wide. "I can hear that you understand what that means. If we have to do it, it's not just turning a few wheels. We're going to be down there cutting and welding in oil and mud up to our ears."

Morrison marched back carrying a four-foot wrench on each shoulder and dumped one at Cullenbine's feet, just inches from his toes. The Englishman didn't flinch. Picking it up by the end of the handle, he raised it horizontally, using only the power of his massive wrist.

McArdle appeared reluctant to take his wrench from Morrison, and his eyes darted to the stairway.

"You look as if you're not so sure you want to do this, Tiny."

"I have to get back to the room," the little Scot said in a voice so low that Cullenbine wasn't sure what he had heard.

"Speak up, boy. We can't all hear you. Did you say you wanted to go back to bed?"

170

McArdle was trembling, though not from fear. "I don't feel good. I've got to do something, you sonofabitch."

"Maybe you should have worn a diaper."

The laughter was on Cullenbine's side; the men were swinging over to him. He couldn't let up. "If you're thinking about something big and hard up your ass, I can offer you this." He slapped the long handle of the wrench. Amazingly, McArdle hesitated. What was he worried about below? Suddenly Cullenbine knew that he mustn't let him get back there. As the Scot moved to lay down his wrench, Cullenbine poked him sharply in the abdomen with the butt of his own weapon.

McArdle realized that he could return to his exploder only over Cullenbine's broken body. It had been a terrible mistake to leave MacCrummon guarding the radio traffic. The capping that Cullenbine had announced was all the tip they needed that the plan was at least suspected on Mavis A. Fat Tom could have slipped back to the room, set off the radio shack and come back shooting. He cursed himself for not having trusted his other three men with more information. They stood together in the second rank, looking at him for any sort of signal, but there was none he could give.

Fat Tom MacCrummon was lying on Tiny McArdle's bed, his eyes wide open. Though he had stripped to his underwear, sweat drenched him from head to foot. It was nothing he had heard through the plug in his ear; there had been only one radio message since Tiny had gone, and that in code. He was dreading what he *might* hear.

Tom MacCrummon had feared only one thing all his life: making a mistake. As a boy he had worked in his father's carpentry shop, and every board cut too short or not planed straight had brought whatever piece of lumber convenient to Big Tom's hand into hard contact with Little Tom's skin. In school he had been a shapeless blob whose every mistake on the athletic field or in class had caused loud jeers and laughter. With his growth and strength came the wild temper of the chronically bullied;

none dared mock him any longer But the damage was done, he was unable to make a decision without agonizing about it. This was the man Tiny McArdle had left with the fate of his country plugged in his ear.

It should have been clear enough: If he heard any warning being sent to the platform, he was to blow the charge to cut the message off before it could be fully understood. And if he heard the platform attempting to call for help, he had to blow that message out of the air, too. But who could tell what a message was going to be by the way it began? The chances of a mistake were immense. A weather report that opened with ambiguous language or an ominous tone meant he might prematurely destroy the radio shack and give the platform the early alert it was meant to be denied. A true warning might reveal its meaning in the first sentence, before his finger could reach the red button. Pushing himself up on one elbow, he brought the electronic exploder out of the pillow and he tested the circuits as he had seen McArdle do. His wet fingers gently lifted the safety shield. Oh, Jesus, was he going to go into the books as the man who made the mistake that lost Scotland to England for the second time?

McArdle rolled the knurled wheel on the head of his wrench, opening the jaws six inches. What he lost in concentrated mass, he gained in reach, and this could be critical in the fight with the much taller and longer-armed chief engineer.

Cullenbine brought the jaws of his own wrench closed. It was going to be power against speed; he put his chances on power.

They began to circle one another, the wrenches held like axes before them, while the men broke ranks and ringed them in a moving swarm.

Forty-pounder fights did not last long; the first man able to bring the jaws-end into solid contact had his win. A blow to a limb caused the kind of bone damage that required wiring, steel pins and surgical shortening. A smash to the torso destroyed organs; kidneys and spleens had to

172

be removed in rags; livers could never be fully repaired; intestines burst and lungs collapsed. Blows to the head were near-decapitations and instant death. Such losers were dragged to machinery-packed areas where making the physical damage appear accidental could be stage-managed.

The techniques of forty-pounder fighting were simple but demanding. The wrench's head was so heavy that it could not be moved with real speed. The lighter handle was therefore used to strike, stab, trip and parry—to create an opening through pain or loss of balance so that the crushing end might be turned and maneuvered to deliver the final destroying blows.

Lustgarten took the call from the radio shack in the conference room. The ranking officers on Mavis A. had spontaneously made the room into a command post when the number of calls they had to make to each other became excessive.

Magnus, still in his bathrobe and sweater, was seated cross-legged on the floor, his lap covered with the thick files of production figures and budgets he had requisitioned from Cullenbine's files. Looking as comfortable as though he were reclining on a couch, Zamke stood beneath an overhead light reading a paperback; he had not moved for hours. Magnus wondered whether this display was for effect.

Only Lustgarten had not occupied himself. Immaculately dressed, and with his cap set squarely on his head, he sat unmoving on the edge of the table until the phone rang. When he picked it up, he held the receiver in a way that turned it into a military field telephone, his elbow at shoulder height as though to clear a horde of junior officers in a crowded dugout. "Yes, I have it. Was the message received in code? Thank you. And please keep this confidential." He hung up and uncharacteristically punched his palm. *"Enterprise* has turned east. Sighted by an IMAPO plane half an hour ago. The ship is coming our way. We shut down immediately."

"That was the agreement."

Magnus thumped the folder he was reading. "Damn. I hate to do it."

"You agreed," persisted Lustgarten.

"Could you radio for permission?" Zamke asked. "That would make it easier for you."

"I'm the one who gives all the permissions that have to do with production."

"Cullenbine already has the men prepared. Please give the order."

"Colonel Lustgarten, I may have gone too fast."

"Admiral, there is no more information we can receive. The next report we get of the *American Enterprise* may be an announcement by our own lookouts that she is in sight and bearing down on us at full speed."

Magnus held up a hand. "There's one more bit of corroboration I think we can get. A good many of the rigs to the northwest of us are equipped with radar. Short range, but good enough to pick up anything reasonably close. We can get them on the radio and ask them to plot any blips. Then we'd have a pretty good idea about anything headed our way."

Lustgarten pointed at a clock. "We have between six and eight hours to prepare. Cullenbine was unsure that he could get the job done in *days,* much less a few hours. We cannot wait."

"We wait," Magnus said. "Captain Zamke, send a message to all platforms standing between us and the ship."

"Many oil companies are involved," Lustgarten said. "You won't be able to code your message."

Magnus shrugged. "What bloody difference can it make?"

"The IMAPO message was relayed through British Intelligence and it was transmitted in code. The enemy still doesn't know we're on to him."

"You exasperate me. If there *is* an enemy, and they do hear our message, how does it worsen our position?"

"I can't be sure, but I *can* tell you that when your adversary knows something about you that he didn't have to know, your position is worsened."

"Have you finished, Zamke?" Magnus asked, with an edge to his voice for the first time.

"Yes. How's this? 'From Mavis A. to all rigs to northwest. Have reason to believe we may come under attack from sea in your direction. Please help us by tracking all sea traffic heading south or west. Try for visual contact. Pass all contact to us immediately.' "

Magnus reached for a set of oilskins. "I'll take it myself. I want to climb up to the radar tower and tell them to look sharp."

McArdle uppercut the butt of his wrench at Cullenbine's chin. The chief blocked it easily and the clash of metal rang through the room.

McArdle flicked short handle blows at the shaft of Cullenbine's wrench, trying to smash the bigger man's fingers and make him drop his weapon. Even heavy gloves couldn't turn away a good hit. But the Englishman was quicker than McArdle thought he would be; with a blocking technique that took little effort he could tire his opponent disproportionately, and this was a battle where your arms dared not grow heavier than those of your enemy.

After raining a series of chops at Cullenbine's right hand, McArdle unexpectedly slid his handle down the platform master's wrench. The blow caught Cullenbine near the left wrist. He grunted in pain and his hand came loose on the tool. McArdle tried to knock it to the floor with an overhand, but caught a thunderous kick on the thigh that just missed cracking the bone. By the time he was reset to swing, the other man had recovered and taken a firm grip on his own weapon. Cullenbine raised his forty-pounder above his head and stepped forward. He hammered the wrench straight down, making no attempt to evade McArdle's block. The full force of the blow drove McArdle back, the shock transmitted to his hands, arms and shoulders making them numb and weak.

175

By the time his strength returned, Cullenbine had recocked his wrench overhead and once more brought it down on McArdle's handle.

The Englishman struck clangorously, again and again, using the hundred-pound advantage of his thick frame to jolt the small Scot's muscles to jelly.

McArdle felt the wall looming close behind him. He knew he couldn't continue to absorb these thunderbolts without a cushioning backstep. Another pulverizing shock sent him retreating once more, and the wall brushed his back. There was no more feeling in his hands. He could hear Cullenbine's gusting breath as the big man readied every muscle in his body for a final stroke.

McArdle pushed his trembling arms out together in a sudden jab. His wrench handle caught Cullenbine across the bull neck and knocked him into a brief retreat, and Cullenbine's wrench remained overhead at the length of his arms. For McArdle, it was now or it was death. Again his arms shot out, this time hurling the horizontal length of his wrench at his enemy's ankles.

Cullenbine's heavy boots would probably have saved him from serious damage, but his reflexes worked faster than his mind; he scissored his legs over the flying steel, destroying his balance and any chance for an immediate finishing swing.

The thrown wrench skittered across the smooth floor, coming to a halt at the feet of one of the crew, who scooped it up and held it out. McArdle pushed himself away from the wall and darted around Cullenbine to try to retrieve his weapon. For a moment, his exposed back was turned to the pursuing Englishman.

Cullenbine whirled the forty-pound monster about his head like a hammer-thrower building momentum and let the wrench fly at McArdle's skull in a whirring blur. It sailed a quarter-inch past the Scot's ear and into the crowd, crushing the shoulder and part of the chest of the man it struck down.

McArdle's hands were already on his wrench when Cullenbine dove for his own, which lay across the body of the fallen worker. But when the Englishman lurched to his feet with both hands on the handle, the head of it would not come free; it was in the strong, tugging grip of one of McArdle's men.

McArdle now aimed his first killing blow. Unable to maneuver his wrench, Cullenbine dropped to the floor beneath it, letting the blow land on the handle, now held at the small end by himself and at the jaw end by McArdle's man. Without rising, Cullenbine kicked as hard as he could at the side of the man's knee. It cracked with the sound of a dry tree limb breaking and the maimed man dropped to the floor, surrendering his end of the forty-pounder.

The thick clothing Cullenbine wore was barely able to save his ribs and backbone from the rain of kicks delivered by McArdle's steel-toed shoes. He swung a leg at the Scot's planted foot and took him down.

Both men scrambled quickly to their feet. With the little man's famed ability to gouge and tear at close quarters, Cullenbine didn't want to be rolling around on the floor and McArdle didn't want to close with the big man's crushing strength.

Again they circled, each estimating that he had the capacity for one more all-out attempt to kill.

MacCrummon's earplug came alive. He heard some procedure numbers and letters, then a voice speaking English in the clear. No code.

From Mavis A. to all rigs to northwest—
Please let it be just a check on wave heights or damage reports.
Have reason to believe we may come under attack—

Cullenbine stepped inside an overhand swing by McArdle so that the Scot's forty-pounder went over his thick shoulder. Then he slipped his wrench behind McArdle's back and dropped its length into the crooked elbows of his huge encircling arms. Cullenbine now had his man pinned to him chest-to-chest by a bar of steel, and his great hands were free. He placed them on McArdle's face and bent him slowly backward over the bar, beginning to stretch the vertebrae of the neck and upper spine.

McArdle had to call on more strength than he knew he had. With one hand and forearm he managed to lever his wrench upward and catch Cullenbine's face neatly, cheekbone-to-cheekbone, in the toothed jaws. Then he thrust the handle away from him, twisting Cullenbine's head a full ninety degrees sideways. McArdle saw that if he could shorten his grip he could increase the arc in which he could twist this wrench; it would probably be enough to snap Cullenbine's neck.

The room started to darken as the hands pressing into McArdle's face bent him further over the bar at his back. He slipped his fingers four inches up his wrench and with the last of his strength pushed it away from him. The pressure on his back was mercifully released as Cullenbine's wrench clattered to the floor.

The platform master turned to relieve the pressure on his neck and tore at the jaws clamping his cheeks. For a fraction of a second, he was vulnerable. Before his face was a foot clear, McArdle slammed the wrench back at him as hard as he could with the heel of his hand. The pointed end of the top jaw slid under the lip of Cullenbine's hard hat and caught him in the center of the forehead. Blood burst through the lacerated skin, and the hulking frame fell backward.

McArdle saw that the man's eyes were still open, but his movements were weak and twitching and he seemed unable to move toward his own wrench. The Scot started to step over him to get back to his room, then realized it would be foolish not to finish off the big man. Disposing of the body would keep the men busy.

The roaring ring of onlookers had grown so tight around the fighters that McArdle could not set himself to swing, so he spun the head and butt of the wrench in a chest-high circle, clearing the room he needed.

—from the sea in your direction—

MacCrummon could hardly hear the voice in his ears over his own moans. His finger trembled over the firing button. He already knew enough; why couldn't he press down?

—Please help us by—

Cullenbine was able to move his head just enough to take McArdle's first blow on his hard hat. He felt the metal shell crush against his scalp and heard the glancing wrench crack into the wooden floor. McArdle was only a dark, pulsating shape above him now. Without being able to see, he could only move his head randomly in a blind attempt to avoid the blow he knew was coming. Then the world leaped under him, smashed against his shoulders and bounced his head on the floor. A short, hard clap of thunder split the air and rang through the vast hall.

Admiral Magnus was lifted off his feet and bounced through the rainy night along the catwalk around the radar tower. Like a fast camera shutter freezing action, his eyes caught the radio shack beneath him exploding into the night in a whirl of debris and white flame. Only the iron railing around the catwalk prevented him from falling onto the helicopter landing deck twenty feet below. He grasped the rail with both hands and waited for the tower with its tall, revolving dishes to begin its long topple.

But the swaying stopped quickly; the main girders had held. He ran his hands over the wetness on his face and held his fingers close to his eyes. Only rain, no blood. Somehow the twenty-foot steel stairway to the tower still stood, though the steps and rail were badly buckled. If the explosion had come three seconds earlier, it would have caught him at the center of those exposed stairs and he would have been a crumpled ball of flesh and cloth sinking in the churning ocean that lay straight beneath the west side of the radar tower.

One of the radar men stepped dazedly out of the darkened radar-control room, and Magnus pulled himself to his feet. "King, have you got power in there? Are the scopes still operating?"

"Yes, sir, Admiral Magnus. It all went dark for a minute and then came up again."

Both men looked up; the radar dish still turned steadily against the black sky.

"Injuries?"

"Just bruises, sir. What about the radiomen?"

"I'll check them. You stay here and look after the radar equipment. Watch those scopes for any traffic bearing this way. If anything shows up, call the conference room, or the observation tower right below you."

Magnus eased himself down the buckled ladder. The two tied-down helicopters—the ones that had brought him and Lustgarten—had been heavily damaged. Rotor blades drooped like broken feathers; holes a foot in diameter were punched through plexiglass and aluminum. Lord, he thought, it was a miracle the gasoline for the copters hadn't gone up. The fuel was stacked in drums on the pad just behind the rotorcraft. A big fork-lift tractor standing in front of the drums had probably helped block any fragments.

The wall of the radio shack that had faced the helicopter pad no longer existed. The surging wind was whipping smoke out of the gutted room, but deep inside fires still burned. Magnus took an emergency lantern and a first-aid kit out of a broken wall box and forced himself to enter.

Two of the three operators on duty were dead, decapitated by heavy charges exploding at eye level. A white hand clutched upward from one of the bodies, the same hand that Magnus had put the radio message into minutes before. A death sentence, it had turned out.

The third man had been in the lavatory. He had survived, but a three-foot dagger of the wooden door had blown through his thigh. Magnus applied a tourniquet and gave the half-conscious man a shot of morphine from a syrette. A quick inspection of the shambles revealed that there was not a usable piece of radio equipment left in the room.

180

The great, scarlet splinter in the surviving radioman's leg made carrying him difficult. Magnus was barely able to drag him up the ladder to the radar room. As he staggered through the door, hands eased the body off his shoulders and a wide-eyed King waved him to the intercom.

Hardly able to draw breath, Magnus managed to identify himself. It was Lustgarten. "Your man King tells me we have lost our radio," the German said.

"Yes, but we still have the radar. I suppose they weren't able to get up here to set charges. The security was a lot tighter than it was in radio. They sent so many personal messages down there."

"We will discuss your security another day. We have a more pressing problem. Whoever did this is on board Mavis A., almost certainly in force and well-armed. They have made us deaf and dumb. Now they will try to make us blind."

"You mean they'll be after the radar, too? Maybe they thought the explosives below took care of us up here as well."

"They'll be up to check that point."

"We have no way to defend ourselves here. Is this equipment really worth anything to us now, Lustgarten?"

"If *they* want the radar out, *we* want it on. Our advantages are so small that we cannot afford to give up anything to them."

"I'll try to get something set up, Colonel."

"Not you. You're needed here. Please come down to the conference room at once. Is there anyone you can trust up there who can be left in charge?"

"King's an excellent man."

"Good. Tell him his luck has run out and leave at once. They will be coming for you very quickly."

chapter 10

Before the echo of the charge faded, McArdle forgot Cullenbine and fought through the milling crewmen to the stairway leading below, his men, Morrison, Frazer and Thomson, beside him. Thomson was dragging along the groaning, cursing man whose leg Cullenbine had broken.

They found MacCrummon weeping on the bed, the exploder fallen to the floor. McArdle, who understood leadership as few men understood anything, lifted the blubbering fat man and hugged him. "You're a beautiful man, Tom."

The effect was instantaneous. Strength swelled back into the fat man like wind filling a slack sail; he grinned and laughed and kissed the cheek of the slight man before him. "I done right, then, Tiny? I done right?"

"We can't do anything wrong today. We'll finish up now. Go get it, Frazer."

Frazer stepped out, returned instantly with the large red fire extinguisher that had been hanging in the corridor and turned it upside down on a table. The bottom of the container had been cut through and was held in place by wax. Thomson dug into this with a penknife and the metal plate was lifted out.

MacCrummon shook the cylinder above McArdle's outstretched hands. Six loaded Colt .45's wrapped in tissue paper fell out. Each had two extra clips lightly taped to the muzzle. McArdle handed the weapons around. When he came to the injured man, who had been placed on the bed, he hesitated. "Chip, the rig is going to the bottom. You've got but one use for this gun down here. If you're going to use it that way, I'll leave it."

"Take it along, Tiny, where it will be the most use. I ain't had a decent bath in months. I'll probably enjoy it."

"Good boy, Chip." McArdle stuck the extra automatic under his belt.

"Will we take the lift, Tiny?"

"They'll have figured out that we're coming. They could jam the lift and cage us like mice. We'll use the stairs and ladders. Don't wave your guns around until I say so."

"It'll be one hell of a climb, Tiny," Thomson said.

McArdle said, "Make it a fast one. I want us all up there in fifteen minutes."

Harold King was an "excellent man," Magnus had said on the phone to Lustgarten. The bald, middle-aged King had assumed the admiral was referring to his ability to run, maintain and repair a complex radar installation, and he would have agreed with the assessment completely. But a moment later, Magnus was leaving him with orders to preserve his tower against an unknown number of armed professionals. Even the seasoned Magnus had made the mistake of believing that competence in one specialty meant skill in others.

In point of fact, King was hopelessly academic. His talent lay in his uncanny ability to remember anything he had read, and to look at a spectacularly tangled wiring diagram and instantly see in his mind every molecule of the electric flow it represented. It was up to the technicians to open the panels and touch the rainbow of wires, for King had a positive horror of tools and all forms of physical manipulation.

"Mr. King," one of the radar men said, "this is insane. He can't give us orders like that. We're not soldiers, we're employees. Unionized employees. I think this should be reported to a shop steward, or that we should resign our positions."

"Billings," King said, "if we do that those men will come up here and smash everything. It's taken us months to get it all working just so. Why, you spent every day of two weeks, including off days, with your head inside that number-four unit. Do you fancy the idea of some idiot coming in here and taking a hammer to it?"

"Well, no. That wouldn't do at all. Perhaps if we promised not to use the equipment? Or we could post a 'Positively Off Limits' sign at the bottom of the stairs? We could even offer to put a guard down there ourselves to keep people out." Although he was barely in his thirties, Billings, might have been the grandfather of all present.

Most of the others nodded and grunted tentative assent to Billings's plan. Like all guardians of delicate and beautiful equipment, they loathed the idea of anyone else touching it.

King hesitated. "Admiral Magnus says it's important to keep the equipment operating. He's been a very decent chap. And he says that the safety of everybody on Mavis may depend on us."

"Not a word about *our* safety," Billings sniffed. "Or even the gift of a cap pistol that we can use to bluff them away."

"Too bad the bloody stairs didn't blow down. There's no other way to get up here. Then we could defend ourselves with a teaspoon."

A blueprint of the radar tower came into King's head, and instantly the stairs disappeared.

"The stairs. If we could get rid of the stairs, we'd be all right."

"We have no way to do that," Billings said. "They're

welded to the deck and catwalk. We'd need an acetylene torch. Anyway, there's no time."

King's mind kept running over his mental diagram of Mavis A.'s upper reaches. What force could oppose the steel of the stairway? Use the revolving radar mast as a winch to rip the stairs away? Impossible; there was no cable to make the connection. The rotor hubs of the helicopters? No, the craft looked smashed; besides, no one up here knew how to start the engines. Then he saw it. "The tractor. There's a deck tractor in front of the helicopters. It's got a good strong tow chain, and it might do."

"That's jolly good," Billings said. "We should try it."

"Can you drive the silly thing?"

"I think I can figure it out. How do I get back up here if I get the stairs down?"

King kicked a large spool lying in a corner. "There's a hundred feet of heavy electric cable here. We can haul you back up."

"Oh, very good. All right, here I go."

While he was the most willing of King's men, Bernard Billings was also the most deliberate. Nature seemed to have left him without the ability to hurry. He picked slowly through the oilskins to find his own; he lit his pipe, which fortunately was already packed. His fellow workers, knowing that he hated to be rushed, remained anxiously silent. Finally he let himself down the stairs and strolled deliberately to the tractor, stopping once for a full twenty seconds to refasten a catch on a boot. Eventually the rain-soaked men on the catwalk heard the roar of the tractor's engine through the wind.

The head- and taillights of the squat little vehicle flicked on, and it began to make its way along the pad to the stairs. Billings backed the tractor into position as though he were jockeying into a tight parking spot in Whitehall. Before he got out of the driver's seat to pick up the chain coiled behind it he turned off the lights and shut off the engine.

"Good heaven, Francis, get down there and help him. He'll take a week," King said.

A man clattered down the stairs and snatched the end of the chain from Billings. "I think we can do it with one pull," he shouted. He ran back up the stairs and wound and fastened the chain at the level of the top step. He raced back to the deck.

"Any time now, Billings."

Billings refired the engine, turned on the lights and ground the tractor into gear. As it started to move, Francis jumped aboard to give it more traction. The chain stiffened and the engine's hum sank to a lower note. The heavily ribbed tires had stopped turning and seemed ready to lose their grip on the rain-glazed deck when something snapped up above. Then the catwalk began to tilt downward, the side supports of the stairway tearing like paper. In another moment, the steps had been pulled down flat, a continuation of the taut chain.

"Let's get the hell out of here, Billings."

"Yes, yes, Francis. You first."

The men on the catwalk had already let down a length of wire. Francis clamped his legs around it and clung with his hands while they hauled him up. As he climbed over the catwalk railing, he saw a darker shadow moving among the gasoline drums behind the helicopters. "I think they're here, Mr. King. Over that way. They must have come up the ladders."

King flung the end of the wire down to Billings. "They're right behind you, man," he called down. "Be quick."

Billings was not in the best condition, and he doubted his ability to cling to the swaying wire. Thoughtfully he brought it around his chest. Or would it be better passed between his legs in some sort of bosun's chair arrangement? If so, what sort of knot would be best?

Now King saw the shadow of the man too. It had stopped, crouching in the rain behind the first row of gasoline drums. A second shadow appeared, this one toward the edge of the platform.

"There's at least two of them now, Mr. King. Why don't they close in?"

"They might have come up in separate groups and are waiting for everybody to get here."

"What the hell is Billings *doing?*"

Billings had decided on a chest sling, but not on a knot. He drew a wire-stripping tool out of his utility belt and cleared six inches of insulation off the end of the wire. This done, he measured the wire carefully around his chest, holding his thumb at the point where the stripped end circled back. He then stripped bare another six inches of wire, returned the stripping tool to his belt and drew out pliers, with which he began an elaborate electrician's splice on the bare wire. This would serve him instead of a knot.

"Billings, you sonofabitch, we're going to leave you there," King hissed.

There were now five separate shadows moving past the helicopters toward the radar tower.

"Mr. King, they're coming."

"Francis and I will haul you up, Billings. The rest of you get inside. If you see we're not going to make it back in there with you, barricade the door as best you can. Close all the ventilators so they can't drop anything in on you. Go."

Billings was almost done with his splice.

"We're going to pull you up."

"No, wait. I'm not sure that this is the proper splice at all." He began to undo the wire with his pliers.

A gunshot exploded out in the storm. King didn't hear the ring of a bullet striking and thought it must have been fired in the air.

A burred and menacing voice barked from the advancing shadows. "All right, you radar people. Hold on right there. Don't move."

"Pull, Francis," King shouted.

Billings had only half undone the splice around his chest when he was jerked off his feet by King and Francis.

"Shit, Tiny," MacCrummon called over the wind,

"they've got the stairs down. Pulled them loose with that tractor. How can we get up there?"

"The same way that one's going. They can haul us."

McArdle dropped to one knee and pointed his .45 at the distant shapes of the men on the catwalk. "Freeze right there and let that line down."

If McArdle had ever in his life done any target shooting with a Colt .45, he would have known that he had made a bad error. The big automatic, made seventy years before to stop machete-swinging Moros at point-blank range, was notoriously inaccurate at any distance.

King saw McArdle's intentions and was determined to thwart them. "Don't stop, Francis. We've got a chance in this dark."

"Not if they've got machine guns."

"We'll know that in a second."

"Or poor Billings will."

Swinging from the end of the wire, Billings saw a row of orange flashes spurt from a spot on the deck forty yards away. Bullets whanged into the metal on both sides of him. He caught the edge of the catwalk, then a rung of the railing, and attempted to swing his legs up. Hands were tearing at his oilskins, trying to get a grip on him. Just above the heads of the crouching King and Francis he saw the paint on the steel wall explode into ugly black blots again and again. With a last violent heave, he rolled under the railing and kept right on going until he was lying against the wall of the radar room. The other two men flung themselves down in the same position, so that the men below could no longer see them.

"Mr. King," Billings said, "can this catwalk deck under us stop bullets?"

"Not rifles or heavy machine guns. But they don't have those, or we wouldn't be alive now."

"What about pistols?"

"Magnums would probably cut through this steel like butter. With less than that, we may be all right. Of course I'm only guessing from what I've read."

They heard voices beneath them. One shouted, "Stand

up and put your hands over your head. We won't hurt you."

"Like you didn't hurt the boys in the radio shack, eh?" King called.

"That was necessary. Killing you isn't. Not at all. I'll tell you what. You don't even have to show yourselves. Just secure the end of whatever it was you were using to hoist that man, then throw the other end down here and we'll do the rest. If you've got any more line, you can let yourselves down the other side and get lost."

King didn't know what he was going to say until he heard himself. "Forget it. We've got guns. You can't get up here alive."

"That's a bluff. Guns aren't allowed on Mavis. Now get that line down here quick."

"Forget it," King yelled again.

"My boys are right underneath you, mister. If I say the word they'll open up your bellies right through that tin you're lying on."

Francis spoke in a low voice. "What will we tell them, Mr. King?"

"Go to hell, you bastards," Billings bawled.

"I knew we should have left him down there."

The men hugging the catwalk tensed their stomach muscles as though this could turn aside steel-jacketed .45's. Each already felt the slugs tearing through him.

There was a ragged volley from below. King could feel the walk bucking under him, but the metal was holding.

Tiny McArdle was trembling with fury. The men above were keeping him from fulfilling his sacred word. "Stop firing. It's not working, and we're liable to need the ammunition. Scout around. See if there's any other way up."

His three men scattered, running along beneath the catwalk, disappearing around the side of the tower. They were back in sight moments later, peering into equipment sheds and scouting through stacked tools. Finally they halted in frustration, and McArdle motioned them back to him.

190

"Nothing," MacCrummon said, "Not a single ladder, not a brace to climb, not a rope to throw."

Frazer said, "If one of us stood on the other's shoulders we might be able to reach the lip of the walk."

"They could lie out of sight until our fingers came over the edge, and then pound them flat with a hammer."

"Is there any way to burn them out, Tiny?"

"In this rain? And the damned tower's all steel."

"What about the gasoline over there for the helicopters?"

"Tom, I think you've got something. We could use the tractor. It's got a fork-lift on the front."

"It'll take a helluva lot of gasoline to burn hot enough in all this weather."

"We've got a helluva lot of gasoline. Let's do it."

McArdle jumped on the tractor and drove it between the helicopters as the other Scots sprinted beside him. When the fork was lowered, they found they could roll two big gasoline drums onto it. They began to stack the drums under the catwalk circling the radar tower.

Peering cautiously over the catwalk's edge, King, Billings and Francis were able to watch the preparations for their cremation.

"Mr. King, I'm not going to let them do that to me. I'm going to surrender and let that wire down," said Francis.

"Well, let's use all the time we've got. It'll take them a good twenty minutes to shuttle enough drums from way over there."

King felt good about his decision; he was being as true to Magnus's orders as he could, and he was saving lives. Whether or not their charred bodies remained in the tower, the radar watch would be over. Even if he and his men had been armed, he thought, he wouldn't have tried to injure the men below. Yes, they had tried to kill him, but that had been his own fault. He had refused what was probably a reasonable request.

He anticipated the reactions of the Scots when he hauled them up to the catwalk: grins, and maybe a little apology from them about the unpleasantness with the guns. For a while he thought about the greeting he would give them. Yielding but dignified? Good-natured but gently barbed?

The volume of shouting on the deck seemed to grow. King took a chance and thrust his head far enough over the catwalk's edge to see what was going on. The Scots were too busy to notice. They already had a half-dozen drums standing in front of the tower. Not quite enough yet. The Scots seemed to have decided that the fuel containers should be stacked two high in order to concentrate the fire. King estimated that twenty drums double-stacked beneath the catwalk would do the job nicely.

Having determined to surrender in a short while, he felt a kinship with the men below. They were all victims of some political circumstance. No longer feeling threatened by them, he pushed his shoulders over the edge to get a better view.

For a moment it seemed that one of the men glanced at him, but he couldn't be sure in the dark. They started to tilt a drum for the prongs of McArdle's fork-lift as he drove forward briskly with the tractor. King could see that they had not lifted the drum's edge quite enough and that the lift had been set a bit too high. He heard himself start to shout, "Watch it!" but it was too late; the sharp fork punched deep into the drum. When the Scots wrestled it off the impaling prongs, gasoline spurted thickly out of the twin punctures. Swearing and straining, they reset the gushing container and got it into place on the second tier. The wind was blowing straight into King's face. It drove the gasoline sloshing down onto the deck back underneath the stack.

King smiled slyly to himself. He had thought up what promised to be a marvelous joke. He crawled along the catwalk until he was beneath a deflated two-man rescue raft bracketed to the wall. With a quick motion, he raised himself and lifted the release handle. The raft fell on the walk in front of him. After a moment's fumbling, the inflation lanyard was in his hand, and when he tugged it, the raft leaped out in all directions. By quick manipulation, he was able to have it standing on its edge by the time it was fully inflated. He located a foot-square waterproof bag that was attached to the craft by a small nylon line, and opening the bag's zipper, dumped the contents out on the catwalk. From the small heap of morphine capsules and first-aid compresses, he took an eight-inch-long metal tube. Then he found the four flares sealed together in waterproof plastic. Shielding this under his body, he opened it with his fingernail, dropped a flare into the exposed breech of the metal tube and resealed it.

In the time it took King to crawl back to above where the Scots were working, his plan changed. His first intention had been to wait until his opponents were clear of the pool of gasoline before setting it on fire. But physical advantage is heady stuff, and now he decided to wait until they were tightly clustered around the point of ignition. He was aware that the scheme could fail; the teeming rain might drown the flare or dilute the gasoline, or the fire could be so small and momentary that it would do no more than infuriate the Scots. Then his chance to surrender himself and his men would be gone. The men below would complete their pyre against all cries for mercy and burn them to ashes. Yet he accepted this. King had found out something known to only the few: The need to be a hero ran as wild and far from reason as the need to be a coward.

McArdle saw that his men were tiring. They had only ten drums in place against the tower—five stacks, each two high—and their breath was already tearing as they clung to the tractor around him. "You drive after we stack this load, Tom," he shouted. Perhaps there was no need to go so fast. Should they slow up a bit and give the poor bastards up in the tower a little more chance to think about surrendering?

He stopped the tractor five feet in front of the stacked drums and the men hopped off. McArdle joined them in wrestling the two drums off the fork. The whole area reeked of the gasoline spilling out of the ruptured drum.

"Hey, look," MacCrummon said, and pointed.

Against the sky they made out the head and shoulders of a man hanging over the edge of the catwalk, not more than fifteen feet away.

"Let him watch. It'll show him we're not fooling," McArdle said. It bothered him to be so close to a man he might have to burn alive. He had gotten tough too fast, he thought. Perhaps even now he could show a little reassuring friendliness. The figure above lifted an arm and appeared about to wave. McArdle freed a hand from the drum he was moving and waved back in a casual greeting.

A red streak appeared to shoot out of the overhanging man and something exploded against the deck in a brilliance of sparks. In an instant a low-running sheet of flame ran across the deck, enveloping the Scots to the knees. For a moment they felt nothing as their soaked boots and trousers resisted the heat. Then someone felt the first caress of the fire on his skin and yelped. They ran wildly out of the burning ring, and the rain quickly extinguished their smoldering garments.

But now the leaking drum blew up in a roaring billow like that of a flamethrower; it barely missed engulfing the Scots, who tumbled back to the edge of the platform. Another drum blew, and its burning river swept past McArdle's men and poured a flaming waterfall over the edge of Mavis A. and into the ocean. The inferno penned the Scots with their backs to the tower and the sea.

Up on the catwalk, Billings and Francis had bolted inside the radar room at the first glow from the deck, but King remained to watch. He was appalled by the speed and power of the flames. He had wanted the men below to die instantly, and when they didn't he was desperate for them to get away. As the roaring circle grew smaller around them, King could feel the heat of the catwalk plates beginning to come up through the soles of his shoes. He had to get inside before the rest of the drums went. Backing toward the door, he felt his legs tangle in something: the wire they had used to bring up Francis and Billings. The loop was still in place. Picking up the coils, King ran back to the end of the catwalk. The Scots were right below him. "H-e-e-y," King yelled. "Up here."

The smallest of the men turned his face upward and pointed accusingly at him. King never lived to hear the shot; the bullet struck just below his breastbone and angled up into his heart.

McArdle watched the man above tumble backwards. Something fell from the walk, and the Scot scooped it up. A loop of wire. It ran up and disappeared over the rail where the man had been standing.

With a mad yell, McArdle slipped the loop over the head and shoulders of the startled MacCrummon. The fat man laughed, and the others swore happily. Fat Tom braced his foot against the side of the tower and pulled mightily on the wire. The other end caught under King's body for a second, then came loose and fell at MacCrummon's feet.

Now the Scots got the last break of their lives. The nearest drums blew simultaneously, turning the men into gyrating torches. As they sailed one by one over the edge of the platform like Roman candles, they thought not of all the thousand sadnesses that had been their days, but only of the cooling, enveloping sea waiting below.

Ninety feet below the waterline of the *American Enterprise,* The Dropper and the O'Driscoll brothers were numb with exhaustion. Between them, they had traveled most of the quarter-mile alleyway that ran along the spine of the ship through its doublebottom, and had carefully placed the plastergel brought down by the crew of the *Enterprise*.

The Dropper had determined the intervals and picked the spots for placement. The brothers, Roland and Eamon, with occasional skilled help from George Barton, had served as his hands, scooping the puttied explosive out of the bags and layering the thick gray ribbons along the steel plates of the hull where it curved up to meet the gigantic oil tanks.

Neither of the O'Driscolls knew anything about explosives, but The Dropper's genius for destruction extended to teaching the art. He showed them what to do, breaking complex tasks into simple parts and assigning them in simple sequences. Operating in this way, he was able to confine his own task to the more sophisticated work of wiring, placing and timing the detonators.

They were almost done. The Dropper was tying some of the last 144-inch lengths of plastic-covered wire into position, and the final strings of explosives had been laid to open the bulkhead into the engine spaces.

"There. All charges placed, all hookups done but the last," cackled The Dropper, pulling a full bottle of Scotch out of his canvas toolbag. "We'll have to run wires up to the deck and hook them to the exploder, but that'll only take a few minutes. A little celebration is called for now."

They flopped down with their backs against the engine-room bulkhead. The Dropper twisted open the bottle, took a good pull and passed it to the brothers.

"You amateurs may not realize what a work of art you have accomplished here," he said. "Take the explosive itself." He poked a finger into the ribbon that passed along the base of the bulkhead. "Nine out of ten would have been happier to use gelignite 60. A fine ammonium nitrate, mind you, but not right for this job." His heel pounded on the steel of the deck plates. "To break steel like this, you need *brisance*. You got that fancy word? *Brisance*. It's the ability of an explosive to *shatter*. When you're blastin' in a coal mine you can always drill a hole in the rock for your charge and enclose it. Then you want *push*." A long, steady push on Eamon O'Driscoll's shoulder almost flattened him. "You get a nice pressure build, and the rock splits open like an overinflated tire. But these charges of ours are sittin' out in the open air. They must *shatter* the steel. We want *this* kind of blow," and he shot a pointed knuckle into Eamon's bicep.

"Ouch, you little bastard. Watch it. I get your point."

"Good. Now you understand why I'm happy to have plastergel. And here's something else." The Dropper picked up a box the size and shape of a mechanic's tool chest. "Somebody else might have done the job with the first lousy exploder that came to hand. Not this boy. This here is the Beethoven Dynamo Condenser Exploder. It has a capacity of two hundred detonators and it never lets you down. Quinn knew from my reputation that I only used the best. He told me he went out and bought this out of his own pocket, using not a dollar of the Army's money. It cost him a hundred and eleven American dollars, and that's a buy. He went after plastergel instead of anythin' else because he knew I like it on the steel. That is a very classy man, and here's to more of him." He took another long drink, and the brothers followed. Half the bottle was already gone.

The Dropper flipped a shiny aluminum tube in his hand. "Think of it, boys. This little Number 8 electric detonator is what's goin' to put an end to all of these millions of tons of steel and oil—not to speak of more millions of hours of work and sweat designin' and buildin'."

The drink was quickly affecting them. They passed the detonator from hand to hand as though they had not been working with others exactly like it for the last fifteen hours.

"You don't understand what a little marvel this is. In this closed end they've pressed a base charge of PETN, a hellish little explosive. That's the flashin' mixture, but by itself it's not sensitive enough. So they sprinkle over it what we call an ignitin' mixture—lead styphnate, lead azide and a bit of aluminum powder."

"How do you set the whole mess off?" Eamon asked thickly.

"There's a bridge wire that runs through it all. When our little Beethoven sends out its electric charge, the wire glows, just like a light bulb. That sets off the igniter that sets off the flasher that sets off the primary. And *that*"—he grabbed a ball-peen hammer and rapped the metal deck plates—"sets off *four million pounds per square inch* of pressure wherever we've got those charges." He pointed to a half-eaten sandwich on the deck. "The fish are going to be finishin' that."

Roland O'Driscoll's voice was a whisper. "Exactly what will happen to the ship when we fire the charges?"

The Dropper was thoughtful for a minute. "I can only say what the steel will do. What the water does isn't my business. How long the ship will take to sink, I can only guess."

"Then guess."

"Well, I'm usin' interval-delay blasting caps. The charges will go off a hundred milliseconds apart. That will help each successive charge work on a weakened area alongside it. I reckon we'll open up about seven hundred feet of hull. Of course a lot of that damage will carry up into the tanks above us to let out the oil. We can't count that in estimatin' the sea water that will come in."

"How long will she take to sink?"

"This can only be a guess, Roland, based on the holes I expect to blast and the space the sea has to fill. At a very conservative guess, I'd say that this barge will be sittin' on the bottom twenty minutes after old Beethoven starts his symphony."

"Will it go down in one piece?"

"That depends on what the waves do once the integrity of the hull structure is broken."

"Will she go down by the head? By the stern?"

"I'm no marine engineer, but there's a good chance that all that water rushin' in along her length will turn her over on her side. Maybe keel her completely over if the water's deep enough."

"Dominic says it's only about a hundred feet deep at Mavis A."

"If he's right then we'll only settle ten or twenty feet."

"What will happen then?"

"Hell, man, you're a sailor. What does a storm like this do to a ship that's lying dead in the water with bad structural damage? Sooner or later it'll break us up; the only question is how fast."

"How long do you think a man could live in this water?"

"It bein' late fall, the temperature is already way down.

198

With regular survival gear, you'd have about an hour. That's out of a book I found in one of the lifeboats."

"An hour. As long as that."

"Now don't sound so disappointed. Anyway, Dominic's goin' to take care of us. You heard him; he's got a plan to get us picked up."

"Nobody's goin' to pick us up."

"Maybe we can get the lifeboats off."

"Impossible."

One more round between the three of them finished the bottle. Each now perceived that the two others were very drunk.

"If we don't get picked up," The Dropper said, "then we're dead men. We shouldn't think about it too much."

"What the hell else should we think about?"

"About forty years in jail, Roland. We've done for a lot of boys in the last few hours."

"But *drownin'*, Dropper. Did you ever think hard about drownin'?"

"I have. And it doesn't sound good. But the one thing I know is that it doesn't take forty years to happen."

"My God, I'm scared. I don't want the water. Drop, if we're goin' into the water, could you shoot me?"

"Hell, no. The sweet Jesus will forgive me for takin' off a few Englishmen, but not for helpin' with an Irishman's suicide."

"Eamon, will you do it?"

"I couldn't, Roland."

The Dropper said, "You might ask Devlin. He doesn't much care who he murders."

The thought of dying by the cold hand of the hairless Devlin made Roland shrink inside. "Shall we finish up, then?"

"No, you're not ready for it. And, truth be told, neither are we." The Dropper giggled. "I think we should go somewhere for a couple of hours, relax and have ourselves a time."

"And where would that be?" Eamon asked. "Bermuda? The Riviera?"

The Dropper managed to focus his eyes on his watch. "I think we should all drop in on my girl. She'll be home alone now, and lonely, I'm sure."

"What bloody girl? Or maybe you've found a comely little Filipino mess boy?"

"You caught a couple of looks at the first officer's wife, didn't you? What did you think of her?"

"Mrs. Browne is a knockout. Absolutely lovely. Now what lie are you goin' to tell us?"

"No lie at all. She's my girl."

"Roland, I think the poor old Dropper's been sniffin' the gel too long."

"I'll tell it straight, and you can listen or not. I went to her place earlier this evenin' and declared I was available. She snapped me up—just like that."

"Just like that."

"Come to think of it, I made her a few promises."

"A yacht bigger than this one?"

"Better: her life. I told her where this tub was goin', and that if she didn't want to join it, she should think about findin' a new romance."

"Jesus, Dropper, you weren't supposed to tell any of them."

"Don't you understand, Rollie, she let me take her. She's sick of that stiff-backed bastard Owen. I could see it clear at the captain's table. She knows we could have a good time together—and that's not even mentionin' not wantin' to drown. I forgot to tell the poor thing that she might have to do so just the same, of course. Now brush as much of the crap off yourselves as you can and we'll go visitin'."

"Dominic won't like this."

"That's why we're not invitin' him. Now take the hardware," he said, motioning to their pile of automatic rifles and grenades. "We don't want any of the crew comin' across that."

"Dropper, we're not interested in sittin' around watchin' you kiss a lady."

"Eamon, my boy, you and your brother are even

younger and handsomer than I am. I'm sure she won't be able to keep her hands off any of us. This is goin' to be the most memorable evenin' of her life."

When Noel Cullenbine came to his feet, his face was a massive black bruise. His eyes were swollen and blood was caked across his forehead. But he was like some mythological beast that had gained strength from its wounds. His mind seemed clearer, his voice louder and his fists harder than they had been before. Hearing the fire klaxon howling, he kneed and slugged his way through the milling crowd in the hall until he reached the locater light box. All the fire-warning circuits from the helicopter pad were blinking. He yelled to his foremen.

Some of the crew were beginning to leave the hall. Cullenbine reached into the box and activated an override that slid shut the room's steel fire doors. Men began to shout and pound at them. Cullenbine jumped up on an exercise horse and roared. "Listen to me, you sons-of-bitches! You'd better get that shit out of your pants and do what I tell you or we'll all be feeding the eels in a couple of hours."

"What the hell is it, Cullenbine?" somebody called. "Is it going to be a blowout?"

"It could be worse than that. We have to be ready for anything. Let me see the firefighting teams." Two dozen hands went up. "As soon as I let you out that door, get your equipment and hustle up to the helicopter pad. It looks like everything up there is burning." He opened the doors. As the men went out, others started to follow. "Everybody else stay put," Cullenbine boomed. "Let's see oil men only. Roustabouts, tool-pushers, welders, rig engineers, the works." Scores of hands rose. "These foremen will break you up into three teams, one for each leg. Get down there into position right now and clear away for a shutdown. I'm going upstairs to find out what's happening. Now move it!"

The foremen plunged into the crowd, calling out names and floor positions, and within a minute the confusion ebbed. The crew seemed relieved to be under command again.

When Cullenbine called the conference room, Zamke answered. "Mr. Cullenbine, I have been waiting here for you. The others have gone up to the observation tower. We are going to operate from there; it's the only place with any visibility. Plase hurry and join us."

Cullenbine stepped out of the elevator, and peered hard into the gloom of the observation tower. In the dim glow of the tall, rain-streaked windows and red battle-lights he spotted Magnus, Lustgarten and Zamke.

"Where have *you* been?" Magnus asked in wonder.

"Losing an argument with a man half my size, mostly. I let McArdle get away."

"Yes. He led an attack on the radar tower after they bombed the radio shack."

"Where is he now?"

"He's dead. All his men, too. King got them, somehow. Extraordinary work."

"Any contact with King?"

"With the tower. A phone line managed to stay open. King was killed in the fight, but we still have our radar."

"The *Enterprise* will be showing up damned soon," Cullenbine said. "Over here, everyone."

They gathered around the etched diagram of Mavis A., back-lit on the table top.

"Let's look at all the physics and possibilities first." The platform master's finger began to trace over the diagram. "The legs of Mavis A. are built to withstand a collision with any ordinary ship. She could even stand up to most of the early supertankers. But a fully loaded *American Enterprise* is the closest thing to an irresistible force that exists. If she catches us squarely, she'll slice through at least one of our legs easily. After that several things could happen.

"If the tanker breaks off a large enough corner of our triangular platform when she takes the leg, the rest of the platform will tilt and slide everything on it into the sea

202

like a tray of dishes. This would probably pull the other legs down too, so destruction would be total. But if *Enterprise* snaps off the leg cleanly below the platform we might have a strange situation. The bottom of the platform is not many feet higher than the ship's deck, so the main deck of Mavis A. might simply sag down and rest on the deck of the tanker. We would be more or less safely supported as long as *Enterprise* remained in place."

Magnus brightened a bit. "What would be the chances of the weight of the platform pinning the ship against the shallow bottom we have here? That would make the difference between a full-scale disaster and something we could live with."

"I can't run calculations on that without knowing the exact dimensions and cargo weight of the *Enterprise*. I'm afraid it doesn't look very good. With her enormous displacement, I don't think even the weight of most of Mavis's superstructure could drive her down deep enough. Of course, the *Enterprise* would be barely skimming bottom here, estimating her draft at between ninety and one hundred feet, and it wouldn't take very much to put her bow in the mud. But it's my guess that our weight won't stop her in time."

"What do you mean by that, Mr. Cullenbine?" Lustgarten asked.

"I believe that even with the weight of the platform bearing on her, the momentum of the *Enterprise* will carry her through to take out a second leg. In which case, the platform would break up and the superstructure would drop into the water."

"Mr. Cullenbine, suppose the ship is neither tightly pinned to the bottom nor able to carry through to the second leg?" Magnus asked.

"Somewhere between the two possibilities, you mean? Yes, that could happen, I suppose. We would be safe for the moment, supported by the ship at one corner as though she were a floating caisson. But then our attackers could simply reverse engines, back out from under us and let us fall of our own weight."

"Would her engines have the power to do that? She'd be reversing from a dead stop."

"Provided the structures were not locked together in the fall, I think she could do it."

"Then the only measures we can take are to try to save the crew and to keep the oil spill as low as we can," Magnus said.

"It sounds as though the best chance for survival will be down in one of the legs," said Lustgarten.

"Quite so," replied Cullenbine. "Going into the water is out of the question."

"But *which* leg?" Zamke asked. "Suppose it's the one that's struck?"

Cullenbine nodded. "Yes. Those elevators in the legs only take fifteen men at a time, and they take about ten minutes for a round trip. We can't wait until the ship is committed to make our move." He tapped the diagram. "But I think I can make a good guess which leg they'll hit. Look. The oil tanks around Blueleg and Yellowleg are filled almost to the top. The weight of that oil can absorb an awful lot of the impact. It could make the difference between knocking us over cleanly and causing big problems. But Redleg is empty, and so is by far the most vulnerable target."

Magnus frowned. "But will they know that?"

"Their planning and intelligence have been very good up to now. We know that they had men aboard. The information about oil storage is known to every man on Mavis who cares to ask. It could have gone back to Edinburgh on any helicopter or lighter in the last week—and I think it did."

"It sounds logical," Magnus said. "So let's put all our money on Redleg being hit. We'll split everybody up into Yellowleg and Blueleg and listen for loud noises. But we have to get the wells capped first. Will there be time?"

"Depends on when the tanker shows up, Admiral. It'll be damned close."

"There may be panic. Would guns help to keep order?" asked Zamke.

"Probably," Cullenbine said. "Too bad we don't have any."

Cullenbine did his job beautifully. It wasn't until the oil men in Blueleg and Yellowleg were in position that he sent the nonoperating personnel—painters, cooks, medics, pilots and engineers—down to join them. Then he had the elevators brought to the top of the legs and turned off, so that even in the event of a panic no one could get out without his permission.

In selecting the crew to work with Cullenbine in Redleg, chance had neglected two men who were badly needed down there: Randy Martin and Bairn Harrison. The work in Redleg had hardly begun when a sling let go and dropped a fifteen-foot-long, thirty-six-inch pipe to the floor. No one was hurt and the thousand-pound pipe fell well out of the way, so it was left where it was—squarely on top of the hatch cover that was the only exit from Sadie's and Gail's steel chamber.

chapter 11

A great green pyramid of sea climbed over the unrising prow of the *American Enterprise* and ran several thousand tons of white water down the weather deck. On the bridge, Captain Cody and Owen Browne watched the boiling foam roll thirteen hundred feet and explode with a dull boom against the bridge house. Spray reached the navigating bridge windows.

"I don't think you can do it, Browne. The seas are getting worse."

"I'll have to stay on the center walk. I'll hitch up to the safety cable. The valves and piping will give some protection."

"That walk wasn't made for this weather—nothing was. You could drown down there without even going overboard. Or you could be crushed to jelly."

"I think we're getting about two waves an hour that aren't survivable."

"Too bad they don't publish timetables."

"I'll check the mixture one more time." Making his way back to the control room, Browne found the row of dials that read out the mixtures of gases in the *Enterprise's* tanks. None of the full tanks gave readings, the needles resting on the safe side of the gauges, but the empty Number One tank's needle was two-thirds of the way into the red danger band. Browne had replaced the inert stack gases in the tank with oxygen sucked in by the ventilation fans, and there had been plenty of time for the sludge pools at the bottom of the tank to produce a large volume of explosive fumes. Only a spark was needed to blow the bottom out of the *Enterprise* beneath Number One.

Browne went back to Cody. "It's all set. In a couple of minutes it will be time for my regular tour of the engine room. I'll show myself to the Irishman down there and start back here. Engleberg will come with me and sneak me off the elevator at the weather-deck level. Then he'll come to see you about some nonsense and head straight back to the engine room. That way the elevator indicator won't tip anything off except for a couple of seconds. I'll get outside easily. They're spread too thin to watch everywhere."

Cody cautiously pulled a half-dozen disposable butane lighters out of his pocket. "I took these out of the store. You might need more than one. I've got tape, too."

Browne rattled the pocket of his uniform jacket. "I already have four of 'em. And tape."

"Goddamn it, Browne, someday I'm going to think that this should have been me."

"Captain, it's likely to be you yet. If I disappear out there, you'll try it, won't you?" He pointed at the lighters in the captain's hand. "You have everything you need. The tank doesn't know that we've agreed I'll do the job. It will explode for you, too."

Cody felt himself flush. He had not really considered that he might yet have to take Browne's place, though the possibility could not have been more obvious. It wasn't that he felt fear; there was simply a resistance to annihilation in his heart and mind. "I'll allow you three quarters of an hour. Then I'll be along."

"The guard?"

"I can take him, I think."

They shook hands, making sure the guard couldn't see them.

"Good luck, Browne." Cody looked hard into his mate's face, seeking a sign of the willingness to die. Somehow, in this seagoing bookkeeper, it was there.

Browne nodded to Cody, waved to the guard and walked unhurriedly to the waiting elevator.

Billings had taken charge of the radar room on Mavis A. He stepped over King's body lying on its back in the center of the room. It hadn't seemed decent to leave him out on the catwalk in the rain, but he would have been in the way of the operators if they had placed him against the walls.

Though the fire had been out for some time, the heat in the room, reflected off the hot steel, was still unbearable. Worrying about the effect of the temperature on the delicate electronic equipment, Billings stood in front of a scope and anxiously checked the sweep. It seemed steady and strong enough, but he could smell overheated insulation. Something wavered at the top of the screen. What was happening?

The sweep went around again; the wavering was still there. Billings watched it for almost five minutes. "It's a blip. There's a blip on the screen. A damned big one."

"The one Magnus's looking for, do you think?" one of the operators asked.

"I haven't got a track on it yet, but I would guess so."

"Will they have us on their own radar yet?"

"Their equipment should be roughly comparable to ours. They have us, all right. We'll see them coming straight for us, I think. Will you get the admiral on that phone for me, please?"

Danenhower, the electronics officer on the *American Enterprise,* supervised all the electronic equipment on the ship, including her radar. He didn't like the way Quinn and Barton were reacting to the new blip on the screen. "What would that be up there, Mr. Danenhower?" Quinn asked.

"That's an oil-drilling platform—Mavis A. First rig in the Mavis Field. Biggest rig there ever was."

"I see. Barton, that was very fine navigation. We're right where we're supposed to be."

"You know all about it, then?" muttered Danenhower.

"As a matter of fact, we do. We picked it as a navigation point for a rendezvous we wish to make. You may now put this picture on the bridge reader. Barton, Mr. Browne is keeping the course. Have Father Costello tell him that he's to make straight for Mavis."

Owen Browne took one of the leather-and-canvas safety harnesses out of the rack over the steel door to the weather deck, wriggled his shoulders into the straps and snapped the buckle shut across his chest. Then he loosened the dogs holding the door shut and eased it back. Immediately it was torn from his hands and thrown back against the bulkhead with a booming clang. A knee-high wall of water burst through the narrow opening into the corridor. When it subsided, the first officer quickly stepped outside and dogged the door tight again. He was now in a world that was as much water as air.

There was a roar from up forward, and five hundred feet ahead he saw a swirl of white sweeping toward him. He found the stout springhook that dangled off the end of a steel cable attached to the back of his safety harness; swiftly he thumbed back the latch and let it snap through one of the eyes on the track overhead. When he moved forward, the line followed easily, the eye riding on a ball-bearing trolley in the track. Tethered overhead, Browne was now moving down a square, steel-lattice walkway that ran to the bow.

The white swirl was on him. He went down, tumbling and suffocating. His legs slid out of the latticework and headed for the deck four feet below, but the safety cable hauled him up short. When the water receded, his cap and one shoe were gone and his jacket had become un-buttoned. A low boom came from far forward; another wave was sweeping down on him. He sprinted forward as fast as he could, with the wire binding a bit in the track.

The wave caught him when he had advanced perhaps a hundred and twenty feet. This time the back of his head slammed against the spoke of a valve wheel. Though he didn't lose consciousness, he found his legs unable to move for some minutes, and he sagged from the safety cable.

A yellow light flared from the direction of the bridge house; the door he had come through was open. How had that happened? Three men came out of the gloom. They, too, made their way forward, but they wore no safety harnesses. They clawed unsteadily, hand over hand, along the railing and latticework.

"I told you it wasn't us who unlocked that door and let that water in," The Dropper yelled over the wind. "There's the one who done it. Looks like a Yank hung up on a clothes rope."

The figures crowded around Browne, and The Dropper peered closely into his face. Even the wind couldn't take away the strong smell of whiskey. "It's that cheeky first officer. What are you doin' out here, Mr. Browne? Not just goin' for a walk in the moonlight, I take it."

"Better check him over," Eamon O'Driscoll said.

They rummaged in his pockets and Roland drew out the four butane lighters and tape. "Maybe he was goin' out for a smoke."

"Funny," The Dropper said, "all those lighters and no cigarettes."

Now Browne was certain that they were all drunk. He broke free and sprinted forward down the walkway. Whatever chance he had to stay ahead of them disap-peared when he ran headlong into the next rush of sea, which caught him chest-high and flung him back into the midst of the Irishmen, who had thrown themselves flat and clung on for their lives. Browne unsnapped the springhook from the overhead track and squeezed his arms and shoulders through the latticework of the walkway, attempting to drop to the weather deck itself and take his chances, but The Dropper caught one of his legs. The first officer dangled headfirst off the walk, his fingertips just brushing the deck, while the O'Driscoll brothers maneuvered through the lattice. One took him in a headlock while the other bent an arm up behind him.

Browne drove his free elbow into an abdomen, and the grip on his arm came free. When he jerked his entangled leg with all his strength, his remaining shoe came off in The Dropper's hand and the leg slid out of the lattice. With both feet now on the deck, Browne battled to break the hold of the arm locked around his head. He was amazed by how well he was fighting them.

An insistent hiss grew in intensity. Browne and Eamon O'Driscoll, the man holding him, saw the tower of sea water thirty yards away and thundering aft. O'Driscoll released his grip and sprinted for the supports of the walkway, the only hold within reach, and Browne followed. They wedged their bodies under oil pipes and cornered braces, knowing that a mere handhold would not keep them aboard. The sea fell like a concrete wall, strangling for endless seconds the terrified bodies beneath it. When it had rolled past, Browne found the tails of his jacket snagged on the sharp edge of a broken weld. By the time he freed himself they were on him again, this time joined by The Dropper, who had jumped off the walkway. The Irishmen, as exhausted by now as Browne, held him down simply by sprawling on him.

"We can't stay here," The Dropper shouted.

"What about under there?" said Roland O'Driscoll, poking his finger at a spot beneath the walk where two abutting flow-control panels and a loop of piping made a roughly sheltered square about five feet on each side. Each of the IRA men grabbed a handful of Browne's clothing and dragged him over the deck into the square. When the next wave hit, the obstructions around them and overhead took almost all of the impact. The water rose chest-high on the sitting men before dissipating, but the force of it was so diminished that they needed only a light hold to stay in place.

"We'll stay here until we get our wind," The Dropper gasped.

"It better not be long," Eamon O'Driscoll said. "We've got to finish wiring the exploder back there."

The Dropper slapped him drunkenly on the shoulder. "The trip back home after pleasant times always seems longer, doesn't it?"

The brothers didn't answer him. He sensed their shame, and it wounded his feelings.

"What's the matter, boys? Didn't you have a good time?"

"Let it alone," Roland O'Driscoll said.

"Oh, let it alone, is it? You were willin' enough to come along as my guests and put your filthy hands on my lovely girl, but now it's 'let it alone,' huh?"

"Shut up, will you?" Eamon barked.

"Oho. Now I get it," The Dropper said. "You're bein' polite to our good Mr. Browne here. My, my, look at that awful expression on his pasty face shinin' right through the dark. I think he's already made a good guess."

Browne started up, but The Dropper put a stranglehold on him and brought his mouth to within an inch of the first officer's ear. "I don't know why you're sharp with us, Mr. Browne, when we all have a lovely thing in common. That is to say, *Mrs.* Browne. We've just come from her, the three of us. Come from her tight, blond little puss, I mean—and some other places, too."

Browne twisted his head violently, trying to sink his teeth into The Dropper's arm, but the Irishman's heavy coat stopped him. The hold tightened. "If you've touched my wife, I'll cut your throats."

"Touched her? I think it was more a matter of her touchin' us. Why, that woman can simply not be satisfied. You're a very lucky young man, Browne."

"You're a lying cocksucker."

"I can't be angry at you for using such a word, because

213

the lovely girl has left me with such a pleasant memory of that act."

"Good God, Dropper, let him alone."

"Eamon, when you praise a man's possessions you praise the man."

The harder Browne fought to rise, the harder The Dropper applied the choke.

"And I want you to congratulate Ethel for me—I can call her Ethel now, can't I? It's a rare girl who can so improve her performance from one get-together to the next. I mean, I though she was a helluva lot better this visit than the first time."

The officer's strength seemed to double; all of The Dropper's force could hardly hold him. "You don't mean that's news to you, Browne? Surely she told you about the handsome Irish lover that's been droppin' by. No? Well, didn't you notice a man had been there? Not even in her eyes? Hey, boys, look here. I think the poor man is cryin' real tears. Maybe I can soothe him down a bit. Listen, Browne. The news isn't all bad. The truth is that Ethel and I have taken quite a shine to one another, so you won't have the awful worry of protectin' her anymore. She's comin' with me when I leave the ship. Now I don't want you to take my word for that. I want you to ask her in person."

The stranglehold was now so tight that Browne seemed on the point of losing consciousness.

"You're killin' him, Dropper." Roland O'Driscoll seized The Dropper's wrist and forced his grip off the struggling first officer's throat. Browne was on his feet like a cougar.

"You let him loose, you crazy bastard. Grab him back," The Dropper screamed.

Eamon O'Driscoll tried to grab the wild-eyed man's arm, but found himself hugged from behind with a grip that almost broke his ribs. "Hey, he's got me. Lend a hand here."

Before Roland and The Dropper could rise from their cramped corner, Eamon was lifted off his feet and carried out of the sheltered square beneath the walk. Owen Browne was a much slighter man physically than the younger O'Driscoll, but the brawny Irishman felt as helpless as though encircled by steel bars. Water began to rise on the deck; it was not a hammering wall, but a great swell sluicing sideways across the ship and it rose to the chests of the two men. Roland and The Dropper, forced to cling for their lives to the walkway supports, saw the two heads on the exposed weather deck rise in the water and drift slowly toward the rail.

"Oh, Christ, they're goin' overboard," Roland choked.

But it was well over a hundred feet to the edge of the deck, and the swell began to flatten before the men were quite there. Their bodies and legs appeared again; there was still deck under their feet.

Seeing that he had not stayed aboard by more than a dozen yards, Eamon O'Driscoll tried desperately to drag the clinging Browne back to the walk, but the officer dug his heels into the deck plates and held him to the spot.

There was panic in Eamon's voice now. "Roland. Come out and help me before we go over. He's mad."

The shout came dimly to the men at the walkway. "Eamon's callin' us, Dropper," Roland said, his arms still wrapped tightly around a support, even though the deck was momentarily clear of water.

"I hear him," The Dropper said, "and the only thing that would get me out on that open deck would be if he was my brother."

"Roland," came the faint shout.

"Oh, God, I can't do it, Dropper," Roland said.

Another wave crossed the far rail, rose rapidly around Roland and The Dropper and reached for Eamon and Browne.

"There they go," The Dropper said. He freed a hand and took a grip on Roland's collar, as though it was necessary to restrain him.

They watched the heads of the men on the open deck rise again and move away. When the wave had run off and the weather deck was again visible Browne and

Eamon were gone. Then a broad, white-foaming wave rose high enough for the men on deck to see its crest. It shouldn't have been possible in the dark and blowing spray, but they distinctly saw the heads and shoulders of the men, still locked together, and heard a high wail, thin and despairing.

Roland O'Driscoll buried his face in the crook of his elbow. His mind saw a sun-drenched morning and heard two little boys laughing as they brought home the family's milk in a cart. Behind the ship, the smaller of the boys sank from the sun forever in a cold smother of fear.

Bairn Harrison and Randy Martin were working on the seafloor at the bottom of Blueleg. The men around them were as packed together as a Brighton beach crowd in an August heat wave. Above the floor, nonoperating crewmen lounged in scaffolding and perched on valves and catwalks. The skeleton of the open elevator shaft ran up a hundred and sixty feet to disappear in the gloom overhead. The elevator itself sat at the head of the shaft, the electrical connections that controlled it from below disconnected.

Because they lived with danger every day for months on end, the men of Mavis A. were not as panicked by the events of the last hour as they should have been. They believed that they had been marooned in Blueleg to make sure they were all available for some sort of task that Cullenbine would soon announce. The shutdown efforts here, they felt, were just the beginning.

Harrison threw down an oxygen cylinder. "I wish we was in Redleg. None of them dummies is going to look after the girls right."

"Suppose the electric wires to the room got cut during the work? There wouldn't be any light or ventilation down there," Martin said.

"They could suffocate."

"They'd have brains enough to come out of there if the air got bad."

"Suppose they couldn't? Suppose it just snuck up on

'em while they was asleep? Or maybe the cover is blocked. We've cleared things off it ten times if we done it once."

"Most of the boys know where that hatch is, and they'd clear anything they saw."

"If things get dicey, they're not going to have a lot of time to think about Gail and Sadie. And you know how it is when a mob is supposed to be looking after something. Everybody thinks everybody else is taking care of it."

"So what do you want to do?"

"Get to Redleg."

"They won't let us use the lift."

"Then we'll climb out."

"That's a hundred and sixty feet up."

"We can do it. We won't have to go up the whole way. After a hundred and forty feet we can get outside to the bracing beneath the deck and can go through it like we used to with the girls. Then we get into Redleg the same way we got out of here."

"It's not going to be the same as those play periods, Bairn. It's a good six hundred feet in the wet and wind, and you can only go so fast through that iron. It'll take a long time and a lot of care."

"We have to do it."

"What if they try to stop us?"

"We won't let 'em see us. We'll get around behind the lift shaft. The light doesn't fall back there. We'll go up the braces real slow and leisurely, like we was looking for an empty spot to wedge into for a rest."

"We should stop up there for a while and get any eyes off us. From there it's an easy step over to the wall rungs."

"Good enough. Let's move out."

The pull of love will send some species of moths to a mate across dozens of miles. Bairn Harrison and Randy Martin were now embarked on a journey far more dangerous and unlikely, but the motivation was precisely the same.

Holding the dripping, shivering Roland O'Driscoll in his arms, Dominic Quinn turned to Cody. "Where was Mr. Browne going, Captain? Why did he fight so hard?"

Captain Cody was covered by the automatic weapon held by Father Costello. "I don't know, Quinn. I thought he was in the engine room."

Quinn turned from O'Driscoll, letting The Dropper lead his friend to a chair. The commandant's handsome face seemed twisted in the shadowy light thrown by the bridge instruments. "I think you meant to sabotage our plans. I warned you against that. For your safety I hoped that I would not have to pen you up during the last part of this operation. I see that I expected too much. Costello, I want all the officers of this ship locked up."

"Where, Dominic?"

"Most of them are in their rooms. Just seal them in. Lock the rest anywhere you can find space. Begin with Captain Cody."

"I want to tell Mrs. Browne about her husband," Cody said.

"Lock him in with her, Costello."

"Don't we need some engineers?" said Costello.

"No," Quinn said, "the engine room is completely automated. Simply keep everything set on full ahead. We can handle everything else from the bridge. If we need anything from the engines, Barton can handle it. Mr. Traskin is a good teacher."

Costello waved the gun at Cody's middle. "Let's go to Mr. Browne's suite." Lifting the metal lid of a chest of emergency tools, he slipped a hammer and a fistful of heavy nails into his pocket.

Browne's suite was dark when Costello thrust Cody inside. The captain listened for the twist of the lock after the thick teak door had been slammed shut behind him, but it didn't come. Instead, he heard the splintery thud of nails being driven. Costello was toe-nailing long spikes through the door and frame.

218

Something moved. Cody found the switch that turned on the lamps.

Ethel Browne was sprawled on her back across a broad table that had been dragged into the center of the room. Her legs hung off the table's edge, and her arms were thrown wide. Except for blue wool stockings pushed down around her ankles and a brassiere pulled above her breasts, she was nude, Cody thought she was unconscious, but when he came closer her eyes turned to him.

The left side of her face was red and slightly swollen. But the skin was not broken, and Cody guessed that she had been slapped repeatedly.

"I'm all right," she said softly, before he could speak. She sat up, removed the brassiere and stockings and flung them from her as though they were filthy. Sitting naked on the edge of the table, she looked at Cody without shame. Except for the tremor in her voice, she might have been speaking to him during a stroll around the deck. "It was Mullins and the two brothers. They let themselves in. They were drunk."

"They'll rot in prison for this, Ethel. Their politics can't cover for them now."

"It wasn't their fault, Captain; it was mine. I was with Mullins before. Oh, my, how surprised you look. Yes, he came here earlier today and promised me safety. He didn't even have to slap me when he took me then. I shouldn't have been surprised when he came back with his friends. Men like to pass around a good thing, don't they?"

Cody tried to shake her by the shoulders, but she was as rigid as wood. "Don't talk that way, Ethel. How we act under pressure like this has nothing to do with the way we are."

He found a heavy thermal jump suit in a closet and held it out to her, but she made no move to take it. "They were playful at first, full of little jokes. The brothers were so shy that I found myself liking them. Then Mullins wanted me to do things for all of them. The other two saw that I didn't want to, and they were trying to talk him

219

out of it. I think it would have been all right—it seemed as if they were going to leave—but Mullins was still in a joking mood. He opened his pants and showed his . . . He was laughing, fooling with me. He said, 'Don't tell me that skinny, white-faced husband has anything like that, girlie.' It was there waving in front of me, and I went after it with my nails. I caught him and twisted and tore the skin. The others pulled me away. I fought, and they had a hard time holding me. Drunk as they were, it drove them wild.

"They put me on that table and did things to me that I didn't know existed. I stopped fighting a long time before they were through. But I know that no man is ever going to touch me again."

Cody slipped her legs into the jump suit. She slid off the table, got into the garment and zipped it up. "Don't tell Owen about this, Captain. I'll do it myself."

"Owen is dead, Ethel. He was trying to blow the Number One tank so we could stop the ship. The three that were here caught him. He took one of them overboard with him. I'm sorry."

The breath eased out of her in a long whimper. "Hail Mary . . . Hail Mary . . . Hail Mary." Her hands clutched at her belly. "There's nothing in me anymore. There's nothing inside that's still alive." She sagged into Cody's arms. "He knew, Captain. When he died out there in the water, he knew I'd been with somebody else."

"You did what they made you do. You expect too much courage from yourself, Ethel."

When she looked up into his eyes, he thought that he had never seen a harder face on a woman. "What did I need courage for? I was going to be saved. That was the deal."

"You keep saying that. Saved from what?"

"This ship is going to be sunk, Captain Cody. No ransom is going to be paid because none is being asked for. They've intended to sink us all along."

"Mullins told you that?"

Her mouth contorted. "It was Ethel's dirty little secret."

Cody went to the door and flung his body against it, but the thick teak hardly even rattled. "Owen could have stopped them. Just a spark in Number One tank and we'd have taken the bottom out of her up forward. I've got to finish the job for him. But how do I get through three inches of teak?"

Deliberately, Ethel kicked over a leather wastebasket near the table. Two khaki-colored U.S. Army hand grenades rolled out.

"Well, I'll be damned," Cody said.

"They took off their weapons when they came in. One of them dropped these in that basket and then forgot about them."

Cody scooped up the grenades. "I'll use one to take the door down and the other to set off the tank." He pushed an end table against the door. "Ethel, shove that sofa out about five feet from the bulkhead. I'll jump behind it after I pull the pin. You get into the bedroom."

She did as she was told.

Cody removed the pin, but continued to hold down the arming handle. Placing the grenade on the table so that it lay against the door, he let the spring-loaded handle fly away. He had four seconds to get himself flat behind the sofa and would have made it easily but for the fact that his foot ran into the open end of the wastebasket lying in the center of the room. He fell full length.

He lurched up and went for the sofa in a bearlike hands-and-feet stumble. When the grenade went off, only his head and shoulders were safely behind the heavy leather. Simultaneously with the noise and the crack of wood he felt a fragment slice the back of his right knee. The leg collapsed under him.

Running out of the bedroom, Ethel Browne almost choked on the sharp smell of explosive. The door had a hole three feet long and two feet wide punched through it. Cody was swearing and clutching the back of his leg with a blood-soaked hand. "I'm crippled. The goddamned thing hamstrung me. I'll never make it across the deck like this."

"Do you think they heard?"

"Must have. They'll have a man down here in a minute."

"Can . . . can I do it?" She picked up the other grenade.

Cody's entire life of command had prepared him for this moment. He wasted not a second dissembling about frailties, difficulties or proprieties. He gave strength with his instructions by making them orders. "Get out that door and use the stairs, not the elevator, to get to the door going out to the walkway along the weather deck. You know where that is. If you have time, take a safety harness and hook up; you were shown how to do that in the drills when you came aboard. Make all the distance you can toward the bow between waves. Run. Try to jam yourself somewhere when the waves hit. When the walkway ends, you'll be right over Number One tank. Try to gauge the waves before you unhook. You'll be at the mercy of whatever seas come aboard while you're out there, so give youself as much time between them as you can. If you get caught by a wave, try to hook the safety harness to any piece of equipment you can find.

"When you come off the walkway, go left or right; it makes no difference. Make straight for the side of the ship, until you come to the edge of the pipes and valves, and there's nothing but flat deck in front of you. Then make your way aft about twenty yards, and you'll find a manhole—a hatch. It's circular, about three feet across. It should be easy to find because it's painted white. There's a long lever set into the hatch. Pull it toward the side of the ship. It will be tight, but you should be able to do it. When the lever has come down as far as it will go, the hatch will be unlocked. Lift it open."

Cody placed her hand on the grenade, her fingers around the handle. "You're going to drop this down the tank. But before you do, put your finger through this wire loop and pull it out of that hole. Don't release the handle

222

until you're ready. You'll only have four seconds to get as far aft as you can. You never know what a tank explosion will do. It can come through the top, go out the bottom or both. Or it might not happen at all." Opening a zipper pocket in a leg of her thermal suit, he dropped the grenade into it.

Ethel went for the door in a crouch and disappeared through the narrow crack as gracefully as though it had been six feet square. As she disappeared, Cody saw that her feet were still bare.

The vast platform overhead shut down what little light the sky mustered. Bairn Harrison and Randy Martin had picked their way through hundreds of feet of cold, dripping girders by feel and instinct alone. Their shins and knees were raw from dozens of missteps, their fingers could hardly close and they shivered uncontrollably in sodden clothing.

Below them, the waves had taken on a new kind of muttering. "Listen," Martin shouted into Harrison's ear. "You can hear the water pounding on the leg. We're close."

"It's about time. I'm ready to drop off here like a frozen fly."

They came to a long, steeply descending girder. "Is this it, Randy? The one that goes down near the door? There's two other girders just like it around here. I can't be sure."

"If we go down the wrong one, we lose twenty minutes. I don't know if we've got that left in us."

"This one is as good as any."

They descended, facing the girder as if on a ship's ladder. After several minutes, Harrison's heel hit the bracing plate where the girder disappeared into the concrete of Redleg.

"We're there."

"Are we near the door?"

Harrison stretched his leg out as far as he could and

223

rubbed his feet over the concrete. His toe hit an iron rung. "*Bull's-eye,* Randy."

"Can you see it?"

"No, but it's there, about ten feet up. There's no other place those rungs go except from the water to that door."

"Randy, your arms are shorter than mine. I'll hold you while you lean out to get your hand on the ladder."

Martin stepped carefully down the girder alongside Harrison, braced his feet in an angle of iron and grabbed his friend's right hand firmly in his left.

"See you around," Martin said and leaned into the blackness. He found a rung, but his near-frozen hand would hardly close around it. He tried placing his thumb inside his curled fingers on the iron in order to create some sort of grip. "Got it. Let go." His other hand was released; he swung his legs off the girder, his feet scrabbling for a rung, and found one just before his grip let go. "Did it. Just."

"Move up the ladder. I'll be right behind you.".

Much taller than Martin, Harrison had little trouble. He climbed carefully for thirty seconds until a hand caught his collar. It was Martin kneeling in the doorway above and helping him up.

Getting to their feet, they hurried through the door opening on the forty-foot tunnel into the interior of Redleg. In the faint gleam of small bulbs, they saw an iron door ahead. When Martin turned the latch and swung it open, light and noise rushed up at them. Far below they saw a boiling swarm of men at work. From a dozen places came the white, sparkling glare of acetylene torches, and Cullenbine's voice floated up to them clearly.

Harrison pointed down to the spot where he knew the girls' chamber to be. "Christ, Randy." His voice was shaking. "Look at the size of that pipe across the hole. We'll never get that moved by hand."

"Maybe a bunch of us could roll it off."

"No room. See how it fell down between that stack of valves and the wall. It'll have to be lifted. How can we do that?"

224

"Make a rig, like we'd do with any other lifting job down there. Use the winch."

"We can't, Bairn. Look, they've got the winch right off its pedestal. It must have been in the way."

"Shit. Well, Cullenbine will have to think of something."

"It doesn't look like he's about to take any time off to help us."

There was a whir overhead, and through the openwork of the shaft that ran down past the door where they stood, they saw the elevator coming down. As it passed them, they screamed at the startled operator. He stopped, and they climbed through the framework and jumped down into the bucket.

"Where the hell did you guys come from?" It was one of the foremen, the only men Cullenbine was trusting with the elevator.

"From Blueleg," Martin said. "How's it going down here?"

"All I can tell you is that we're shutting her down fast. Nobody's telling us why yet, but I know it's not good. I've never seen Cullenbine in such a state. Anything that gets in his way—bam—it finds itself on its ass twenty yards away. The way he's pushing us, we'll all be dead in another hour."

"How close to finished are you?"

"Damn close. I don't know how the man does it."

"Listen, mister. We need help."

Martin's next words came out unheard as the clamor of the general alarm filled the leg. They didn't know it, but their time was almost gone.

"No question about it. They're the lights of a ship, the biggest damned ship there ever was." Magnus was peering with a set of night binoculars through the observation tower windows.

"We've sounded the alarm down in Redleg," Lustgarten said. "Cullenbine will have to bring his men out, finished or not."

"How long, Admiral?" asked Zamke.

"I'd say she was about five miles off. Probably making top speed, which would be twenty knots in clear sailing. The wind and sea might slow her down. If they cross us up and come straight in to take, say, Blueleg, we've got fifteen minutes. If they've got their mind on Redleg, as we hope, they'll have to swing wide around us. Quite wide, in fact, if they want to line up to take two legs in succession, starting with Red. For a hull that size to take on such a maneuver in this weather, we could add twenty to twenty-five minutes. If they go for Redleg, we may have as much as forty minutes."

Zamke beckoned to Magnus. "Mr. Cullenbine is on the phone."

Magnus took the receiver. "Cullenbine, we've got them in sight. Radar tracked them to us in a straight line. There's no doubt about what they're after now."

"How many minutes?"

"There may be none. They're coming north-northwest. If they take Blueleg, the closest to them, there's only a quarter of an hour."

"Admiral, if they take Blue, we're as cool down here as anywhere else. How long until they line up on Red?"

"We've just figured it at forty minutes."

"I need about forty to finish."

"Then you wouldn't have time to get out."

"And if we don't finish, half the oil in the whole Mavis Field will go into the Atlantic."

"Your lives are my responsibility. Come up."

"No, Admiral Magnus, I don't think so. We're going to try to finish."

"The men won't stay."

"The men won't know."

"That's not fair, Cullenbine."

"If they get wet, I'll get wet with them. There's no more time to talk."

Magnus heard the line go dead. "Cullenbine's going to stay down there and keep at it."

"Good man," Lustgarten said.

"What about us?" said Zamke. "Shall we go down in one of the legs?"

"We can afford to wait until the ship is committed. After that—well, I don't mean to be overly dramatic, but I think I'll stay here. It will be a sight I'll only see once." Magnus smiled. "When I saw the *Bismarck* roll under, I thought that it was the peak moment of my life. I felt as if I'd gone down with her, and that everything after that adventure would be downhill. And it was. But now I have something to live for that could be even greater, haven't I? Yes, yes, it's quite too good to miss. I'll stay here."

Lustgarten snorted. "They say that certain attacks on the Somme were led by unarmed English officers kicking soccer balls. I must say that I never understood such silliness, but apparently it's in the national genes."

"We shall miss you, Colonel," Magnus said.

"Not at all. If there *is* any chance to save ourselves, we'll see it from this spot, not by hiding blindly under the sea. The gods take an interest in great situations. We may yet feel their hand."

"Teutonic conceit," said Magnus.

chapter 12

Ethel Browne had been luckier than her husband. She had barely missed being caught—for the second time—by the same men.

When The Dropper and Roland O'Driscoll came from below unrolling their wire, they found the door to the weather deck standing open and seas smashing inside. They knew they had left the dogs unfastened when they came back inside after their struggle with Browne, so now they swung the door shut, dogged it properly and went on with their work.

The Dropper had chosen this spot to set his Beethoven exploder because it was convenient to both the deck and the bridge, and it seemed to him a good departure point for any rescue operations that might develop. By the time he had finished wiring the Beethoven, Ethel Browne was more than halfway down the walkway to Number One tank.

Ethel was already starting to tire when the sea broke her arm. Seeing the wave coming, she threw herself flat on the walk, locked her elbow around a support and tucked her wrist under her other arm. The sound of the water sweeping down told her that this was a wave far larger than any that had yet struck her. It fell like an avalanche, choking her for an excruciating time. The pull of the water as it ran off pivoted her body around the arm locked to the support and broke the bone above the elbow. At first there was no pain, but she felt the snap. When the wave had receded she pulled the arm free with her other hand and continued moving forward.

By now the thermal suit was drenched and heavy, and each time she dropped for a wave it was harder to rise. After a while she felt something catching under her foot; when she looked down she saw that a thick flap of skin had been sliced loose from the bare sole. After a hundred yards it began to hurt, a startling and all but unbearable pain. Another surging wave jammed the ends of the broken bone in the arm together, forcing it into a nerve.

She screamed, but the sound was inaudible over the tumult. Another sea fell on her before she could recover herself, and then another. She kept a count of them for a while, but finally lost interest. Trying to pray, she couldn't remember any words; trying to sleep, she was frightened by the dreams edging in on her. Like a child looking for a more comfortable position in bed, she rolled on her side. Something was under her leg, adding to the pain; pulling at it, she came awake. The grenade. *The job.* She always did her jobs. She grabbed a projecting rail above her head and somehow pulled herself erect.

There was a light on the bow. She was closer than she had thought. Keeping her eyes riveted on the glow, she fought ahead, moving faster and more desperately, as though she could outrun her agony.

Now the light in front of her seemed to break into bits, to became two, five, a dozen, some of them red, green and blue. At last she could identify their pattern: They were the lights of Mavis A. The *American Enterprise* was not going to fail.

Barton was at the helm of the *American Enterprise* while Quinn, The Dropper and Roland O'Driscoll stood behind him watching the same lights.

"We can take her straight in from here, Dominic," Barton said.

"I want to hit the leg to the south, George," said Quinn. "We can go through it more easily because the tanks around its walls are not filled with oil, or so my technical friends have told me."

"This isn't a rowboat on a lake in the spring. It'll be the best part of half an hour bringing her around to come in from the south."

"Can you do it, George?"

"I don't know. I've never steered anything like this."

"We took you along because you were the finest all-around seaman available to us. I will rely entirely on your judgment. If you feel the maneuver to the south is too difficult, we will continue just as we are. Our chances from the south are the best, but we must look to our limitations. What do you think?"

Barton was quiet for almost a minute, then spun the wheel. "The south it is."

Quinn patted Barton's back. "Good. It will be easy to know we've got the right leg. It will be painted bright red."

Billings waited a full ten minutes past what he was certain was a change in the bearing of the blip on his radar screen before calling the observation tower. "Captain Zamke, target ship has made a definite twenty-degree change in course. I am now plotting that she will pass us safely to the west."

Zamke held the phone in one hand and squinted through his binoculars. He could not yet visually confirm what the radar room was reporting. "Radar reports that the ship is swinging away to the west. Admiral Magnus, does that tell us anything?"

"How many degrees have they gone off?"

"About twenty, Billings makes it."

"That would be about the deviation they would need to begin a circling maneuver."

"Like coming around us to make an approach to Redleg?"

"Exactly."

"If they are, at least Cullenbine may have time for his shutdown. I'm afraid the other legs are well behind him." He spoke again into the receiver. "Billings, watch the target carefully. We believe they're going to circle us to the west and come up from the south in a run against Redleg. We'll probably lose sight of them visually for a while, so we're depending on you."

"Yes, sir. Target in track," Billings said and hung up.

Lustgarten smiled thinly. "Why the hell do we keep calling *them* the target?"

Barton's new course took the *Amercian Enterprise* within a half-mile of Mavis A. Even at that distance, the size and complexity of the platform was apparent. Quinn and The Dropper stood in the open on the port bridge wing, crouching against the driving rain and watching the rig slide by. The sight seemed to return The Dropper to his customary high spirits. "Will you just look at that thing! A whole city up on stilts. Oh, what a nice splash it's goin' to make when we hit it. Barton's a lucky man to be at the wheel. I once ran a lorry into a bakeshop window because I couldn't resist the splatter, but this . . ."

"There are men on there—scores of them. Don't you feel anythin' about them?"

"Hey, Dominic, *you* dreamed this up, not me. We're goin' to get in the history books, you'll remember."

"Yes, I suppose I'm bein' soft. And for what we're goin' to do, the cost won't be high—no more than you'd lose in patrol activity on a quiet day of any war."

"Maybe. But if somethin' happens to me, it's goin' to seem the same as if the whole world got it. The plan about the rescue boat isn't goin' to work, is it?"

"They've been gone for hours. I think the others know that, too."

"What's to save us, then?"

"The *Enterprise* might not break up."

The Dropper looked at the mountains rolling beneath them. "And my mother might die childless."

"That's it," Cullenbine boomed. "Start moving up by gangs. The A gang first. Get down in the other legs."

"Why the hell won't you tell us what's going on, Mr. Cullenbine?"

"We handle it. Easy. *Easy.* Don't overload that elevator."

Harrison and Martin found themselves caught in the noisy rush. The work gangs were not really panicked yet, but their imaginations were beginning to wake up. There were still some jokes, but men who were crowded away from the elevator bucket were increasingly ready to use their fists to stay close.

Cullenbine was speaking to the observation tower. "All shut down in Redleg. We're getting out. Get the elevators running in the other legs so that these men can get down in them."

"Thank God," Magnus said. "According to our radar, the ship's coming in almost dead from the south, which means Redleg is the primary target. They'll almost certainly try for a second leg on their momentum, but we can't tell which one yet."

"We've got time to get out, then?"

"Barely. You have an estimated twenty minutes before impact."

"Okay. The first load of men is moving topside." He looked up to find Harrison and Martin standing in front of him, covered with sweat despite the sharp undersea chill.

"Mr. Cullenbine," Martin said, "we've got two women down here. They're stuck. You must help us get them out."

"Women. Christ, I don't believe it. Show me where."

Cullenbine ran behind the two Scots to where the pipe lay across the cover. Harrison squatted down, directing an emergency lamp, and pointed. Only a ten-inch arc of the cover was visible beneath the pipe. "There's a room down there. Steel-lined."

"Is the ventilation okay?"

"Yes, Mr. Cullenbine. I've checked it."

Martin said, "Do you think if we got enough men over here we could lift the pipe?"

"Never. Even if we could, there's no room to roll it off, and they couldn't lift it high enough to clear the garbage on each side. This is a job for machinery."

"Can we get the winch remounted?"

"We'd have to move it into position, rebolt it below the pedestal and hook it up electrically. Then we'd have to rig a block, run cable through it and get the sling under the pipe. It's possible, but never in twenty minutes—and that's all we've got, boys."

"Why goddamn it?" Harrison screamed.

Cullenbine pointed to the side of the leg. "Because a ship's bow maybe a hundred and fifty feet high is going to come in here."

"We can't leave them to die down here."

"Harrison, we can't save them."

"*You* can do it, Mr. Cullenbine. You always know a way." There were tears in Martin's eyes.

Cullenbine prowled around the pipe. He noticed a short length of two-inch bar protruding on the far side. Dropping to his knees, he squinted beneath the pipe, his cheek against the floor. "We've got a little break. The pipe fell on a piece of reinforcing bar. She's off the floor a little—probably enough to snake a good-sized cable underneath."

"What the hell does that mean when we don't have a winch to take up the cable?" asked Martin.

"Maybe we don't need the winch," the platform master said. He was looking upward to where the elevator was rising through the open shaft, carrying what seemed an overload of men. "When the last of those guys are out of here, we can use that elevator as a haul."

"The lift?"

234

"Sure. We can rig a block from that cross-girder up there. The angle's pretty good—perpendicular enough to drag it free. We'll have to wind the cable off the winch drum by hand. That'll be a bitch. Then we'll run the cable through the block, get a sling under the pipe on one end and a hook into the bottom of the elevator bucket on the other. Wait a minute. We'll need a second block at the bottom of the shaft to clear the cable from the shaft's side trusses. But shit, that's no problem, and when that elevator goes up, the pipe will go up too."

Harrison leaped into the air. "Mr. Cullenbine, you're a fucking genius."

"Right now I wish I was a gorilla instead. The three of us are going to have to do everything by hand before it gets damp down here. Harrison, start pulling the cable off that drum. Martin, let's find a way to get up on the girder with that big block over there."

"Mr. Cullenbine," Harrison said, "there's one more thing."

"Yeah?"

"If the girls don't get out, then we don't get out either. I mean none of us."

Cullenbine started to redden at the threat, then decided that he liked the sentiment. He laughed. "Hell, Mom always said that the whores would get me one way or another."

The *American Enterprise* was now close enough to Mavis A. for George Barton to be able to make out the colors of the legs. His steering had been good. The leg at the corner of the platform directly over the bow of the ship was painted a brilliant red.

"Dominic," Barton said, "I'm goin' to try to line us up to take the yellow leg too."

"If we can hit both of them they'll have no chance."

"I think we can do it."

"Is The Dropper down at the exploder?"

"Right. With O'Driscoll."

"The others?"

"Devlin's in the engine room, and Costello is making sure that the crew stays bottled up."

"You're less sentimental than I am, George. Shall we free the crew before we hit?"

"Dom, that would only deny them the chance to die in a nice, warm bed."

They stood watching; Mavis A. stood less than a thousand yards ahead. An unusually large sea fell across the bow and thundered aft.

Ethel Browne ran out of breath. She fought inhaling for endless moments and finally drew in a full breath of water. Then she was in the clear again, the sea running off beneath the walk. She coughed, and vomited sea water. The only reason she was still alive was that when she had seen the monstrous wall of water looming ahead she had the quickness of mind to slide her legs through the ironwork and secure herself by the crooks of her knees. Now her legs felt as if they had been shattered, but she found she could still move them. Again she used her good arm to pull herself to her feet. A fearful look over the bow told her that no big sea was imminent.

She had no more strength to fight another wave like the last one. Unsnapping her safety cable from the overhead track and holding the hook in her hand, she bent, stepped through the framework of the walkway and fell to the weather deck.

Because she landed squarely on her back in several inches of water still washing over the deck, she was not badly hurt. Dimly remembering Cody's instructions, she stumbled toward the side. When she was almost there, a quartering sea came at her. The first two pipes she tried to snap her safety cable onto were too wide for the hook; only at the last moment did she find a small eyebolt set in the deck and slip her hook on it.

This sea did not cross the ship, but ran off the same way it had come. As it did so, it pulled her to the end of the cable, so that she was no more than twenty feet from the side. Then she noticed that she was at the edge of the tangle of piping running from the centerline of the weather deck. She stood up and strained her eyes through the darkness. There it was, not fifteen yards away: a splash of white right where Cody had said it would be. The manhole.

A devastating dizziness came over her. She fell to her knees to rest, and could not find the strength to rise. Her fingers clawed at the release buckle; the safety harness fell open and she shrugged out of it. Nausea from the pain in her arm sent spasms through her. She dragged herself toward the manhole, all the while imagining that over the bow at her back there towered a leaden gray cliff of sea that would kill her. She crawled unseeingly, until her forehead struck a combing so sharply that she felt the skin tear open. Rolling over onto her back, her eyes stared blankly at the ragged gray and black of the sky. To stop felt good. So good.

But there was the job. Pressing down hard on the deck with her hand, she sat up. Inches away from her face was a slightly concave circle of white, from which protruded a long white lever pointing at the bow. Her head became clear again. That lever had to be moved toward the side of the ship. That would be toward her. Bracing her knees against the side of the combing, she grasped the lever as close to the end as she could and tugged with all the strength remaining in her good arm. The bar remained frozen in place. Cody had said a woman could do it. Ethel looked forward. A great, dark slope was beginning to build. There was no way she could get back to the safety harness and into it in time. A stack of foot-thick piping ran fore and aft behind the manhole. She climbed up over the combing and pulled herself across the cover to the inboard side. The spacing was perfect. She laughed, hysterically and delightedly. When she placed her back against the piping, she could brace her bare, bleeding feet against the lever with her legs half bent.

The dark shape was standing straight up over the bow. Ethel put everything she had left into the straightening of her legs. The lever moved a few inches, slowly at first, and then so rapidly that it flew straight to the side.

Again climbing down off the combing, she crawled across the cover and grasped the end of the lever. At the first tug, the cover came open a foot and then fell closed as it slipped from her fingers. She pulled again, this time managing to put all of her back and legs into the upward jerk. The cover fell backward loudly.

Ethel found herself looking down into a black hole from which belched a dizzying rush of fetid fumes. The wave seemed only yards in front of her, climbing vertically up into the sky. Reaching into the pocket of her thermal suit, she brought out the grenade. It seemed unbearably cold and heavy in her small hand. She squeezed the handle, grasped the pin in her teeth and pulled. It came free. She felt a powerful spring trying to twist the handle out of her fingers.

Ethel held the grenade squarely over the dark hole. She could not miss. The wave crossed over the bow. She felt the grip of life tighten around her, trying to bring her back, and as she dropped the grenade she called Owen's name in a high, weak voice.

Magnus and Lustgarten put down their binoculars; there was no longer any need for them.

"I was on the sea for something like fifty-five years," Magnus said, "and the thought of sleeping under it isn't one bit more appealing now than it was at the beginning."

Zamke said, "I cannot swim. I have never set foot into a body of water, not even a swimming pool. My mother thought it was dangerous and passed her fear along to me very nicely."

"Good," Magnus said. "You won't be able to struggle uncomfortably long."

Still half a mile away, the *Enterprise* already seemed to fill the observation-tower windows, and they could plainly see the ocean rushing under and over her blunt, onrushing bows.

Suddenly those bows seemed to thicken, as though a

238

huge fist were being made. A fiery volcano erupted, shooting a column of flame and debris into the sky and painting the bottom of low-lying clouds red. A shock wave boomed against the windows of the observation tower, and fragments could be seen raining down over the ship as the glow of the explosion faded. For a minute, fires blazed from the forepeak of the *Enterprise,* but a great wave smashed over it, and the flames disappeared except for isolated flickers.

"She's blown up. Good God, she's blown up," Zamke yelled.

"What was it," gasped Lustgarten. "Mine? Torpedo? Aerial bomb?"

"It didn't look like any of those," Magnus said. "From the flame, I'd say it was a gas explosion. One of her tanks may have gone."

"How could that happen?" Zamke asked.

"It could be an accident. It could be something they meant to happen after the ship hit us; perhaps it went up too soon."

"Will they sink?"

Magnus had the binoculars trained on the bow. "I'm afraid not. She still has considerable way. But the bow is badly deformed, and I'll bet that the bottom is blown right out of her up forward. She'll be shipping one hell of a lot of water, even if she doesn't sink."

"Will that help us?" asked Lustgarten.

"It could knock some speed off her, and—depending how fast she's shipping water—it could drag her bow down into the mud. She can't be clearing by more than a few feet here."

"Could it stop her?"

"Not completely, I think. But enough to give us some kind of chance."

Quinn and Barton waited for their eyes to readjust to the darkness. Finally they could see the damage. Far up at the bows, a jagged fence some twenty feet high had been thrown up across the deck: steel plates that had peeled back as the fist of the blast punched through.

Quinn tried to keep his voice even. "Tell me what's happenin', George."

Over the heaved plates, Barton at the wheel still had the platform in sight. "The Number One tank has exploded. It was empty. That means explosive gases. Somehow a spark got in there."

"We're sinkin', then."

"We're settlin'. We can be pretty sure that the bottom under the tank is out, and we'll be shippin' water pretty fast. There are devices to close watertight doors when the water hits a certain level, but if this is some kind of sabotage by the crew, they might have knocked out the system."

"What about the hole in the deck? It's huge."

"And we're takin' hundreds of tons of water every time we bust through one of those big seas."

"We've got to make it to Mavis."

"We'll make it. But we're losin' way already, and I think we're startin' to drag bottom some, even without the hole. It's not as sure as it was, Dominic."

"We'll do it. If there's a God in heaven, we'll do it."

Magnus gave orders that the crew be told what was happening.

He had underestimated them. After a brief flare of near panic, they accepted the situation for what it was: another of the hammerblows of life that had driven them out of warm, safe rooms ashore to place them at the mercy of man-killing waves and winds. They probably would have been less calm if Magnus had made it clearer that the legs might not stand when the platform was hit, or that the ship might destroy a second leg.

An eye beneath the sea would have seen a wound on the bottom of the *American Enterprise* far greater than the one that had sunk the *Titanic*. It was not long fore and aft—barely a hundred and fifty feet—but it

240

stretched almost two hundred feet across the beam. With the heavy cargo of oil weighing down the hull more than ninety feet below the surface, the fantastic pressure caused the water to geyser up into the hole. The explosion had taken out the first line of watertight doors in the double-bottom, so not only was the space in the empty Number One tank being filled, but a good part of the considerable volume of the double-bottom itself.

For a few hundred yards the *Enterprise* skimmed the undersea sand unimpeded except for occasional higher ridges and the hydrodynamic drag on the misshapen bow. Then she began to drag along the scraps of sand formed by the raging bottom currents of the North Sea and plates loosened by the blast broke free and fluttered away like leaves.

Now the bow struck an unusually high ridge of sand. Weakened frames in the forepeak gave way and the entire lower bow crumpled backward. Seams opened all along the hull, and bubbles could be seen where the water found openings. Still, it seemed that the earth itself could not restrain the energy stored in all the tons of the hurtling *Enterprise;* the high ridge was flattened and the misshapen bow continued on its fearsome way.

But after another two hundred yards, it was beginning to plane down into the mud. The ship was soon barely making five knots. If there had been a mile and a half to go instead of less than eight hundred yards, there would have been no collision.

If the lights had been turned on in the bridge of the *Enterprise,* Mangus could have made out the figure of the helmsman. "We've about six minutes," he said. "If anyone wants them, there are some rubber rafts stored outside."

Nobody moved.

"Where's Mr. Cullenbine?" Lustgarten asked. "If we are not immediately drowned, he would be a good man to have with us."

"You're right," Magnus said. He made a call, spoke

briefly and hung up. "They say he stayed behind with a couple of men. He's still down in Redleg." A call to Redleg brought no answer. "I'll put it on the public-address horn down there." He flipped open the circuit.

Cullenbine recognized the voice on the horn as Magnus's.

"Cullenbine. Attention, Cullenbine. Redleg will be hit inside of six minutes. Come up at once."

"We're not going to make it, damn it," Martin said. "Even if we had them in the elevator right now we'd barely do it."

The blocks had been fixed in place and the cable hooked to the bottom of the elevator. They had brought the other end around the pipe, and were now fastening a shackle.

Cullenbine swung a hammer so quickly that it became a blur. "We'll have this connecting pin through in a minute. There may be time to lift the pipe off and get the girls out, but there'll be none to get the shackle or blocks unfastened so that the elevator can move all the way up. So listen carefully. When I hook this shackle up, I'm going to get in the bucket and run the elevator far enough up to pull the pipe off the cover. Martin, you drag the girls out and get them to the shaft as quickly as you can. Harrison, use this hammer to knock the connecting pin out of the shackle; I'll let the pipe down to take the strain off. Then you run for the shaft too. I'm going to raise the elevator high enough to slip the cable out from under the pipe and get that open shackle moving up until it hits the first block. It won't be able to go through, but I think the empty elevator will have enough power to tear the two blocks off their fastenings, and then there'll be nothing left to stop us. I'll drop down to get you and we'll take off."

"Even then——"

"Done," Cullenbine roared. Throwing the hammer to Harrison he bolted for the elevator and vaulted over the wire rail into the bucket. Immediately he began moving

242

up, first quickly, then slowly as the strain tightened the cable.

Harrison and Martin had worked in the oil fields long enough to have sense of the direction of strains and the strength of various riggings, and they knew that this jury rig was chancy. They had rigged the blocks hurriedly, using whatever wire and technique that had come to hand. If they had underestimated, the blocks would tear loose and leave the pipe in place. If they had overcompensated, the pipe would lift away, but later, when the opened shackle caught in the blocks, the elevator would not be able to tear them loose and the bucket would be anchored to the bottom of the shaft by the cable.

The wires fastening the block to the cross-girder stretched and seemed about to snap like rubber bands when there was a clank.

"She moved, Randy. The pipe moved."

The pipe was dragging sideways against the cavity in which it lay; they had been unable to rig the cable to pull it straight up. Would the pipe ride up over the imprisoning metal alongside, or would the angle be too severe? Suddenly the pipe seemed to spring ten feet off the floor. Before the Scots could shout their elation, the freed tons were swinging straight at them as the cable headed for plumb. As they flung themselves flat, the giant pipe scythed the air a foot above them. Before it could swing back, they had rolled out of its way.

They ran for the cover. There was a slam behind them as Cullenbine dropped the pipe back to the floor, but above the reverberation they could hear the Texan screaming at them. "Harrison, you sonofabitch, get that connecting pin off." It was a voice to obey.

"Get 'em out, Randy. I've got to get the shackle." Harrison scrambled back toward the pipe.

Martin found the handle of the hatch and pulled up. A stinking wave of heat rushed out of the chamber below. The lights were on, and he found himself looking at two upturned faces, paper-white and with eyes so wide that they seemed about to burst out of their sockets. The girls were seated on the floor, below the hatch, holding each other's hands, their clothes, even their money-stashed pillowcases, forgotten in their panic. They wore identical robes, faded and ragged.

Randy Martin couldn't restrain a sob of relief, and he could barely bring himself to speak. "It's all right now. I'm here. Bairn, too. Even Mr. Cullenbine is helping. That's a funny one, eh?"

They seemed turned to stone, and for an awful moment he thought they were dead. He dropped down into the chamber; kneeling, he embraced them both, kissing their necks and cheeks, and they all began to cry.

With three blows, Harrison hammered the connecting pin out of the shackle, then signaled to Cullenbine, who was peering down from the bucket. The bucket began to rise. The cable came taut and pulled out from under the pipe without difficulty. Then the shackle ran up to the cross-girder and caught in the first block. Above, the elevator came to a stop, and up at the top of the shaft the motor strained loudly enough to be heard by Harrison down on the sea-floor. The block stood out from the girder and the cable trembled, but still the wire fastening held. How long before that strain burned out the motor? No more than thirty seconds. Did they *have* thirty seconds?

Harrison heard his name called weakly, and turned to see Sadie and Gail weaving toward him. Martin was climbing over some pipes behind them.

"Not here. Go for the lift," he shouted, pointing to the base of the shaft.

Then they heard a sound no man had ever heard before. It was as though, for the first time since there had been an earth, the very sea had turned to flee some terrible force greater than itself. There was a drumming against the south wall of Redleg, strangely highpitched and alive. The air itself thrummed and seemed about to shatter.

"Sonofabitch, what is it?" Martin called to Harrison.

"The ship Cullenbine told us about. She's on us."

Cullenbine lowered the elevator five feet, slammed the control lever to "up," and the cable came taut with a metallic snap. The block shuddered and several strands of wire broke. Cullenbine did it again and again. It was dangerous, a good way to jolt the elevator crooked and jam it in its shaft, but he heard the noise too; there was neither time nor choice.

He could see the four upturned faces at the base of the shaft. Should he tell them to start climbing up the frame? No use. They wouldn't get fifty feet. Again the elevator slammed upward, and this time there was a noise like the strings of a piano being struck with a sledge hammer.

"Watch it," Cullenbine shouted.

The block sprang off the cross-girder and flew across Redleg on its cable, to land almost at the feet of the waiting Scots.

Cullenbine kept the car going up at full speed. He had a far more direct pull against the second block, which had been fastened almost directly below the bucket, than against the first. There was a shock, and again he heard the harsh piano chord. Now the car was climbing freely. He reversed and started it down again at full speed.

The shattering scream of the sea being squeezed between ship and leg now began to drown out even the tortured howl of the elevator machinery.

Cullenbine felt the floor of the bucket shiver and slew sideways. The descent slowed; metal dug into metal. He flung the control handle to "stop."

"Shit," he screamed. He called over the side to the people below. "The pulling warped the bucket. It's sticking in the tracks. I'm afraid that if I force it down, I'll get it stuck for good."

"We'll climb up to you on the frame," Martin called.

"No time. The girls can't move fast enough. You'll have to get on the cable. Stand on the blocks at the end. We'll find a way to get you off when you reach the top."

"What does he want us to do? I don't understand," Sadie Buck said.

"Let's go," bawled Cullenbine. He started the bucket

up again, and when the slack was out of the cable and the blocks barely rested on the floor, he stopped. "Climb on."

"We'll tie 'em on, Randy," Harrison said. The two men slipped off their belts and helped the girls step up onto the blocks. Then each cinched his belt around his girl and the cable, and climbed up on the block beside her.

Martin shouted upward, "Okay, Mr. Cullenbine, take it away." The elevator bucket began to move, and in a moment the four Scots were rising through the shaft.

"You're goin' to get her, George," Dominic Quinn shouted. "You're goin' to hit her dead on."

"Yes, she's a goner. Quick, now, Dominic, get me the fire ax out of that rack. I can't leave the helm."

"An ax?"

"After we've smashed into her, I'm goin' to chop Mr. Traskin out of his cabin. I can't leave him there. There aren't enough men who care about engines anymore."

Quinn placed the ax next to Barton. "So there's still such a thing as a sentimental Irishman."

"Brace yourself, Dominic."

"Will there be much of a shock?"

"I don't know. Nobody's ever done this before."

So huge was the mangled prow moving toward him that Magnus could not grasp the reality of its motion. It seemed to him that Mavis A. was drifting rapidly down upon some storm-battered headland. "It's going to be a direct hit. They're very good."

When the elevator reached the top of Redleg, Cullenbine stepped to the framework of the shaft and started climbing down to where the Scots hung suspended. He shouted at them to start the cable swinging, but the sea drowned his voice, so he pantomimed by waving his arm in a wide arc back and forth. They quickly understood, and by the time Cullenbine had reached their level, the four of them, working like children on a swing, were arcing back and forth across the elevator shaft. Martin stretched out his hand; Cullenbine caught it and barely resisted the backward swing of the weight of four people. He pulled until Martin and Harrison were able to grab the framework and reduce the strain.

One by one the Scots stepped off the block and joined Cullenbine on the frame. They let the block swing away and began to climb as only the pursued can. They were just tumbling into the elevator bucket when there came a crack as though the world had split down the center. Looking down, they saw the south wall of the leg below appear to flap for an instant like a window shade in a whipping breeze. The web of a whale-sized spider started at the center of the wall and in an instant spread up and down the hundred and sixty feet from floor to roof. Then the concrete became oatmeal and fell away in dusty grains, each grain weighing tons. The water didn't so much tumble in as jerk across in a straight cliff. Above this white-foaming mass was a jagged immensity of torn red-and-black iron.

The five people in the bucket felt the roof above—the main deck of Mavis A.—begin to sag, and all the concrete of Redleg around them seemed to vanish at once. Caught in its framework, the elevator was hanging out in the empty night.

Miraculously, all the floodlights on the roof of Redleg remained on, illuminating a sight that the watchers could scarcely grasp. With numbed wonder they saw the weather deck of the *American Enterprise* sliding by below.

Cullenbine couldn't make himself heard above the terrifying roar, but the Scots could see him waving upward, his lips forming the words, "Climb out."

For all its bulk and power, the *American Enterprise* shuddered and slowed as she plowed through the hundreds of thousands of tons of Redleg's concrete, and then took much of the weight of the sagging platform on her deck. There was no question that her deformed bow and the gaping hole in her bottom were taking a decisive toll.

Beneath the sea, the prow of the *Enterprise,* now beaten wider than the beam of the ship and as flat as an anvil, sought the fatal collision with Yellowleg. But the bow was against the bottom and rapidly shoveling itself deeper—three feet, five feet, eight feet. There was nothing more that could be torn away; the great keel itself was driving into the mud.

Braced against the windows of Mavis A.'s observation tower, the men had maintained their footing despite the great impact and the drop of the platform onto the supertanker's deck.

Magnus, who had been fantasizing what it would be like to watch the sea coming up through the windows of the falling tower, felt a ludicrous twinge of disappointment. "The corner held. Our deck is resting on hers. And she's lost way—"

Lustgarten was at Magnus's shoulder. "Is she going to get Yellowleg?"

"I don't know. She's so long that I can't tell how much of her has gone past us."

"Listen to that steel being chewed up. I've never heard anything like it."

Magnus watched one of the ship's towering kingposts approach the edge of the leaning platform. He waited for the post to shear off like a blade of grass, but after a minute it still stood; the gap between it and the platform deck wasn't closing. *"She's stopped. That big, murderous bastard has stopped."*

Zamke let out his breath explosively. "Shouldn't we be doing something?"

Lustgarten waved at the wheelhouse of the *Enterprise.* "The man on that bridge is the one who should be doing something, and you can bet that he's going to start soon. Magnus, what's his next move?"

Magnus scratched his cheek. "He's planing down into the mud, so there's no use trying to drive forward. Backing out is another thing, though. If he started right now, before the ship could take any more water, he might just be able to do it."

"And let our own weight snap us off Yellow and Blue-leg."

"Exactly. What I would do now if I were the man on that bridge would be to reverse my engines. Go full astern. Right *now*."

The engines, Dominic Quinn thought. *We've got to reverse the engines*. His throat burned to shout the order, but George Barton had already left the helm to free his friend Mr. Traskin. With a flick of his hand Quinn could send the order from the gleaming console before him to the automated engines below—if only he knew which handle to select and which way to move it. Should he guess? No. He could cripple their position irretrievably. He told himself to be calm. Barton would return in five minutes at the most.

Mavis A. was at their mercy now; nothing could make any difference. Yet something in him cried out at the wait. A lull in battle always turned disastrously against the side with the advantage; it gave the reeling enemy a final chance.

The intercom chimed and flashed. That would be The Dropper wanting to set off his charges. No, Dropper, not quite yet.

Lustgarten said, "If there were a way to keep her from backing out from under us . . ."

Magnus nodded. "In the shape she's in, it wouldn't take much to hold her. If even one of her anchors had let go when she hit, she'd be stuck."

Excitement entered Zamke's voice. "Maybe you have it. We could board her. Look, our deck is resting on her. We could just *stroll* on. Then we run forward, free one of her anchors—"

"That won't work," Magnus said. "Getting to her bow along that torn-up deck would be an hour's job in broad daylight and without those seas. Working with nothing but our hands, we'd have to find and free an anchor weighing Christ knows how many tons from a forepeak that's been crushed like a tomato can—not to mention freeing twenty fathoms of chain."

"Then we're finished."

"Maybe not, Lustgarten," Magnus said. "There's one more way."

chapter 13

The miserable loneliness that overtook men caught alone in the vastness of the *American Enterprise* was getting to Dominic Quinn. The sheer volume of the darkness on the empty bridge seemed to overwhelm the feeble lighting of the instrument panel. He had the unreasoning feeling that if those lights went out, the blackness would grow woolly and tangible, smothering him where he stood. The wind howled outside the rain-lashed window, but the air on the bridge was musty and dead. He shuddered.

A thousand feet ahead, a string of floodlights continued to flare at one side of Mavis A. Half the platform was now starkly outlined against the night. Like the list of a sinking ship, its tilt could be seen clearly. The upright booms of the enormous cranes at each corner were at least fifteen degrees off vertical.

Quinn spun the focus on a pair of binoculars. At first he saw nothing; then through the rain he picked out a group of figures running along the superstructure. *They're abandoning,* he thought. A waste of time; they'd be better

251

off taking their chances on the platform. He looked for other swarming figures in the floodlights, but saw only that one group of three. Wait. There was a second group. One, two, three, four, five . . . that was all. They were standing on the corner of the platform's main deck, the section that lay over the ship. Quinn saw that they could walk just a few feet and be able to step onto the tanker's deck near the center walkway. He seized his Kalashnikov. The crew of the platform could now board the *American Enterprise.*

His binoculars picked up the first group again. When he had first seen them, they had been high up on the platform; by now they had come much lower. They were racing down the outside stairs level by level. To join with the group waiting below and then rush the tanker's bridge? Where was that goddamned Barton?

Cullenbine and the four Scots couldn't catch up with their senses. From the crumbling nightmare inside Redleg, they had clawed their way out of the elevator and up twisted stairs to the main deck. Now they found themselves standing not with empty sea beneath them, but on the deck of a ship so huge that they seemed the size of mice. Looking a thousand feet down the deck, they saw a bridge structure the size of an apartment house. There were lights on the bridge wings but no human figure under them.

Cullenbine looked over his shoulder. The superstructure of Mavis A., still somehow awash in light, leaned over him; it was badly out of plumb, seeming about to topple. He saw figures running down its stairs, which ended where he and his group were standing.

Zamke, the first one down, yelled against the wind, "Cullenbine. You got out."

"Maybe I shouldn't have bothered. It looks as if you guys are headed for the water."

"No. We're going to try to keep the ship from reversing herself."

252

Magnus and Lustgarten ran up, panting. "Cullenbine," Magnus gasped. "Thank God. We need you badly."

"What's your idea?"

"I thought perhaps we could get this crane above us operating. If we can drop the hook down onto that tanker's deck and get a firm hold before she picks up too much way, we can probably keep her under us."

"I don't know," Cullenbine said. "The tilt in the platform has probably slid the crane off its rotation bearings. I don't think she'll swing. But maybe she won't have to. If we lower the boom a bit, its tip will be squarely above the ship's deck."

"How will we set the hook in her?"

"I'm not sure. You could get down on the ship, but that hook weighs five tons all by itself. Even with Lustgarten, Zamke and the two Scots to help, we couldn't do much."

"We'll do what we can."

"Is the hook tied down, Cullenbine?"

"Uh-uh. It's held tight under a bracing girder. All I have to do is slack off and she'll float away."

"Are you sure you can operate that crane?"

"I designed it."

"All right, I'll get down on the deck with the Germans and the Scotties."

Cullenbine turned to the women. "Go someplace safe." He fished a flashlight out of his pocket and handed it to Sadie. "But go where you can keep a watch straight down the ship's deck toward the bridge. If you spot anybody coming forward to where we're working, signal us with this light. A series of blinks will do fine. Make sure I see it, up in the cab of the crane."

"You think they'll come after us?" Magnus asked.

"With everything they've got, Admiral."

Cullenbine looked up to the cab of the gigantic crane. He would have to climb a forty-foot steel ladder to get there. Magnus followed his gaze.

"Watch your step, Cullenbine. I wouldn't want to have to scrape all that education off the deck."

Quinn was watching Cullenbine go up the ladder and into the crane when Barton came up behind him.

"Trouble, it looks like, Dominic."

"There's a man up in that crane, and some others down on our deck. Here, have a look."

Barton took the binoculars.

"They're not doing anything, just waiting. Maybe grouping for something."

"I don't think we have any more time, George. I want you to try to get us out from under that platform right now."

"Right." Barton turned to the console, punched the engines to "All Stop," and the *Enterprise*'s two forty-five-foot propellers stopped driving the ship against the mud.

Quinn was looking through the binoculars again. "Something's happening." The boom of the towering crane was moving, its tip being lowered in the direction of the ship's bridge. The hoisting cable, a massive hook at the end, hung free. "They're going to try to snag us, George."

Under Barton's hand, the engine controls moved to "Full Astern." Again the propellers began to turn. It took several minutes until they were at full power, pulling against the sucking mud, the platform's weight and the fearful inertia of hull and cargo. For a time nothing happened. Then, from far forward, the Irishmen heard the grind and shriek of separating steel. Quinn drew a deep breath. "We're moving out. Mavis will fall."

Noel Cullenbine had the best seat in the house: the operator's cockpit of the crane. From forty feet above the tanker's weather deck, he looked down out of floor-to-ceiling windows on a scene too sprawling for his eye to take in all at once.

On the ship, directly below him, Magnus, Zamke, Lustgarten, Harrison and Martin gyrated, trying to position themselves beneath the descending hook. Behind them a quarter-mile of barren deck stretched to the white loom of

254

the bridge house, seen hazily through the whipping rain like a grave marker. Beyond the ship's sides, the sea still churned and leaped, but with the *Enterprise* no longer boring into them, the gale-flattened waves had stopped sweeping across the deck.

Concrete and metal began to pop and whine like an artillery barrage as the ship started to reverse. Cullenbine just managed to halt the lowering boom before the enormous hook bounced on the deck. The men below strained to catch it and turn the open end to the ship's bow.

As the *Enterprise* slid backward foot by foot, Cullenbine looked down into the torn hull where the corner of the platform had laid back the steel. He could see Magnus kneeling at the edge of the tortured metal, trying to find a firm enough hold for the hook.

The chasm of ripped deck between Magnus on the ship and Cullenbine on the platform began to widen. After seventy-five yards of backward movement, the ship was plainly beginning to gather momentum. Cullenbine felt his feet tremble on the pedals that operated the boom.

Suddenly an enormous, arching deck support that crossed the ship's beam appeared from under the platform. It seemed thick enough, though its center had been half buckled by the weight of the platform.

Cullenbine saw Magnus giving the signal to lower the hook. There would be greater control doing so with the cable than with the boom. He moved the cable-speed control to its lowest setting and started the revolution of a take-up drum that had the diameter of a subway tunnel.

Perversely, the closed end of the hook had swung to face the approaching support. Just before it hit the hook, Magnus wigwagged Cullenbine to stop lowering. The support and hook came together with a sound like the collision of buses. The hook struck on its closed side, and for a moment it seemed as though it would slide over its target. But the ship did not yet have sufficient way, so the hook flipped around on its own axis and slipped over the support.

Instantly the crane began to tilt, its massive cables under ferocious strain. Despite its size, the deck support seemed to vibrate like a banjo string. Its buckled section, which had been pressed straight down toward the keel, now began to point forward. It bowed, and then the hook pulled through the metal as though it were butter.

"Damn," Lustgarten said. "That finished us."

The hook, still on the cable, swung wildly among the wreckage on the forward deck of the still-moving ship.

"There will be one more," Magnus yelled.

"One more what?"

"One more deck support. Bigger than the one that just went. It braces the anchors, too."

"The explosion probably got it."

After they had watched the corner of the platform recede for another minute, Zamke spotted something in the lights. "It's there. You can hardly see it under all the plates that are wrapped around it, but it's *there*."

"A wonder," said Lustgarten.

"The wonder I'm looking for, Colonel," said Magnus, "is a way to get the hook on it through all that metal garbage."

Lustgarten shouted, "Look at the oil."

A section of deck that had been ripped open down into Number Two tank had come into view, and a huge lake of oil lay glittering under the floodlights of Mavis A. The hook swung directly above the black expanse.

Lustgarten laughed. "Mr. Cullenbine is like a little boy ready to go fishing. A pole, a line, a hook, and now a lake."

Suddenly the hook ran down and plunged into the oil, and ten seconds later the cable stopped running.

"What's Cullenbine doing, Admiral?"

"I can only guess, Lustgarten. But I figure we've got that hook about sixty feet down in that thick oil, so we'll have some things going for us we didn't have before. We've lessened the swinging and have the hook down below any loose metal that can knock it aside. Not only that—look, the oil is streaming out the cable; that hook is

256

coming up to ride just below the surface of the oil. We've got the best angle we'll ever have for that support to pick up the open end as it moves past."

The shredded steel surrounding the support contacted the cable. The angle created by its dragging in the oil helped the steel strands slide over sharp edges without being cut.

"Here it comes," Lustgarten said.

The black, glistening hook rose out of the oil as the moving ship slid the cable over the support. The men on the deck could see only a blunt, solid hump—its back. The position was perfect. The hook caught a crumpled wedge of loose metal, which split open to form a guiding pathway. The support was so thick that the hook's mouth almost missed swallowing it.

Once more the gigantic crane leapt forward under the massive pull of the *American Enterprise*. The web of cables supporting the boom sang in the storm like angels, and somewhere welds began to pop loose.

Zamke shrank back. "The boom is going to snap. We've got to get clear."

"*Hold,* you bastard," shouted Magnus.

It was as though he had intimidated the machine. Seconds later, the gap between the men and the platform had stopped widening.

Zamke gave a whoop and flung himself, laughing, into Magnus's arms. Lustgarten pounded everyone he could reach on the back. The Scots whistled piercingly.

Over Zamke's shoulder, the admiral saw a light blinking rapidly on the platform—Sadie's signal. "We have to shorten the celebration. I think somebody's coming who wants that hook out of there."

Looking toward the *Enterprise*'s bridge house, they saw one, two . . . three . . . four hurrying figures. Even at this distance, they were seen to be moving in the stiff, unswinging way of men who are carrying weapons.

The approaching men were Punchy Devlin, The Dropper, Father Costello and George Barton, their leader.

Dominic Quinn remained to watch on the bridge, while Roland O'Driscoll, whose nerves Quinn no longer trusted, sat below with the Beethoven exploder. He had been given instructions by The Dropper on how to proceed if necessary.

Barton set the pace. Like all seamen, he was a master at matching the energy to the job, and he had quickly seen that a run would exhaust his men long before they reached their objective. As they went forward at little more than a trot, he saw that the men ahead had spotted his approach—as he had intended them to. They had begun to retreat through the wreckage of the forward deck, making their way back to the platform, just as he had hoped. For one thing, he had no wish to kill anyone; for another, it was a sign that they were unarmed and unable to resist the freeing of the hook.

Punchy Devlin was not at all pleased that there might not be anyone to kill. As he advanced, his fingers moved over the heavy Kalashnikov as though over a beloved baby.

Father Costello was in good spirits; he had a dramatic streak in him, with a special weakness for playing soldier, and now he saw himself as one of a line of red-coated infantry marching on some French position. He had often thought that if he had not chosen the Church, he might have gone as a soldier or actor. It was still a secret dream of his to become a Ballylannon Mummer, one of those tradition-steeped actors who played out the martial history of early Ireland with precise drill and wooden swords.

The Dropper trotted in a cold fury. The thought of opening seventeen hundred feet of hull with a turn of his wrist had come to possess him. He understood that Roland O'Driscoll was no longer in shape for any close work, and that Quinn's decision had been a correct one, but the potential loss of his great moment left him bitter. Well, if he couldn't break up ships, he could break up people.

The men ahead of the Irishmen made slow work of climbing through the wreckage of the bow. By the time they had all returned to the platform, their pursuers had reached the end of the undamaged deck.

Not knowing whether the party from the ship intended to open fire, Cullenbine's men flattened themselves on the platform. The range was long, but bullets could reach them. The men on the ship were within the floodlights' arc, the yellow and orange of their weather gear glowing brightly.

"They're slinging their guns," Lustgarten said.

"That means they're going to climb through the junk and try to get aboard Mavis," said Magnus.

"What will they do when they get here?"

"Depends on whether we try to stop them. All they want is to get up into that crane and slack the cable off so that they can free the hook and get the *Enterprise* moving again."

Having seen Sadie's signal, Cullenbine had rushed down the ladder, and now he joined the others.

"Can anyone think of a way to fight them?" Magnus asked.

"Sure," Cullenbine said. "Set up a heavy machine gun, say an M–60, behind that little steel shed over there. The only problem is that we don't even have a BB gun."

Lustgarten felt the exhaustion of thirty-five years of wars overtaking him. He rested his cheek on the cold, wet steel of the deck. Just before he closed his eyes, he saw that he was lying on a white-painted stripe. It floated aimlessly in his head, his policeman's mind not quite able to dismiss it. Finally he heaved himself half-erect and scanned the deck around him. There were other lines, forming a pattern. They were not precisely parallel, seeming to open out somewhat in the direction of the sea. The steel shed that Cullenbine had mentioned stood behind a curved white stripe that joined the other stripes. *"A trap field."*

"What's that, Colonel?"

"Cullenbine, isn't this a trap field we're lying on?"

"Yes. Part of the crew's recreation program. When the weather is good we fire clay pigeons out over the sea and the men can bang—" Cullenbine slapped his forehead. "The trap guns."

"The Irish are getting nearer," Magnus said. "We have to hurry."

Cullenbine pointed to the steel shed. "They keep the guns locked in the trap house."

"There's a good-sized padlock on it."

"I see a good-sized crowbar lying over there. Grab it, somebody, and let's get to that house."

Bent double, the six men ran to the trap house. The Irishmen were hidden from their view by a heaved-up section of the ship's plating.

Martin slipped the sharp tip of the crowbar into the hasp of the lock and twisted until the staples popped loose.

Cullenbine squeezed through the small door first. With his bulk inside, there was hardly room for anyone else, but Magnus and Lustgarten followed. "Feel around for a light."

Magnus found the switch and a naked bulb flared. A large electric trap-thrower stood at the center of the house facing a port now closed over with a latched-down shutter. A stack of black-and-yellow clay birds was in the loading sleeve. Behind the trap, a tarp crossed by a curving zipper covered a four-foot square on the wall.

"This better be it," Cullenbine said. He pulled the zipper open to reveal a rack holding fifteen Remington Model 870 pump-action shotguns.

"Let's see about ammo." At the bottom of the rack were two drawers. When he tugged at them they opened sluggishly. "Ah, enough for a long war." There were about fifty boxes of shells.

"They don't happen to have a couple of boxes of double-oh buckshot in there, do they?" asked Magnus.

"All trap loads, I'm afraid. We're going to be able to make a lot more noise than holes."

Cullenbine pulled a gun out of the rack. "Hey, here's a break. They've all got Poly-Chokes."

"What's that?"

"It's this gadget on the muzzle that looks like a silencer. You turn it to control the spread of the shot. By closing it all the way—like this—we can concentrate the shot into a smaller pattern and have some stopping power even with these light loads."

"Me and Bairn don't know anything about shooting," Martin said.

"Then get ready for the shortest course you ever took." Cullenbine handed each of the men two shotguns and two boxes of shells. "Load up two guns, everybody. There's liable to be plenty of blasting and not much time to reload. Now watch: Just hook your fingertips on the lip of this slide under the receiver. Pull the slide open against the spring until you hear a click and the slide stays open. Now press in one shell at a time, like this. There's another spring inside; just push against it until the shell clicks in place. Push here and the slide springs shut. You can load five shells."

"Suppose the ammunition gets wet out there?" asked Zamke.

"The shells have plastic cases; they're practically waterproof."

"What range do they have?"

"I've done quite a bit of shooting," Magnus said, "and I can tell you that thirty-five yards would be extreme."

The knowledge that their formidable-looking armament had no more range than a light pistol depressed them for an instant, but their spirits would have fallen even further if they had known the capability of their opponents' weapons. The Irishmen were each armed with a Kalashnikov AK–47 Automat, the Soviet Army's primary assault rifle. It carried thirty rounds of 7.62-millimeter rimmed cartridges, and on full-automatic fire it could hold a six-inch group at a hundred yards; other submachine guns did well to maintain a twelve-inch group at that distance. Against this the men on Mavis A. had as their only advantages the ability to deliver fire from up to six different locations and the possible elements of concealment and surprise.

The problem was exactly to Lustgarten's liking; he took command as easily as though it were 1944. "We must get ourselves ready before they have us in sight again. I think they'll head straight for the crane, and they'll expect us to make our stand from there."

"What's wrong with that?"

"No cover, for one thing, Cullenbine."

"The dark underneath the cab is good cover."

"The dark doesn't stop bullets. They'd just fire at our muzzle flashes, and we'd be dead."

"Not if we were down on our bellies and waited until we couldn't miss."

"There's no such thing as 'couldn't miss.' But I don't mind that position being lightly held. You, Admiral Magnus, will suffice."

"I'm not going to be much good against them, Lustgarten."

"That's all right. I want the main resistance to come from an ambush on the ship itself, and from flanking fire behind the trap house. You two"—he pointed to the Scots—"I want you to get down on the *Enterprise* and hide yourselves separately in all that metal. Fire when you've gotten as close to them as you can. Hit them if possible, but don't worry if you don't, just as long as they're distracted from what we have behind the trap house. When one of you begins to shoot, the other must open fire as well, whatever the target. Remember, I want distraction. Now hurry."

The Scots ran for the edge of the platform, separating as they entered the glare of the floods.

"Is there any way to turn those lights off, Cullenbine?"

"Not fast enough to do us any good."

"Then please stay deep in the shadows under the crane, Admiral. Go now, please. Mr. Cullenbine, you come with Zamke and me behind the trap house."

When Barton's men picked their way around the last of the heaved-up plates and had the platform corner in view again, they saw no one. Under the harsh floodlights, the deck gleamed bare in the blowing rain.

Barton searched for places of concealment. For his own force there was none once they reached the deck of Mavis A. They would be crossing open, brilliantly lit deck until they reached the crane.

For the defenders, the terrain was better. The darkness beneath the huge crane could hold a regiment, and there was no way of knowing what equipment they might have dug in behind. Barton saw a small house, ahead and to the right; it could easily hide several men, inside or out. He thought this unlikely, for it was too exposed; it was not the kind of place amateur defenders would have the nerve to hold. Actually, he thought, the best defensive position would be right here on the bow of the *Enterprise*. The wreckage presented many spots for a surprise assault.

The Dropper was impatient. Perhaps he could still get back to his explorer in time if they did the job quickly. "What do you say, Barton? Let's get at it."

"Easy. They could have something ready for us."

"With what? If they had guns they wouldn't have scooted away when they saw us comin'."

"I agree. I think that hook was their last card. But let's move ahead as though it wasn't. I don't want us climbin' up on Mavis bunched together or all at the same time. We can't see what might be behind that small house over there, so Costello and Devlin, get over that way to the right. Watch for surprises as you go. Leave about a twenty-yard spread between you, and don't climb up on the platform until you see my wave. Dropper and I will move apart and head straight for the crane from here. We'll get up on the platform before you, and you two will cover us with your guns until we're about halfway across. If we haven't drawn any fire from behind us or from the flank by then, we never will. We'll flatten out and wait for you to come up and join us. Then I'll go for the crane with all of you covering. Got it?"

They all nodded. "Make sure the selector on those AK's is in the middle position. We'll be wanting full automatic fire if anything goes wrong."

Everyone checked his gun. Devlin and Costello moved off to the right, and Barton and The Dropper picked their way straight ahead.

Squatting in the shadows beneath the crane, Magnus had a perfect view down the tilted deck of the platform to the bow of the tanker. He saw that the two Irishmen closest to the crane had reached the edge of Mavis A. and had stopped for a moment, only their heads and shoulders visible above the platform's edge. The other two had swung wide and were still moving. They would be close to the trap house when they came on board, and it must be that that they were covering. Whoever was leading the attack was smart. There were going to be no massed bodies to fire into.

The two circling Irishmen had almost reached the platform when Randy Martin attacked them. He appeared on a twisted pile of plates aiming a shotgun and visible from his boots to his sandy hair. The range was still long. *Stay down, you silly sonofabitch,* Magnus groaned to himself. Then Bairn Harrison appeared with a shotgun on the opposite side of the second group; he also, was too far away, standing erect and totally visible from the knees up.

Martin got two shots out of his wildly wavering gun, each missing by yards, before Devlin and Costello cut loose with their AK's. The Scot seemed to rise on the stream of bullets and disappeared in a backward cartwheel. The stuttering roar of the assault rifles drowned out the feeble bang of Harrison's shotgun, which he was firing at the backs of the distracted Irishmen as fast as he could pump the slide. He missed three times before The Dropper, behind him, aimed carefully and caught him from forty yards away with a six-round burst to the base of the spine. The shotgun sailed away and Harrison died before it hit the deck.

When Barton saw that his enemy was armed and ready to resist, he knew that audacity was an indispensable part of his attack. If the defenders were as inexperienced as he thought, they had to be pressed.

He whistled for The Dropper to follow him. Using chunks of crumbled concrete as steps, they scampered from the ship up to the platform and sprinted straight for the crane. They were almost into the shadows before Barton remembered the plan. He fell to the deck and yelled for The Dropper to do the same, then waved for Costello and Devlin to join them.

The men behind the trap house were ready. When they heard the Scots begin to fire, Cullenbine peeked out to see them die. He was dismayed at the ineptitude of their positioning and fire, but realized that their deaths might have gained something. The two Irishmen who had been attacked now only had eyes for the bow of the ship; they had not even glanced at the trap house since the firing.

Zamke hurried over from the other corner of the house and tugged Cullenbine's sleeve. "The others are going for the crane."

"We can't do anything about them with these light guns. We've got to get some of theirs." The platform master pointed in the direction of the Irishmen still on the ship. "Heavy stuff. Did you hear it?"

Lustgarten scurried up. "They've stopped. They're waving our two up. Get ready." He peered out again.

The two were coming up on the platform, but they were *backing* up, covering the wreckage behind them for further ambushes.

"Perfect," whispered Lustgarten. "The close one is easy. Almost point-blank. You take him, Zamke. Cullenbine and I will take the other. Move when I do."

Lustgarten estimated that the Irishmen would be in the best position by the end of a ten count. *Ein, zwei, drei* . . . He motioned for Cullenbine and Zamke to get ready . . . *vier, fünf* . . . Zamke went to the far end of the house, setting his second gun upright at the corner. He would step out from there . . . *sechs, sieben, acht* . . . Lustgarten and Cullenbine positioned their extra guns and tensed themselves . . . *neun, zehn.*

Lustgarten sprang into the open. The pale face of the closest Irishman, barely five yards away, turned to glare at him. His features were twisted with hatred, and he had terrible hairless brows. But Punchy Devlin was not the colonel's target. Lustgarten forced himself to look past the dreadful face and sighted across the platform thirty yards at the backward-moving figure that was Father Costello. Cullenbine and Lustgarten fired at the same instant. Costello staggered but didn't fall.

As Lustgarten worked the shotgun's slide for a second shot, he could see Devlin's AK coming up out of the corner of his eye. Off to Lustgarten's right, Zamke fired. The breath exploded out of Devlin as the charge caught him between the shoulder blades, and he fell, choking and trying to claw the AK around to Zamke. Cullenbine planted his foot to pin the assault rifle to the deck and fired again at Costello. The shot went wild, as did a second shot by Lustgarten.

Costello came at them in a clumsy run, firing as he came. But although the AK weighed a hefty ten-and-a-half pounds, it climbed rapidly on automatic fire, and its stream of bullets cut the air above them.

Lustgarten, Cullenbine and Zamke now stood in a ragged line, firing at Costello as if he were a charging rhino. They were close enough to see a shiny stream of spent shell cases pouring out of the AK's receiver.

As Cullenbine's shotgun clicked empty a red rose appeared on one side of Costello's face and he seemed to smash into the deck, like a man diving headlong into a swimming pool.

"The guns!" Cullenbine cried. "Get the guns."

Zamke ran for the fallen Costello and retrieved his AK, while Lustgarten snatched Devlin's from beneath Cullenbine's still-planted foot.

Costello managed to get to his hands and knees, and

266

floundered brokenly to the side of the cursing Devlin. "The rites, Punchy. Do you want the rites?"

The words sent Devlin into a loud, choking laugh. "From the looks of that old German, I'm goin' to need 'em." Costello turned the one good eye in his ruined face in time to see Lustgarten center the muzzle of his AK on Devlin's chest and fire a coughing burst; it hit Devlin so hard that it flung his arms and legs out wide.

"You *pig*," gasped Cullenbine.

Lustgarten moved the muzzle to Costello's neck and looked at Zamke. He had never seen his aide so wide-eyed.

Zamke understood the hesitation perfectly. "No, thank you, my Colonel." He seemed about to throw his gun away.

The colonel fired, and the would-be Ballylannon Mummer slammed dead against the deck.

In the second that he should have been looking at the other Irishmen, Lustgarten searched the eyes of Zamke and Magnus. They told him what he was. He felt oddly shocked that they didn't understand, but before the full chill of the awareness could reach him, two bullets crossed through his body, taking him squarely in the lungs and heart.

Barton and The Dropper had watched it all. Agonized, they had held their fire for fear of hitting Costello while he made his clumsy charge. Then it had appeared as if the ambushers were rushing out to help the wounded men, but it had been only to take their guns and murder them. At the moment Costello died, the surviving Irishmen had braced their elbows against the deck and squeezed the triggers of their AK's.

The tall, uniformed man went down first, seeming to drop as if through a trap door. The other two began to retreat to the shelter of the trap house, one heading for the near side, one for the far. Instinctively, both Barton and The Dropper aimed their fire against the closest man, the second of the uniformed men. The two lines of bullets caught Zamke against the steel wall of the house; he flapped against it a moment like a rug being violently beaten and then slid down.

Moving like a panther, the third man—the Irish could see that he was huge, with thick black hair—was able to make it behind the house before they could shift their aim.

Barton groaned. "He can get one of those guns and take us from behind. Get him before he can do anythin', Dropper. I'm goin' for the crane."

They exploded to their feet, The Dropper pounding for the trap house, Barton driving hard for the ladder to the cab of the crane.

Magnus knew that he was invisible to the light-blinded Irishman who was bolting toward him. Picking the point in the shadows that was closest to where the man bound for the ladder would pass, the admiral began to move toward it. He would have had a shot of no more than six feet if he had held his fire, but he was too anxious, and began to blast his shotgun at Barton before he was within easy range.

Barton dropped to one knee and raked the AK's fire into the blackness beneath the crane. Magnus felt thunderbolts whistling past his ears and prepared to die. Then there was silence. The AK was still swinging in the Irishman's hand, but it had stopped flashing and barking. Empty.

Magnus had stopped firing after four shots. For all the wild pounding in his breast, his head told him that, shaking as he was, he could not hope to hit the man at anything but arm's length, and that his palsied hands could never reload in the dark.

He saw a piece fall off the kneeling man's machine gun. The clip; he was reloading. The man's hand fumbled under his weather gear. Magnus lurched out of his prone position and stumbled toward the Irishman on feet so numb that they were all but out of control. His only chance was to get to the man before he could reload and slaughter him.

The grotesqueness of the moment flashed over Magnus as he realized that the capstone of a life spent climbing the heights was going to be in trying to do a job that any Liverpool street thug could have done better.

Barton had been impressed by the simplicity of operation of the AK–47, especially its ease of loading under battle conditions, but now, with this ancient, uncoordinated-looking man loping toward him with a shotgun, the job became horrendous. His hand seemed to search with all the leisure of nightmare for the extra magazine he had tucked into his waistband under the blouse of his weather top. When he finally found and withdrew the heavy, banana-shaped clip, it seemed to move toward the bottom of the AK's receiver in slow motion. He inserted the magazine into its slot, forward end first, then pulled up the rear end until the magazine catch clicked to signal its engagement. Over the wind he could hear the approaching man grunting. Barton reached to the right side of the receiver, pulled and released the operating handle. But as he started to raise the AK, he found it entangled in a pair of thrashing legs. The Mavis man had overrun him.

Both men fell together in a panting heap, each close enough to throttle the other, but neither wanting to release the terrified grip he had on his own weapon. They rolled apart and struggled frantically to bring their guns to bear from the prone position, Magnus with his single round and Barton with his thirty.

Barton's muzzle crossed flesh first. The gush of bullets struck Magnus's legs so squarely that the force pivoted the admiral on his hips and left him lying head first, facing Barton like a soldier perfectly positioned for range firing. It was from this stance that he fired his one remaining shell and nicked Barton just beneath the chin at a range of four feet. He had, in effect, cut the Irishman's throat.

Barton's hands slid off the gun and reached for his bleeding neck; he rolled onto his back, his chest heaving desperately.

Magnus pulled free the drawstrings at the neck and

waist of his weather gear and tied one tightly around the top of each bleeding thigh. The floodlights seemed to be going dim. Just before he slipped into darkness, he saw the arm of the dying Irishman next to him rise slowly into the air and wave toward the crane. As he went under he thought of the dead Ahab waving from the flank of the breaching Moby Dick.

The Dropper, flattened against the trap house, saw Barton wave. *Come on,* he was saying. That meant there was nobody left defending the crane except the man The Dropper was chasing.

Cullenbine was inside the trap house, not behind it as The Dropper suspected. Having dived behind the house a bare step in front of the splatter of bullets from Barton and The Dropper, the platform master had only an empty shotgun; all the other guns were lying out in the open. He had shouted for Zamke and received no answer. Had there been a gun left in the rack inside? Maybe. He ducked inside the door.

When Cullenbine slammed the door behind him, he found himself in darkness. He felt for the light switch where he remembered it to be, but found nothing. When he tried to open the door again to let in some light, he couldn't find the handle. Swearing, he thought of the hinged port through which the trap-thrower fired the clay birds. It had been fastened by sliding bolts at the top. Feeling the outline of the port, he ran his hands along the edge until he found the bolts, drew them back and let the port fall outward with a reverberating clang. Mistake? If anybody was after him, they knew he was inside now.

By the light from the floodlit deck coming through the open port, Cullenbine saw a single shotgun left in the rack. He pulled it free and snapped open the bottom drawer. There was a spilled box of shells, and he was reaching for them when a shadow fell across him. He turned to see The Dropper framed in the center of the port, the Irishman's AK pointing straight at his chest.

Cullenbine felt the small, fierce eyes directly on his. No, the man wasn't seeing anything yet; his eyes were still adjusting to the darkness inside. He had perhaps five seconds. His spine seemed to be turning to water. He put a hand on the trap-thrower to steady himself, and felt something square and uneven under his hand: the control box for the thrower. His fingertips found two low-set buttons, side by side. One to turn on the trap's power supply, one to release the birds? He wasn't sure.

The Dropper was squinting harder through the port now, a hand above his brow, trying to shield his eyes from the glare of the floodlights. Gradually he was able to make out the shape of the thrower and the man behind it. He tucked the AK under his arm and gripped the barrel hard, his palm pressing down, so that the gun wouldn't climb on the burst.

Like a man lifting a hand to ward off an onrushing locomotive, Cullenbine pressed the buttons under his fingers. A steel arm swept out of the side of the thrower in a hissing arc, and at the end of its swing released a clay bird made of silt and pitch. The bird was saucer-shaped, four-and-a-half inches in diameter and weighed only three-and-a-half ounces, but when it hit The Dropper across the eyes, it was traveling just over a hundred miles an hour. There was a splattering puff of red and black, and The Dropper fell from Cullenbine's view and the world of living men.

chapter 14

Dominic Quinn, standing on the bridge of the *American Enterprise,* had watched it all through binoculars. He could see each of his men sprawled and dead: Barton lying close to the crane with the man who had run at him; Costello and Devlin crumpled close to the small house, next to the man who had butchered them; and now The Dropper, somehow struck down as he chased a man into the house.

Quinn wondered whether he and Roland O'Driscoll, who was still waiting below with the exploder, could successfully rush the crane. No one else had come out of the shadows beneath, and the man next to Barton seemed dead or too badly wounded to worry about. The two Mavis men who had sprung the ambush in the wreckage on the bow were certainly finished; he had seen how the bullets flung them. The first uniformed man to be shot had not moved since he was hit, and the fact that the second had not appeared from behind the house indicated that he too was done for. Before he died, had The Dropper killed the man he had chased into the house? If so, the *Enterprise* might still be freed.

A door in the house opened, a tiny, dark square in the whipping rain, and a figure stepped out, moving catlike. It darted over to where The Dropper lay, picked something up, and in another moment had disappeared behind the house.

That's it, Quinn thought. They had a man alive and armed with an AK–47; the position behind the house was now virtually impregnable. He and O'Driscoll might try grenades in a pincer movement, but if they were caught the charges in the supertanker's hull would never be detonated.

So it was to be another magnificent failure, like the Post Office in '16. Well, if it was no worse than that, they hadn't done badly. There would be many a lusty song about Dominic Quinn and the North Sea Gunmen, and a verse or two about the million barrels of oil that were about to go into the water. Yes, they would remember him for a lot of years.

Quinn took the elevator down and found Roland O'Driscoll squatting with his back to the door leading to the weather deck, the Beethoven exploder cradled across his lap.

"It's now, Roland. Our friends are all gone. Dead for Ireland. Mavis still stands, but they'll be a year gettin' this blown-out wreck out from under it. Open the door, boy. We've waited too long for this not to see it."

When O'Driscoll didn't move, Quinn dragged him out of the way, undogged the heavy door and swung it open. They had started through it when a rush of clammy wind bore in on them, followed by a horizontal column of water that came through the opening like a charge out of the mouth of a cannon. Both men were flung down the passageway behind them. When the wave was spent and the water ran sluggishly back through the door, they struggled to their feet, coughing up water.

"Christ," Quinn gasped, "I didn't think it could get any

274

worse out there, but it's doin' it. Even dead in the water we're takin' seas."

The water was still about their ankles, but they could see the half-submerged exploder lying on its side near the door. O'Driscoll splashed to it desperately and gathered it into his arms like a lost child.

Quinn ran his eyes over the machine quickly. "All the wires are still in place. Lucky we don't have to worry about it bein' wet. The Dropper said it would fire no matter what." Looking into O'Driscoll's face, he saw that of a stranger. His friend's eyes seemed to strain in their sockets, and muscles jumped in his cheeks.

"Better give me the box, boy. I'll do it for you. You're not feelin' well. You tell me if I'm doin' it right."

But when Quinn tried to take the exploder out of O'Driscoll's arms, the man clutched it to his chest with all his strength. He had gone for the box not to see if it had survived the wave, but to keep it from Quinn.

"I can't get at it while you're holdin' it that way, Roland," Quinn said, trying to keep his voice gentle. "If you can just clear the little crank for me . . ."

"I can't go back in the water, Dominic," O'Driscoll said. The voice was so much more shrill than normal that Quinn could hardly believe it to be his friend's.

"We might not have to do that at all. I think she'll settle in one piece. Part of the ship is actually restin' on the bottom now, remember."

"I've been helpin' The Dropper. He said he was settin' the charges not just to sink her, but to slice her up, too. And I know these supertanker hulls. They're like folded paper. Tear through the fold in one place and they have no resistance at all."

"We can't know that for sure."

"*I* know it. Once the frames are broken, that ocean will dismantle us. We'll be sittin' here watchin' her go to pieces around our ears. The lights will go out and we'll go into the water."

Quinn tugged at the exploder as hard as he dared without precipitating a scuffle, but he couldn't budge it. "Roland, Roland, Roland," he said sadly. He took his Webley revolver out of his pocket and holding it flat against his palm, whipped its weight against the side of O'Driscoll's head.

O'Driscoll dropped to his knees, and Quinn caught the exploder as it tumbled free. The bloody, upturned face had the look of a frightened child who had toddled to a parent for comfort and been cruelly cuffed. The eyes swam with tears.

Quinn's heart broke at the sight. Choking back a sob, he squatted next to O'Driscoll and kissed his forehead again and again. But he could not find the sorrowing words that he sought, and he felt the trust of the man he loved slipping away.

His mind strove for a gesture of conciliation. Feeling as if they were small boys again, he did what a small boy might do and handed the Webley to O'Driscoll. "Listen, Roland, I'll never forgive myself for hittin' you. If you want to clip me a good one back, go on and do it. I've got it comin'."

But O'Driscoll, his mournful expression unchanged, simply knelt there, holding the big revolver loosely by the barrel.

Another wave jetted through the open door from the weather deck, but now the Irishmen were far down the passage and the water only swirled around their waists.

Quinn stood up and moved for the door, helped by the sea that was now sucking out. "Roland, come and watch with me. It's the moment that will help put Ireland back together again. A great day for the millions of us."

Bracing himself in the door, he looked out. Past the ironwork around the walkway, he saw the receding prairie of the weather deck, its far end resting under a huge, tilting birthday cake lit by strings of garish white candles. He wondered whether the roar of the explosions would be heard above the shriek of the wind. Would there be a fire, with them burning to death in a world composed more of water than of air?

He found the crank at the end of the Beethoven. "Is this the thing here, Roland? Should I just give it a twist?"

O'Driscoll was now alongside him, and Quinn looked into the barrel of the Webley.

O'Driscoll held the revolver on the middle of Quinn's chest, just above the exploder. "You can't drown me, Dominic."

"Then, my friend, we'll finally sleep together. Forever, under—"

"No."

"Courage, Roland. They'll bless us for a thousand years."

"No. Drop the thing right now. I'll shoot you, Dominic."

Quinn looked at O'Driscoll for a moment, gauging what strength remained inside this fear-wrung man, and wondering how much was left inside himself.

Now there was granted to Dominic Quinn something that comes only to few: a desire to change the course of the fates that is greater than all the gifts of life. He might have twisted the crank without warning, before Roland could react, but that would have been the act of an untrustworthy friend. Instead he tapped the crank with the tip of a finger. "Now, Roland, is this the thing?"

O'Driscoll nodded slowly.

"Then here it goes, my love. You do what you must."

In that instant Quinn saw the light of thought flicker out of O'Driscoll's eyes. The commandant tried to deflect the gun muzzle with his hand, and the last thing he felt was the sting of burning powder against his palm as the .455 ripped through it on the way to his heart.

The weight of the Beethoven, still locked in one arm, caused Dominic Quinn to fall forward, face down into the water. Whimpering like a run-over dog, O'Driscoll stooped quickly, grabbed him under the arms, pulled him erect and tried to stand him on his feet, as though this might bring the man back to life.

Not far from the door there was a stair; O'Driscoll dragged Quinn's body there and laid it on its back on the steps. He stared at the wound, touching it, running his fingers around its warm, wet edges.

Quinn's flag for the new Ireland was tucked into O'Driscoll's waistband. He shook out its folds and laid it over his friend's face and body. Standing stiffly at attention, Roland raised the revolver into the air and fired the traditional three-round IRA salute to his fallen comrade. Then he placed the muzzle of the Webley against his chest at the exact position of Quinn's wound and pulled the trigger.

The next wave to flood the passageway was an unusually large one. Quinn's body was washed off the stairs and swept along with O'Driscoll's. When the sea rushed back out the door, the pretty green-and-orange flag was riding its surface, spread out and seeming to flap in the current. As though it were guided, it floated straight out of the *American Enterprise* into the gray dawn. It was never seen again, joining the flags of a thousand other republics that had died before they could be born.

epilogue

The day was perfect—sunlit, cloudless, the kind of summer morning that made you forget that the tranquil surface below could ever tower ninety feet high and smash ships and men as if they were water bugs.

The government helicopter hovered a thousand feet above Mavis A., which looked as colorful and peaceful as a tropical island in the sparkling sea.

Seated behind the pilot, Noel Cullenbine and the London *Times* reporter looked down through the plastic bubble at the platform's crew working in their shirtsleeves.

"You've done a phenomenal job in only nine months, Mr. Cullenbine."

"We're very proud of it, Mr. Teague."

Teague had a notebook open. "Would you mind giving me some background? What was your first priority?"

"The first thing, of course, was to free the *Enterprise* and drain her oil off. It was a tricky job in the fall weather, but we did it without spilling a drop."

"It seems to me that the most remarkable part of the

operation was the small amount of oil that was spilled. Do you agree?"

"That was important, but the truly important factor was how little production time we lost. Think of it: we had Yellowleg and Blueleg back at work within three months. The entire rig will be back in full production within thirteen. The production loss in sterling has been serious, but nothing we can't handle."

"Am I correct in saying that towing the *American Enterprise* across the Atlantic was one of the greatest feats of seamanship ever?"

"That's exaggerated, but it *was* a remarkable performance. Only the dry dock where she was built could handle her, and the towing company had to rewrite the book."

"How about dragging that floating dry dock out here and sinking her under Mavis A.?"

"Tough, but the distances were short and we could slip between the bad weather. What we had to do was more or less cut-and-dried: get the dock here, sink it low enough to slip under Mavis alongside the *Enterprise,* then sink the dock to the bottom, roof her open space with steel and supports, and use every big hydraulic jack we could buy, build or steal to take the load off the *Enterprise*. We were lucky that the clearances we were working with were relatively modest."

"The danger of the sea breaking up the ship must have been in your mind all the time. Why did you wait until the platform was lifted off the deck before you lightered off the oil?"

"Well, the only part of the ship that was structurally damaged was the bow up to the Number Two tank. The naval architects told me that this didn't necessarily compromise the integrity of the rest of the hull, and that made waiting a good gamble. To have pumped the *Enterprise* out with her bow stuck under Mavis would almost certainly have caused the stern's buoyancy to break the ship's back."

"You almost make it sound easy."

"It's occasionally easier to fix something than to destroy it."

"I assume you'll be beefing up your security."

"Oh, yes. I'll show you." Cullenbine leaned forward to the pilot and signaled him to take the helicopter higher.

"The admiral is still pretty bad, I hear."

"Yes, but they think he'll be off those braces one day. He has to be grateful that he got off as cheaply as he did."

"Have any of you changed your minds about accepting your medals?"

"Not unless Her Majesty's government changes *its* mind about including Martin and Harrison. The Germans' families feel the same way."

"But surely you understand the government's point about not giving the Scots any heroes to rally around for secessionist purposes?"

"I understand it perfectly, and I also know that it's a perfect crock."

"Still, you've passed up a great honor."

"Magnus is the only one who might mind. I think he would have liked one more shiny medal to go with that magnificent chestful he already has. But he knows it would have been fakery for us to accept anything. We weren't being brave or fighting for England or the West; we were fighting for our lives. Even rats do that. I'd favor posthumous medals for the Brownes, though—or the Irishmen."

"Terrorists?"

"I suppose that's what they were, but think of the scope of their scheme. Its daring, its cunning, the skill and courage they needed to bring it as close as they did. And though they killed a lot of men, it was no more than the plan required. They weren't wasteful of lives."

"With respect, Mr. Cullenbine, I don't like that sort of talk. Besides which, it's rubbish. They were out to murder everyone on that platform down there, and everyone on the ship as well."

"The storm was probably more than they expected. They couldn't get anyone off—not even themselves."

The reporter's voice was cold. "Sir, I may have to write about this strange turn of heart. How do you explain it?"

"I can't, really, except to tell you that the best doctors were working to save Magnus for weeks, and that he came to loathe every one of them. The IRA's were working just as hard to kill him, and he came to respect them. I guess it's just a closer relationship."

The helicopter reached five thousand feet and Cullenbine signaled the pilot to level off and begin to make a wide circle. For a radius of ten miles around Mavis A., a half-dozen white crescents cut the gleaming blue water. "Those are the new *Agamemnon*-class patrol boats. There are only a few of them now, but as the field develops, we may have as many as thirty in operation."

"I understand they're well-armed."

"Especially when you consider they're only seventy feet long. Each has three *Jellicoe* surface-to-surface missiles. Three of those boats could take out another *Enterprise;* one of them could fight a destroyer to a standstill."

"Mind if we go down and get some pictures? You chaps have been pretty fussy about visitors over the last few months."

"That's all over now. We've got our defenses pretty much the way we want them. Besides, there'll be a hundred boats and helicopters going through here every day from now on, and we have a lot more Mavises on the drawing boards. We'll never be able to sift the good guys from the bad guys among the workmen, so from now on it's a matter of keeping our eyes open."

"Who do you have to watch the closest?"

"The vicious, the crazy and the brave."

As Cullenbine's helicopter dropped down to wave-top height to photograph Mavis A. and various *Agamemnons*, a second helicopter, somewhat larger than the government machine, hovered above the platform.

A tall, thick-boned fat man with a flaring brush of curly white hair occupied the seat next to the pilot. Two younger men, both gaunt and gray-skinned with the pallor of prisoners, leaned over his shoulder from the back seats. The pilot flew the craft with its nose tilted down so that his passengers could see Mavis A. clearly.

"Quinn was a perfect example of how one devoted man might bring down an empire. He was also a perfect example of an idiot who decided he wanted to keep all the heroics to himself, and ended up bollixin' what should have been a brilliant operation." The fat man was obviously in charge; the others took pains not to interrupt.

"Yes, Padraic. But it was magnificent," one of the gaunt men said.

"Being dead and failed is never magnificent. Who knows that whatever finally stopped him couldn't have been gotten past with a few more men and guns? Or perhaps it was a failure of sentiment, one that another commandant might have overcome. You know, it's my experience that Irishmen fail not so often with their guns as with their sentiment."

The helicopter swung aloft for another quarter hour, and then the fat man rapped the bubble. "There's the weakness: the helicopter landin' pad. One big chopper could put enough men, guns and explosives aboard to take her. Just ape the paint job on any of those company birds. No radar to fool or anythin' else."

"It sounds too simple."

"So did Quinn's plan, Tim."

"When?"

"Not now. We'll wait until they've got a few more goin', then hit 'em all at once."

"It's not as easy as you make it. There's months of preparation."

A look of happiness settled on the fat man's face. He spoke with his eyes closed. "Timothy, you're in charge of the technical plans. Bernard, you do the recruitin'. I'll choose the commandant and coordinate. There'll not be another word of this until you hear from me again, probably some time at the end of November."

He waved to the west, and the helicopter tilted and swept away. The men inside had ten thousand thoughts. Not one of them was of dying.

BESTSELLERS

☐	THE EYES OF LOVE—Charles Beardsley	04482-9	$2.50
☐	GIDEON'S DAY—J. J. Marrie	04475-6	$1.75
☐	PASSION CARGO—Marilyn Ross	04463-2	$2.25
☐	TENDER BETRAYAL—Jennifer Blake	04429-2	$2.25
☐	SILENCE IN EDEN—Jerry Allen Potter	04430-6	$2.25
☐	SISTERS AND STRANGERS—Helen Van Slyke	04445-4	$2.50
☐	RAPTURE—Rosamond Royal	04359-8	$2.50
☐	FREEWAY—Deanne Barkley	04385-7	$2.25
☐	THE SIBYL CIPHER—Simmel	04395-4	$2.25
☐	CROWN IN CANDLELIGHT —Rosemary Hawley Jarman	04396-2	$2.25
☐	VENOM—Alan Scholefield	04378-4	$2.25
☐	WOMEN WHO WAIT—Elaine Bissell	04415-2	$1.95
☐	FAT CITY—Leonard Gardner	04388-1	$2.25
☐	LOVE STORIES—Martin Levin, editor	04172-2	$2.50
☐	THE MANNER MUSIC—Charles Reznikoff	04337-7	$2.25
☐	THE ICE AGE—Margaret Drabble	04300-8	$2.25
☐	DEATH OF AN EXPERT WITNESS—P. D. James	04301-6	$1.95
☐	TIM—C. McCullough	08545-2	$1.75
☐	A BRIDGE TOO FAR—Cornelius Ryan	08373-5	$2.50
☐	CHILD OF THE MORNING—Pauline Gedge	04227-3	$2.25
☐	EARTHLY POSSESSIONS—Anne Tyler	04214-1	$1.95

Buy them at your local bookstore or use this handy coupon for ordering: